1991

EYELIDS OF MORNING

Whose house I have made the wilderness, and the barren land his dwellings. Job 39 :6

EYELIDS OF MORNING

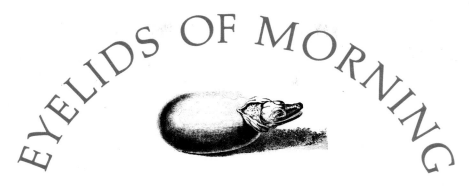

THE MINGLED DESTINIES OF CROCODILES AND MEN

Being a DESCRIPTION of

The Origins, History, and Prospects of
LAKE RUDOLF
Its Peoples, Deserts, Rivers, Mountains and Weather

A NARRATIVE OF OUR INVESTIGATIONS INTO THE NATURAL HISTORY, HABITS, AND MODE OF LIFE OF THE FEARSOME NYLE CROCODYLE, MOST FORMIDABLE OF REPTILES, THE LEGENDARY LEVIATHAN

Including a full, authentic and
thrilling account of the stirring explorations and discoveries of
Count Samuel Teleki von Sjek, as chronicled by his companion and fellow stalwart,
Lieutenant Ludwig von Höhnel, in which the fabled
lake of Rudolph was brought to light

REPLETE WITH ASTOUNDING INCIDENTS, WONDERFUL
ADVENTURES, MYSTERIOUS PROVIDENCES, GRAND ACHIEVEMENTS AND GLORIOUS
DEEDS IN THE PURSUIT OF KNOWLEDGE

ENLIVENED WITH STORIES OF Heroism and unparalleled Daring, marvelous Hunts and incredible
Adventures among savage Saurians, giant Fish, monstrous Behemoths and strange and curious Tribes

and Comprehending
Whatever is Curious and Remarkable in the Works of ART or NATURE

A full descriptive Account by ALISTAIR GRAHAM
a n d
Divers Illustrations by PETER BEARD

The WHOLE enriched with upwards of 220 PHOTOGRAPHS,
16 magnificent COLORED PLATES, 165 well-executed Engravings, and numerous MAPS, being all finely
drawn according to the latest DISCOVERIES
For the use of all GENTLEMEN, MARINERS, MERCHANTS & Others who delight in
TRAVEL and ADVENTURE

Chronicle Books • San Francisco

First Chronicle Books edition 1990

Layout and design by Peter Beard and John Brogna

Printed in Japan

Library of Congress Cataloging in Publication Data

Graham, A.D. (Alistair D.)
Eyelids of morning : the mingled destinies of crocodiles and men : being a description of the origins, history, and prospects of Lake Rudolf, its peoples, deserts, rivers, mountains, and weather... a full descriptive account / by Alistair Graham and divers illustrations by Peter Beard.
   p.   cm.
   Bibliography: p.
ISBN 0-87701-539-2 (pbk.). ISBN 0-87701-554-6 (hard)
1. Crocodiles—Rudolf, Lake (Kenya and Ethiopia) 2. Crocodiles—Kenya—Mythology. 3. Reptiles—Rudolf, Lake (Kenya and Ethiopia)
4. Reptiles—Kenya—Mythology. 5. Rudolf, Lake (Kenya and Ethiopia)
I. Beard, Peter H. (Peter Hill). 1938- . II. Title.
QL666.C925G7 1988
333.95'09676'27—dc19   88-16131
                                                  CIP

BOMC offers recordings and compact discs, cassettes and records. For information and catalog write to BOMR, Camp Hill, PA 17012.

Distributed in Canada by Raincoast Books
112 East Third Avenue, Vancouver, B.C. V5T 1C8

10 9 8 7 6 5 4 3 2 1

Chronicle Books
275 Fifth Street
San Francisco, California 94103

LEVIATHAN

Canst thou draw out leviathan with a hook? or his tongue with a cord which thou lettest down?

Canst thou put an hook into his nose? or bore his jaw through with a thorn?

Will he make many supplications unto thee? will he speak soft words unto thee?

Will he make a covenant with thee? wilt thou take him for a servant for ever?

Wilt thou play with him as with a bird? or wilt thou bind him for thy maidens?

Shall the companions make a banquet of him? shall they part him among the merchants?

Canst thou fill his skin with barbed irons? or his head with fish spears?

Lay thine hand upon him, remember the battle, do no more.

Behold, the hope of him is in vain: shall not one be cast down even at the sight of him?

None is so fierce that dare stir him up: who then is able to stand before me?

Who hath prevented me, that I should repay him? whatsoever is under the whole heaven is mine.

I will not conceal his parts, nor his power, nor him comely proportion.

Who can discover the face of his garment? or who can come to him with his double bridle?

Who can open the doors of his face? his teeth are terrible round about.

His scales are his pride, shut up together as with a close seal.

One is so near to another, that no air can come between them.

They are joined one to another, they stick together, that they cannot be sundered.

By his sneesings a light doth shine, and his eyes are like the eyelids of the morning.

Out of his mouth go burning lamps, and sparks of fire leap out.

Out of his nostrils goeth smoke, as out of a seething pot or caldron.

His breath kindleth coals, and a flame goeth out of his mouth.

In his neck remaineth strength, and sorrow is turned into joy before him.

The flakes of his flesh are joined together; they are firm in themselves; they cannot be moved.

His heart is as firm as a stone; yea, as hard as a piece of the nether millstone.

When he raiseth up himself, the mighty are afraid: by reason of breakings they purify themselves.

The sword of him that layeth at him cannot hold: the spear, the dart, nor the habergeon.

He esteemeth iron as straw, and brass as rotten wood.

The arrow cannot make him flee: slingstones are turned with him into stubble.

Darts are counted as stubble: he laugheth at the shaking of a spear.

Sharp stones are under him: he spreadeth sharp pointed things upon the mire.

He maketh the deep to boil like a pot; he maketh the sea like a pot of ointment.

He maketh a path to shine after him; one would think the deep to be hoary.

Upon earth there is not his like, who is made without fear.

He beholdeth all high things: he is a king over all the children of pride.

Job 41:1-34

DEDICATED TO
ALL

Heroes

Missionaries,

AND

Martyrs,

THEIR
PERILS, ADVENTURES AND ACHIEVEMENTS

CONTENTS

THE FATE OF THE PEBBLEWORMS

The ancient Greeks called them *kroko-drilos*, "pebble-worms"—scaly things that shuffle and lurk around low places.

For the most part man gets on with crocodiles about as well as he did with dragons; and just as he did with dragons, he will banish them from all but the remotest parts of the earth.

At Lake Rudolf we found one of those distant lands where dragons still roam at will, but this does not mean that it will always be so, that mankind is content to let it be. In the face of man's inexorable expansion, Lake Rudolf will one day fall and its dragons be subdued, for civilized man will not tolerate wild beasts that eat his children, his cattle, or even the fish he deems to be his. That would be regression into barbarism.

But there are people who care about crocodiles. They care because these beasts are a part of nature, part of the fast disappearing wilderness whose uniqueness can never be reconstituted. Such people are loath to see that wilderness go before man has established beyond all doubt that it is in his best interests to dispose of it. Just because wild animals are a relic and a symbol of the savagery we mean to rise above does not mean that they have nothing else to offer the hungry, lonely soul of civilized man. Those who bemoan "the rape of the wilderness," who feel we are losing something irreplaceable, may have something real to tell us. We cannot dismiss their ideas as selfish fantasies until we know for certain they are nothing else.

So it seemed to us on Lake Rudolf that rather than abandon the world's last great crocodile population to the whim of man, to be exterminated in the name of inevitability, we might first inquire a little into their lives. By doing so we believed that their fate, already in the clumsy hands of man (to whom even his own fate remains a mystery), might be cast with deliberation and care, in whatever way seemed most reasonable in the light of the facts. Perhaps as a result of our work the existence of crocodiles, which has been a fact of nature for 170 million years, would take on a renewed significance; or it might be what we would only confirm their "uselessness" in the lives of men.

Thus it was that the Government of Kenya contracted Wildlife Services to study the crocodiles of Lake Rudolf. My partner Ian Parker and I had recently left the Kenya Game Department to form this private enterprise, which offered research and management services to the conservation agencies. The chance to study a population of Nile crocodiles, never done before, was something both of us had dreamed of. As it happened, Ian had to go off on another project, and it was Peter Beard who shared most of the time, and the work, at the lake with me.

Crocodiles had only recently been promoted to game animal status from their traditional position as vermin and came low on the Game Department's list of priorities, but eventually the survey was approved. We were to describe the essential biological facts of the Rudolf crocodile population...fix a value for the ratio of males to females, find the proportion of the whole population represented by each age group, study the rate of individual growth, their food and manner of getting it. We were to estimate their potential for reproduction and account for the agencies of mortality that limited their population. We hoped to discover why the population distributed itself around the lake the way it did and what effects man's planned intervention would have.

Since most of the data could be obtained only from an examination of the animals themselves, it meant a prolonged crocodile hunt. We collected 500 crocodiles as a statistically valid sample of the lake's population. We found ourselves spending most of the time grubbing about the carcasses of dead crocodiles measuring and observing and bottling parts for the laboratory.

To many people the pictures here of dissected crocodiles will appear as so many repellent "death images," and our activities altogether dubious. But scientists cannot let susceptibility to imagery or sentiment cloud their vision, for if they do they will cease to make impartial observations. Death, after all, is as common as birth, and at the point of discontinuity will even prevail. If there are death images in these pictures it is scarcely surprising, but you will not find in this book a crusade to eliminate crocodiles. On the contrary, you might catch a hint of a rather wistful daydream in which man in his wisdom and omnipotence grants asylum to a few crocodiles and other "vermin."

Sentimentally oriented preservationists will probably not find this account of our time at Lake Rudolf much to their taste. Not only are there too many pictures of crocs lying on their backs with their toes curled up, but we apparently did nothing but seek impartial information. We showed few signs of feeling sorry for the crocs, neither did we praise them. We forgot to denounce poachers and scold public indifference. Most suspicious of all, we failed to call for the outlawing of crocodile-skin handbags and alligator shoes.

To many sentimentalists the preservation of animals is a romantic cause to which they dedicate themselves in the secret hope of one day attaining to martyrdom. Theirs is a world of heroes and villains, no less among the animals than among the men. Heroes do that which men dream of, and with a flourish. Wildlife biologists equipped with firearms and mathematical probability more closely resemble villains, the bandits of sentiment and fancy. Population biologists can not afford themselves the luxury of getting involved in the lives of individual animals when it is the destiny of the whole species that concerns them.

It is unlikely, then, that our tale of Lake Rudolf will find a place on the Conservation Shelf beside the lion cubs, the fur-and-feather Schweitzers, and the orphans. Even if we desired this it would be no easy task, for there is nothing romantic about crocs, nothing cuddly. The potent symbolism of evil and terror that they hold for most people makes them outsiders.

In any case, the blind preservation of wildlife is too irrational, too much a part of neurotic compulsions arising out of inverted aggression and crippling sentiment, to be a realistic justification for "saving" crocodiles. The adoration of nature, conveniently packaged as it is today, is too often the worship of a lost childhood by disillusioned adults whose struggles toward a regained naïvité are often grotesquely successful. Nevertheless, we do share with preservationists a belief that somewhere in the wastelands and their wild animals lie beautiful things and truthful things, spiritual utilities that we will come to treasure more and more as the pace of life hastens and the space for life diminishes.

In our time on the lake we occasionally had the privilege of being able to sink for a moment into the solitude of nature, to touch the wilderness, and to know of creation. But such moments are rare and will never be ours simply because we wish it, like a love-gift from mother nature. We must work to make such experiences possible; we owe to ourselves to seek the truth about animals before fixing their destinies.

ALISTAIR GRAHAM

Nairobi, 1973

CHAPTER 1 A LAKE IN THE WILDERNESS

A most desolate and forlorn place—a case of Noachian Hydro-
phobia—monument to the Peace Corps—famine within famine—renewed acquaintance with McConnell,
fisherman & oracle—names my boat the Curse—a
paradox or two—plans laid for voyage across the lake—abundance of crocodiles on
the other side—a solitary fisherman.

Ferguson's Gulf is a barren spot in a wasteland of sand that morning after morning is whirled into a choking, blasting duststorm by a hot east wind gusting up to fifty m.p.h. The pounding mornings subside into sultry, brooding afternoons when the gulf dissolves into a mirage of burning air that leaves one breathless and weak. Nothing grows except tatty doum palms along the riverbed, scrubby bushes, and along the water's edge some spike grass with needle-sharp leaves. From a distance the pale brown water is marvelously refreshing to the traveler's eye; but it turns out green and greasy to the touch, and smells of rotting fish.

My immediate destination was the village of Kalokol, which sits on the bone-dry sand of the Kalokol riverbed where it feeds (on the rare days when water runs down it) into Lake Rudolf. At this point there is a two-mile-wide bay made by a long sandspit running northwards, parallel to the mainland, partially shielding the patch of water known as Ferguson's Gulf. Nobody seems to know much about Ferguson or what he did that his name stayed behind him, and looking at his gulf I could think of little good to say for it.

Not much happens at Kalokol. About a mile from the waterline is a low, sandy ridge, the ancient beach of a once deeper lake. Stuck on this rise, out in the open sand, is a tiny cluster of buildings exposed to the full force of the blasting wind. It is a missionary station, and we sometimes wondered if its cheerless position was due to an unconscious "Noah's Phobia," or fear of rising waters, that led to the choosing of the highest available ground; certainly there is a shed behind the station that contains a boat.

Down near the water's edge in a muddy extension of the gulf is the half-sunken remains of a Land-Rover. It is a monument to the Peace Corps, emissaries of hope from Technolopolis who from time to time astonish the Turkana with their earnestness. The mud is deep beneath the Land-Rover. Soon it will sink forever and be forgotten; in the meantime Turkana urchins atop its cab angle for catfish.

I arrived at Lake Rudolf alone on June 4, 1965. The lake had a reputation for being a difficult place—awkward to get to, uncomfortable when reached, and dangerous if meddled with. It lies in the Great Rift Valley just south of the Ethiopian highlands where they give way to the desert of northern Kenya—a 180-mile-long trough, 6 to 30 miles wide, of slippery green water, brackish enough to make one vomit and vindictive enough to make one hate. It can look innocently beautiful, glistening seductively in the morning sunlight; or ominous, like a huge brown slug

above:
Submerged monument to
the Peace Corps

opposite:
Landing near Bob
McConnell's hut on
Ferguson's spit

aestivating in the crippling afternoon heat when even the flies are torpid.

There are those who would hear this in astonishment saying that Lake Rudolf is a fabulous place, so exciting and wild. In fact, looking at things from the Turkana's standpoint—and they are the only inhabitants of the west side of Rudolf—excitement and wildness were the last sensations one might feel. Gazing at the heat-warped surroundings, I saw a few dull black vultures glide over the Gulf and turn and have another look. It was out of the question that they saw anything discarded from Kalokol that was worth stopping for, for the Turkana had had nothing anyway. What the vultures saw were dead people.

In 1924 the Government established a famine relief camp at Kalokol to give food to the many Turkana who were dying as a result of a severe famine. The camp was a great success, and in subsequent years more and more Turkana became famished until gradually a permanent village of professional needy developed. Children were born and raised there who grew up knowing only a life of plenty in a mythical famine—a twisted parody of existence in a land where real and desperate hardship is commonplace.

Not so long ago the Government decided that it was high time the famine ended. So that the community, by now several-thousand-strong, should become self-sufficient, they stopped issuing food and told the campers, who had over the years taken to intermittent fishing, to get down to it and feed themselves from the teeming lake.

What this meant for the older people was a hastened end to already flimsy lives. They had

come to the camp because the only other prospect was a miserable death. And they died i the camp these same deaths they hoped evade.

Occasionally, through this fly-blown, win blown Golgotha strode arrogant warriors, visit ors from the near-desert to the north and we that was the true home of the Turkana. The had left their herds of cattle and goats for while to see for themselves the remarkable sig of their own tribesmen living permanently one spot—not only that, but on the shores of th brack-water catching and eating fish. For th Turkana are true nomads, wanderers who sco settled, communal life, warriors who tend liv stock and dream of heroic battles. But the harsh homeland, though it stretched hundred of miles, was too small for them, even thoug the whole tribe numbered less than 200,000. T Turkana were overcrowded, and the poor ones, pushed so to speak to the fringe of th tribe, up against Lake Rudolf, were sufferir for it. The warriors saw this and returned their families with sad tales of terrible wretc edness.

The Turkana didn't really blame the Gover ment for the famine camp, and certainly not f closing it—that at least put an end to one kir of humiliation. Their bitterness was really f the destiny that pushed them against this brac ish lake and corrupted their warriors in fishermen. Warriors wet themselves with bloo not water.

What the vultures hungrily watched were th skeletons lying where they had dropped— front of their huts, at the stagnant water's edg or just out on the scorching sand. They sa it was starvation that killed them; but everyo: knew it was despair. "Such a shameful dea does not justify a burial," the Turkana said.

Ferguson's Gulf teems with fish life, for th hot shallow water, lush with algae, is an optim habitat for several species of commercial exploitable fish. So that the famine campe might prosper from the bounty at their feet th Government sent an expert fisherman, B McConnell, to show them how. McConn found that the Turkana already knew everythir there was to know about fishing, or so they to him. Since they resented the whole idea of fis ing anyway, it was difficult for them to adm its exponents. But after a while McConnell car to be respected by the Turkana. Though he do not own large flocks of goats, nor many wive he occupies the exalted position, for one destitute, of a mighty soothsayer whose opini is sought in the settlement of nearly all importa matters. If McConnell doesn't think it funn

it doesn't pay the Turkana to think it funny. What he says goes: "Catch more fish!" and everybody is out angling; "Rain!" and it rains.

The evening of my first day on the lake I sat with Bob McConnell outside his palm leaf dwelling on the tip of the sandspit that forms the mouth of the gulf. His house faced west, where every afternoon hot red sunsets burnt out the remnants of the day leaving delicate cool evenings that one savored as something specially valuable. All morning the frenetic wind had pursued and pummeled you; the afternoon heat had clutched at you; but the quiet evening enveloped you as if you had stepped into it from the tortuous day. You settled in your chair, dug your toes into the sand, and vowed "to take there the life the Gods send you." McConnell would gaze impassively at the sun and say nothing. He had already been there a long time already and spoke neither of the life of the Gods nor of leaving.

All the discomfort and ugliness of the day dissolves into the luminous evening. All is calm yet alive, and the pace of the people hastens. Sounds are clear and images sharp, for things are seen better when they can be heard too. A boat to set nets is launched with its own personal sounds: shouts and quiet dialogues, full of expectancy and vigor. Oars clump against wooden sides, rhythmic but not monotonous, for frequent interruptions are essential for the fishermen to make some particularly fine point or converse with the occupants of another boat. A blind man could sit and trace the course of a dozen activities, so clear is the air and conductive of sound. The water is dead flat and still; the smack of a fish is startling.

All the time the activity increases until, as darkness blots out the last smudges of light, there are people and boats everywhere. The Turkana love the evening, unfolding with the warm vibrant night that promises talk and laughter, life and love. Far beyond midnight there are whispers and screams, laughs and tears. Then the wind returns, early sometimes, or late, surreptitiously pooling all sounds. Eventually every noise is sucked up into the tyrant's hiss, and you are alone again.

Sitting outside the house on the spit, McConnell and I discussed the various relationships between men and animals that brought him on the one hand to draw fish from the lake, and me on the other, as he put it, "to count crocodiles."

I was on the lake representing my firm, Wildlife Services, on contract to the Kenya Game Department. We were to assess the biological status of the lake's crocodile population to help the department shape a policy towards an animal traditionally despised as a pest, though technically a game animal nowadays (and therefore worthy of conservation). McConnell was curious to hear why such interest was suddenly being shown in such low-ranking game. After learning that the idea had in fact originated from Wildlife Services, Bob observed that the Game Department was probably only humoring us; at least we were out of their hair up at Rudolf. Certainly the Department wasn't prepared to support the study materially. We were to finance it wholly out of what we could get for the skins of the five hundred crocs to be killed for investigation. Though this meant that money would be very short, it suited us, because we felt strongly that such investigations should support themselves.

But what McConnell really wanted to know was how we thought the crocs on Rudolf fitted in with the growing fishing interests there. The traditional outlook of fishermen towards crocs is one of enmity. Many years ago an old croc hunter, Eric von Hippel, was employed by a commercial fishing enterprise on Uganda's Lake Kyoga to exterminate crocodiles so that fishing could be improved. Von Hippel interpreted the situation unequivocally when he reminisced:

The local fishermen could not . . . have done better, or shown more tenacity, under the lash of the legions of crocodiles which at that time (1939) still held our lakes in their absolute and unchallenged sway . . . [I] could only watch with incredulous fascination as the scaly robbers, operating in packs of many hundreds, were forever tearing up, and feasting on the contents of all and any fishtraps set anywhere within their apparently limitless reach, while balancing their diet with anything else that would happen along, such as human beings, livestock, dogs, game

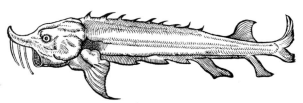

animals, and even birds on the wing . . . these crocodiles must be tackled with the utmost determination, or else commercial fishing by any method whatsoever would remain impossible.

We are inclined to dismiss such descriptions as sensational and exaggerated; but there's many a fisherman who *feels* that way about crocs.

As people interested in the rational handling of wildlife affairs we naturally disputed the fisherman's traditional view of crocodiles as unmitigated pests. If economic worth was the criterion by which things were being judged, then it was narrow-minded to exterminate crocs before finding out if they could be turned to good account. World demand for curiosity goods such as croc skin was increasing, while the supply was dwindling. The Okavango swamps in Botswana had been cleaned out. The Uganda Game Department had virtually exterminated crocs from that country, except for a population of about 2,000 in Murchison Falls National Park. The last few Ethiopian rivers with good croc populations, such as the Omo, were being ruthlessly hunted. This increasing scarcity of Nile crocodiles all over Africa meant an ever-rising value on their hides. Perhaps Lake Rudolf's crocs could be intelligently exploited rather than wiped out. The lake was as yet hardly fished—except by the small Turkana community at Kalokol and other places down the west shore, and by the El Molo over on the southeast shore at Loingalani—so there was ample opportunity to try croc harvesting. There was no reason per se why crocs *and* fish should not both be exploited. It would require only adaption of technique and outlook, plus competent scientific monitoring, to ensure maximal yields and forestall mistakes.

The technical aspects were easy enough. It was in the matter of outlook that problems could be expected. In the human concept of ownership lay the key to understanding. Ownership in the original sense is the claim to food, the instinct to gain control over food resources. It was a concept that evolved with communal living, particularly where there was a tendency to settle. For gregarious, sedentary communities to function harmoniously it was essential that basic food resources be *demonstrably* owned. The ownership of cultivated crops and domestic animals is unequivocal. But ownership of wild, unconstrained animals and plants is impossible. They are therefore instinctively regarded as free for

opposite:
Famine camp at Kalokol

following pages:
Turkana children
Lone hippo
The east shore

all, common property.

In the case of fish it is their invisibility that excepts them from the rule of demonstrable ownership. No one can claim specific individuals; this very anonymity combined with the apparent ubiquity of the fish not only denies claims but facilitates sharing. What is owned among fishermen is the right to fish, and the devices for catching.

The appeal of fishing is also bolstered by other features: the docility of fish, their palatability, their fecundity, and the fact that they are protein, the most prized of all foods. There is also the element of chance. There is always the gambler's possibility of an exceptional catch, of pulling up something unexpected.

Fishing is an ancient and honorable occupation; it may even have been the very first settled human cultural mode. That it became acceptable at all to the Turkana was remarkable. For the Turkana treasure their heritage of nomadic pastoralism, and typically scorn anything less than life as warriors and herdsmen. It was only the chronic, sometimes incredible, hardship of existence in their barren wilderness that forced the poorer, more desperate members of the tribe to resort to the lowly practice of fishing. To ask that they further humble themselves by catching crocs was asking a lot.

But all this was hypothetical. No one yet knew what the possibilities of cropping crocodiles were. In fact it was remarkable how little we did know of crocodiles. Until very recently our fund of facts about the species was accurately summed up in this paragraph from *Voyages to Africa*, written nearly three centuries ago, in 1698, by someone signing himself "T. C."

This River abounds not so much with Fish, and there is but one good sort called a Variole, but there are a vast number of Crocodiles in it, who no doubt devour the Fish; this is an Amphibious Creature, living at pleasure in the Water or on Land; the Head of it is flat above and below, and the Eyes of it indifferently big, and very darkish; they have a long sharp Snout, with long sharp Teeth, and no Tongue to be perceived; the Body large, and all of a bigness; the Back covered with high Scales like the Heads of large Nails, of a greenish Colour, so hard that they are proof against a Halbert; their Tails are very long, covered over with Scales, but the Belly is white and pretty tender; it has four short Legs, with five Claws on the foremost Feet, and but four on the Hinder. It grows as long as it Lives, and some are about 20 Foot from Head to Tail. These great ones many times snap young Children at Land, and sometimes put up their Noses, and pull People out of their Boats in the River; so that many go with Spikes to prevent them putting up their Noses; and it is dangerous to Swim where their Haunts are. But that they Weep when they have taken their Prey, is, from what I can find, a Fable. To take these Creatures, they make a great many Pits by the River Side, and cover them with rotten Sticks, so that passing over, the Sticks

142,209

give way, and they fall in; then Men let down a Rope with a running Noose, to muzzle their Snouts, and so they drag them up and kill them for their Skins, which they sell to Strangers for good Rates; none but the Moors will eat of their Flesh.

It was not until Dr. Hugh Cott of Cambridge published his detailed monograph on crocodile natural history in 1961 that our appreciation of the species advanced significantly beyond T. C.'s. Cott had made many new observations on crocs on his journeys round Zambia and Uganda. His data on individual crocs paved the way for our attempt to grasp an overall picture of a croc *population.* We still knew nothing of crocodile population dynamics—their food and shelter requirements, the scale of births and deaths within a population, the factors influencing natality and mortality, the structure in terms of age and sex, and so on. Why, for instance, did three-quarters of Rudolf's crocs concentrate on the northeast shore, avoiding almost the whole of the west shore except at one or two places, such as Ferguson's Gulf?

In order to solve these problems we planned to work on the east shore. This side of the lake is quite different from the west side, where Kalokol is. It is uninhabited by humans, except for the small El Molo settlement in the south. Occasional nomads reluctantly water their stock in the lake in dry years—otherwise the east shore is deserted. The nomads of the hinterland are wild, unpredictable people likely to turn bandit. At the time of our survey the region was also menaced by *shifta*—roving outlaws hostile to Kenya and sympathetic to the neighboring Somali Republic, which has long claimed much of northern Kenya. Because of the risk of banditry we planned to keep as mobile and unencumbered as possible while on the east side, storing gear when not in use at Kalokol. This meant crossing the lake every month, for skins had to be sold regularly in order to keep going. We planned to collect specimens alternately from two areas, Moite and Alia Bay.

Since money was a limiting factor equipment and supplies had to be cut to the bare minimum. One aspect of the work was imperative—continuity. Interruption of the collection of consistent data from regular, comparable samples of crocodiles through a twelve-month cycle would ruin the project. This obligation of continuity was to tax us harshly. At times the Turkana's notion of a malevolent lake-spirit actively working to block one's progress seemed entirely reasonable; it was impossible not to curse the lake for its innumerable obstacles and discomforts.

Since we would have to do everything ourselves, except skin the carcasses, we expected

to be kept busy. For most of the survey a friend and fellow crocophile, Peter Beard, joined me on the lake. He took over the exhausting, time-consuming daylight hunting, undeterred by the equally long, tiring night hunts that he also helped with. His apparently limitless energy and enthusiasm were indispensable catalysts to a sometimes flagging project; somehow he managed to turn each mishap into a laugh.

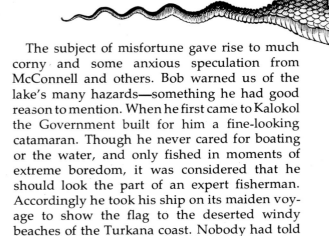

The subject of misfortune gave rise to much corny and some anxious speculation from McConnell and others. Bob warned us of the lake's many hazards—something he had good reason to mention. When he first came to Kalokol the Government built for him a fine-looking catamaran. Though he never cared for boating or the water, and only fished in moments of extreme boredom, it was considered that he should look the part of an expert fisherman. Accordingly he took his ship on its maiden voyage to show the flag to the deserted windy beaches of the Turkana coast. Nobody had told him that someone in the landlocked Fisheries H.Q., more knowledgeable than the boat's designer, had replaced the craft's inboard engines with outboards, modifying in the process the two stern sections. As a result the boat shipped water in a following sea—a circumstance that sank it quickly and very nearly drowned McConnell and his crew.

My own boat, a nineteen-foot converted lifeboat laboriously hauled up from Mombasa on the coast, was, McConnell thought, the very opposite of a lifesaving device. After seeing how long it took to make it seaworthy, Bob began referring to it as The Curse—a name that stuck fast for the rest of its short life.

On rational grounds the information we sought about crocodiles was justification enough for the quest. We stand poised to condemn crocodiles to obliteration, or to captivity and decay in national parks and zoos, or to indifferent dissolution—yet we know scarcely anything about them. Though this seemed unreasonable, it was really a personal opinion, not necessarily of relevance to the situation on Lake Rudolf. McConnell was not disparaging the project when he demanded to know its purpose and its place in the affairs of Lake Rudolf. (Or, when he once said ''I'll tell you all you need to know about crocodiles.'') He was a realist who observed that fishermen were thriving without anyone having first studied their fish for them. Why, he wanted to know, did I wish to disrupt events with facts about crocodiles? The Turkana did not care if crocs laid hard-boiled eggs or

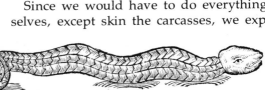

swam upside down. In their world there were quite literally only two important facts about crocodiles: they were evil and they were edible. It would not alter things for the Turkana to redefine crocodiles in biological terms.

As we sat talking in the night we often heard distant gunshots echoing across the gulf. It was the Game Department Scout out killing crocodiles. His job was to "control" crocodiles to protect the fishermen and their gear. Since crocodiles, in Kenya, are no longer vermin but "game" animals, they are legally state property. As such, the state is responsible not only for their protection from the public, but for their good behavior towards the public as well. Discipline among game animals is ensured by "controlling," *i.e.* punishing them. Since it is impossible to identify the specific culprits in the case of marauding crocodiles, the Game Scout simply shoots at them indiscriminately. In this way two or three hundred crocs are controlled every year in Ferguson's Gulf; altogether several thousand have been shot since the Fisheries Department set up shop there.

Hence the paradox: A sportsman may shoot a maximum of two Rudolf crocodiles there after establishing, tortuously, his bona fides. Alongside him the Game Scout is expected to kill as many as he can, by whatever method he pleases. The Turkana, living among the crocs, but neither sportsmen nor gamekeepers, may not molest crocodiles at all.

These aspects of game preservation led us on to the topic of conservation in the wider sense. Already there was talk of alienating the northeast shore of Rudolf as a game park. Bob wanted to know if it was really as game savers that Wildlife Services was coming in to study crocs. I denied any such mission, having no sentimental impulse to "save" crocodiles. If they needed saving it could only be from some disaster common to man as well. Fixation on the problems of crocodile destiny (as defined by humans) seemed like a displacement off the main issue—our own destiny. Those who take wildlife seriously are too often driven before a sentimental despair whose nature is so obscure as to make them defy all reason. The preservation of wildlife is an epic of contrariness—an oscillating love-hate affair of arbitrary laws, impractical ethics, quasi-research, exterminations, rescues, management programs, poaching and anti-poaching and so forth. Those who would advance a rational outlook on wildlife, calling for an objective assessment of wildlife in the light of practical human interests, are taken for cynics and denounced as saboteurs. Yet the intransigent demand of emotional game savers—that wildlife must not be touched by man—seemed a hopeless, almost suicidal ideal in the face of inexorable human expansion.

This impartiality towards crocs was not likely to endear our project to the conservationists. A great deal of what masquerades as wildlife research is really self-indulgence on the part of donors and acceptors of "grants" concerned, consciously or not, more with bolstering the myth of a pristine, totally unfathomable nature than with explaining its workings. In the words of Thoreau, "At the same time that we are earnest to explore and learn all things, we require that all things be mysterious and unexplorable, that land and sea be infinitely wild, unsurveyed and unfathomed by us because unfathomable." Bob's earlier remark about counting crocodiles touched on a little-recognized but significant aspect of the Mowglian mystique of conservation. To many animal lovers there is something ominous about an intent to count, something they intuitively dislike, an impertinence. Such difficult-to-pin-down sensations are not peculiar to conservationists. There is an ancient myth about the evil of census taking: The Old Testament tells how King David was provoked by an angry God to census Israel. His lieutenants were horrified. "Why does the King wish this thing?" Sure enough, after the census the Lord visited a pestilence on Israel, killing 70,000 people. As an indirect way of discrediting King David in the eyes of his subjects, tempting him to a census was unbeatable.

The fear of being counted, or of counting, has to do with the primitive belief that misfortune is an active force in the external world waiting to punish the wicked. As such it can be invoked by one's enemies, or inflicted by a malicious deity. To count people is to expose them and therefore to render them vulnerable. To count is akin to touch—and to touch is to want. The instincts involved are possessive, *aggressive* ones. To *know* another's details is to reveal a covetousness.

Conservationists cherish a fantasy of communion with a mysterious nature. As such they fear objectivity. Under these conditions science is employed to rationalize the sentiments, not to ferret out the truth. Luckily both Lake Rudolf and its crocodiles were still remote from the temples of preservation, so at least the work could be done in peace.

Nevertheless, on the eve of our departure for the east shore to begin work I felt a sense of deep, though indistinct, misgiving. What we were about to do would probably help dispel those very qualities of the wasteland that are so delicate and valuable. The conservationist who desperately tries to re-create and preserve an unfathomable nature—perhaps he is better off in his defiance of reality. When Thoreau concluded "It is not worth the while to go round the world and count the cats in Zanzibar," he touched on a fundamental truth. It would probably gain neither myself nor anyone else much to count the crocs on Rudolf. It would bring the avarice and vandalism of technological man a little closer. It would take away some of the wildness and privacy of the place. It would add to our knowledge of a little-known species of animal. But in the course of time it would take its due place as just another ripple on the tidal wave of human expansion.

In the late afternoons after working on the boat we would walk around the spit thinking ahead and planning. Far out in the gulf crocodiles could often be seen, but only as distant black specks. These crocs, contrary to their species' habit, rarely came ashore, for one seldom found their telltale tracks and belly marks on the beach. No doubt the Turkana's hostility kept them warily afloat, apparently none the worse for forfeiting the many hours of rest on land that crocs normally take every day. Here and there as one gazed across the gulf schools of flatfish would suddenly start jumping, ruffling an acre or more of calm water with their seemingly random eruptions. There was no evidence to suggest that their leaping was the result of attacks from predators, or was related to their own plankton feeding. It often struck me how little we know about even the most familiar animals; though flatfish are the chief commercial fish in the gulf, and their jumping an everyday occurrence, its function remains quite obscure.

Sodden cormorants hung themselves out to dry on the tattered fronds of drowned palm trees in the gulf, their throats wildly shivering as if with a dreadful ague; beneath them waded big, solitary goliath herons, impeccably neat and dry. Most afternoons a lone hippo eased out of the murky water onto the shore below Bob's thatched hut, to crop the tiny patch of spike grass there. It grazed confidently among the children playing in the sand, surrounded by an undrawn but unequivocal circle of respect.

We often walked to the end of the spit where an old man fished, always in exactly the same place, at the very point of the spit where it curls round into the gulf. He had his own method of fishing, one that only a Turkana could conceive of or employ. He simply stood at the water's edge and threw a spear into the lake,

retrieving it by a rope tied to its end. At first I was curious and looked over his shoulder, so to speak, in the hopes of seeing the fish I presumed he saw. But then I realized there was nothing to be seen in the gray-green, turbid water. He simply assumed that one day a fish would swim by at the instant his spear drove in, to be impaled on the inevitability of its own destiny.

The old man never tired, or lost faith, and he was very dignified. It seemed to me that he had refined the art of fishing down to its essential elements, and I could think of no better method to suggest to him.

CHAPTER 2 BASSO NAROK, THE BLACK LAKE

*Astir betimes—a desolate land—volcanic districts—
a poison-spitting snake—a startling hunting episode—on the shores of Lake Rudolf—
an aquatic race—remains of a catastrophe—trials during a hurricane—
curious fish—a melancholy event—
an exultant tribe—fabulous elephants—rapacity of a vulture—a gladdening
feast—vexatious disablement—grateful recompense—forbidden to go further—physiography of Lake Stefanie—a successful hippopotamus hunt— no
posho!—forced to plunder— a tragic scuffle—
anticipation and realization.*

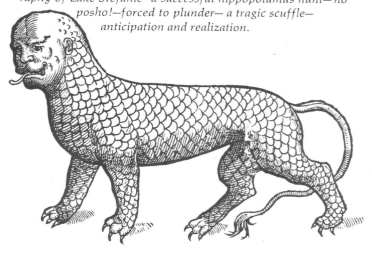

On the eve of my first crossing of Lake Rudolf, I thought back on the historic exploration of Teleki and von Höhnel in 1888 to locate Africa's last great lake. Though my destination, Moite Mountain, was only twenty-eight miles by boat from Kalokol, it might have been another country (indeed the Turkana said it was) for all the resemblance it bore to the relatively civilized west shore. It was from Moite that the discoverers of Rudolf set off on what was to prove the most desperate march of an altogether formidable journey. In the seventy-seven years since their caravan struggled along the lake shore the country has become a little drier and, in a rare reversal of the usual trends in Africa, even less used by humans. So I would see it as Teleki and von Höhnel saw it, a fact that sharpened my curiosity about their journey and imparted a sort of agelessness to the terrain; it was exciting to be able to peer into the circumstances of an historical adventure.

Ludwig Ritter von Höhnel was a young naval lieutenant whose connections in Austrian society enabled him to accompany the wealthy Count Teleki's expedition as geographer and recorder. Von Höhnel described their exploits in the aloof, constrained kind of narrative that is so characteristic of the nineteenth-century explorers. To perceive the immensity of their adventures we have to illuminate their accounts with our own imaginations—the veracity of which is heightened if at the same time we can scan the identical physical surroundings.

Explorers of unknown Africa were strange men, in a way. Driven by irresistible urges to penetrate and "discover" the menacing, mysterious, yet inviting wilderness, they were at the same time tremendously cautious and reserved.

Actually there are sound psychological reasons why the first explorers of an area apparently exercised so little imagination. "Let them wander and scrutinize the outlandish Australians. I have more of God, they more of the road." Thoreau's neat misquotation touches upon the enigma of why they said so little about so much. For them there *was* too much of the road. Their tasks were so laborious, their fears so horrifying, and disaster so omnipresent that they could not afford to see or feel more than was absolutely necessary. They were bound to repress sensation and concentrate all their energies on a single, often banal, goal. If they had not, they would have been overwhelmed.

Daniel Schneider, in *The Image of the Heart* and later writings, points out that contrary to what has been supposed, the mind *does* have an image of internal organs, particularly the heart. This image is monitored by a system—the paraconscious—that warns of imminent danger and protects the heart from sudden shock. This shield is strongest when unknown dangers are prevalent. Though the explorers performed prodigious feats they did so only along narrow, relatively *predictable* paths. That which was wholly unknown and terrifying was fended off by the paraconscious shield. The open road was too much for them; they had to set up their own limited lanes of progression. Hence their disappointingly deficient accounts. It *had* to be that way, or the wilderness would have been too shocking, too overwhelming. We who follow them have the trails blazed; we can risk looking about us, safe in the knowledge that there is no longer anything totally unknown to be afraid of. We can unleash our imagination for we will not be shocked at what it brings out from under the stones.

Many times we passed through the same territory Teleki and von Höhnel had traveled to the lake. Only on rare occasions did we gain insights into the terrors of starvation, isolation, sickness and death that must have accompanied them every day. Our camps were often where theirs had been but there was much difference in the dimension of our positions. Today, with the advent of fishing camps and fisherman tourists there is a world of difference between what these recent visitors see and what Peter Beard and I saw.

Teleki began to turn the dream of an African expedition into reality early in 1886. At first he planned only a hunting trip to Lake Tanganyika. But von Höhnel spoke of the unknown country south of the Ethiopian highlands where, legend had it, there was a great lake. It took little to persuade Teleki, and planning a journey of several years, they set off from Zanzibar on January 23, 1887, in search of the legendary lake.

To carry their food and equipment they hired 668 porters, guides, and bodyguards. Their successes would be in no small part due to one of their guides, Qualla Idris, upon whom they placed immense reliance. Only twenty-four, he had already been to America, "was for six years one of Stanley's truest and most faithful followers in the Congo," had traveled to Europe with Stanley, and then had guided an expedition

Teleki losing 97 lbs.

to Somalia. How many men his age in this day of jets and cars have experienced a fraction of such adventure?

From Zanzibar they sailed for Pangani in the Sultan's steamship, the *Star*. After a miserable night on board, soaked by rain, they were shipwrecked at the mouth of the Pangani River, leaving von Höhnel "not a little exercised in my mind as to whether this mishap at the outset was or was not a bad omen for our journey."

They reached their initial objective, Lake Baringo, after an eventful seven-month safari. On this 500-mile leg they drew their first blood hunting African game, and Teleki found time to climb Mount Kenya to the snowline, about 14,000 feet, the highest ascent made up to then. While traveling through Kikuyuland they were three times attacked by large bands of warriors against whom they had to fight for their lives. Lake Baringo, then the most northerly stopping place for caravans, was noted in Zanzibar as a place of peace and plenty. They looked forward immensely to their arrival there, planning to rest and provision themselves for their journey into the real wilderness of the north. They had no means of knowing that 1887 and 1888 were to be exceptionally bad famine years; thus they arrived at Baringo, only to find it famished and dejected. To cap it, von Höhnel fell seriously ill with dysentery.

They spent several months at Baringo trying to accumulate enough food to go north. Eventually they were forced to send Qualla back into hostile Kikuyuland with a force of 117 men to buy food. He returned with enough for them to make a meager start. But at this point von Höhnel's worsening dysentery led him to despair of his life. (Later he would collapse again at another crucial stage in their journey.)

All this time I was chained to my bed . . . on January 24 there seemed little hope of my recovery. On the evening of that day I felt a strong desire for sleep, and thinking that my wornout spirit was about to

be loosed from my emaciated body at last, I closed my weary eyes, convinced that I was falling into my last long unconsciousness. I woke again about 4 o'clock the next morning, but it was a long time before I realized that I was still alive, and I asked myself again and again, where am I? Am I really not yet dead? Then I remembered that the Count had stood before my bed the evening before, asking me how I felt, and I had answered, all hope having left me, that I was near my end. After that a grey veil had shrouded everything from me, and I had died. But how was it now? Had I indeed awakened in eternity? But surely that was a cock crow I heard. Was I to live after all? For a long time I could not believe it, and yet when I called to Chuma he appeared.

Now they were delayed while von Höhnel recovered. Of their original 668 men only 238 remained. Many had deserted and a number had died of disease or fighting the Kikuyu. On February 9 they felt able to start. They had food for only two weeks, but despite that and their poor condition, everyone set off in high spirits with ''much enthusiastic shouting,'' for there is even in the most timid an exhilaration at the start of a long journey. But, as if enough omens had not already been received, an alarm was raised of an impending attack from the Suk, a nomadic tribe from the northwest. The caravan turned back to Baringo to defend itself, only to discover that the alarm was false. Nothing dampens spirits more than false starts, and in contrast to the elated crew of the day before, it was a subdued caravan that finally left Baringo the next day for the unknown.

Of the country to the north they knew very little. That it was hot, dry, and uninhabited was common knowledge. How far and in what direction one had to go before again meeting people no one knew. A speculative sketch map drawn by Joseph Thomson in 1884 showed a ''large salt lake, about 100 miles long,'' and another smaller lake, stuck in a blank tract of country. The distance was said to be about 150 miles. That was all.

Leaving Baringo they climbed east out of the Rift Valley onto the Lorogi plateau, then marched north towards a chain of mountains. These they named the Mathews Range after General Mathews who had done much to help them in Zanzibar. This was their first geographical discovery.

Here began the first of a series of grueling marches that were to test their stamina to the limit. Heading for a vaguely described area called Barsaloi they struck a dry riverbed in which they hoped to find water. They dug all night, in many places, before they found any; and it seeped into their holes so slowly that it was a whole day before everyone had drunk. Their really hard times were just beginning.

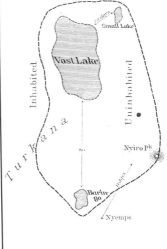

Samuel Teleki von Szek

This was a crucial stage. They had come to a virtual desert. The threat of thirst made an immediate decision imperative. Approximately fifty miles away loomed the outline of a mountain, which their guide called Nyiro, where people were said to live. It was the only place likely to have water, but to get there meant a dry march of at least two days. The men were already weak and dispirited; though Teleki very nearly turned back he finally decided to go on, well aware of the risks. Starting at 2:30 on the morning of February 26, with each porter carrying an almost incredible eighty to one-hundred pound load, they marched with only two short stops until eight that night. The country, as expected, was absolutely dry and deserted. They did thirty tortuous miles in eighteen hours that day. Next morning they faced the same prospect; and now the men began to fail, first one and then another crumpling under his load. Seven hours and nineteen miles later they found water in a slimy swamp in the foothills of Nyiro. It saved their lives. By sending water back to those who had collapsed the caravan gradually collected; but four men died that day, and the survivors were at the limit of their endurance. They had covered forty-nine miles in fifty-nine hours, carrying back-breaking loads. They had crossed the desert to Mount Nyiro, but the place they had come to seemed uninhabited and altogether hopeless; nor had they any means of telling if they were on the right track.

But the next day they did come across some people who proved friendly—indeed they could hardly be otherwise, living half-starved on the

**Fellow stalwart
Ludwig Ritter von Höhnel**

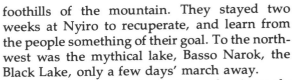

foothills of the mountain. They stayed two weeks at Nyiro to recuperate, and learn from the people something of their goal. To the north-west was the mythical lake, Basso Narok, the Black Lake, only a few days' march away.

Having accumulated about ten days' supply of food, they set off.

The scenery became more and more dreary as we advanced. The barren ground was strewn with gleaming, chiefly red and green volcanic debris, pumice stone, huge blocks of blistered lava and here and there pieces of petrified wood. There was no regular path and we had to pick our way carefully amongst the scoriae, some of which were as sharp as knives. And this glaring monotony continued until 2 o'clock. The good spirits which the thought that we were nearing the end of our long tramp had filled us in the morning had long since dissipated . . . and we were disposed to think the whole thing a mere phantasmagoria.

The void down in the depths beneath became filled as if by magic with picturesque mountains and rugged slopes, with a medley of ravines and valleys, which appeared to be closing up from every side to form a fitting frame for the dark green gleaming surface of the lake stretching away beyond as far as the eye could reach . . . full of enthusiasm and gratefully remembering the gracious interest taken in our plans from the first by his Royal and Imperial Highness, Prince Rudolf of Austria, Count Teleki named the sheet of water, set like a pearl of great price in the wonderful landscape beneath us, Lake Rudolf.

The date was March 5, 1888.

They must have been tremendously excited. It was over a year since they had left Zanzibar and here at last was a fantastic discovery, a fitting reward for their determination and toil; a somewhat dubious objective had become a reality. And the inviting, cool, green water below them dispelled the spectre of thirst.

But the lake was to prove hostile to those who disturbed its tranquility. It was still a day's march to the lake shore over frightful terrain.

Narrow valleys were encumbered with stones and debris, or with deep loose sand in which our feet sunk making progress difficult. And when the sun rose higher its rays were reflected from the smooth black surface of the rock, causing an almost intolerable

glare, whilst a burning wind from the south whirled the sand in our faces, and almost blew the loads off the heads of the men . . . although utterly exhausted we felt our spirits rise . . . rushed down shouting into the lake . . . clear as crystal . . . and, bitter disappointment; the water was brackish.

Another man had died on this leg and the physical and mental condition of the rest was bad. Theirs was an epic discovery that would forever associate their names with Africa; but the plight they now found themselves in was, if anything, worse than before. They had come, uninvited, to a bitter desert, shunned by all other forms of life. They had food for only eight days. Knowing what lay behind them, they could not turn back. Von Höhnel, who kept a diary of their journey, makes no mention of this, nor of their ideas for ultimately getting back, but it must have been a recurrent worry. Although they saw many fish in the lake they were, inexplicably, unable to catch them. They had to drink the nauseating salty water, for there was no other. Of wild animals there was no sign. Yet this was what they had come for, to battle with nature and to prevail; to explore, discover and succeed, and their resolve did not fail them, though it faltered.

It is in the record of their marches that one sees them beginning to waver. For the most part Teleki was a single-minded man who led the expedition as if he were commanding a military force. But in the next week he permitted two exceptions to his choice of route along the lake shore, deviations that were time-wasting and fruitless, and in retrospect difficult to understand. The first was a sudden march inland towards Mount Kulal, where they vaguely hoped to "improve their prospects." They soon abandoned the idea, but not before they saw something that did little to improve their peace of mind. "We came upon a regular heap of camel's bones. There must have been the remains of some two hundred animals in one pile, and although the bones were already bleaching in the sun, there was still an odor

Desert feast, from Teleki's photograph

of putrid flesh upon them. We were at a loss to understand how such a number of animals could have fallen in one place, for the natural position in which the skeletons lay proved that they had not been carried here, but had lain as they fell." Arthur Neumann, the first to follow Teleki's footsteps to Lake Rudolf, eight years later came across the same bones. The sight depressed him greatly too, and he wrote apologetically that he suddenly had grave doubts about his position and for the first time in all his wanderings, felt really frightened. The wind and isolation and feelings of death at the end of a dried-up world started to reach him.

Teleki's second detour was nearly fatal. On March 9 his party camped at Loingalani Springs, the only fresh water along the east shore. On the thirteenth they passed the symmetrical, conical hill called Por, on which inscrutable abstract rock engravings are to be found.

At this point von Höhnel's journal provides another insight into their state of mind. He wrote: "We collected most of our facts relating to the extent of the lake and the course of its shores, a duty which, it will be readily understood, we rigidly performed in our anxious and precarious position." To the explorer, knowing where he is relative to where he has come from is perhaps the most important contribution to his peace of mind. The ultimate in hopelessness is to be lost. So long as he knows his position there is always hope. That is why von Höhnel so carefully took his sightings—in the interests of confidence, not cartography.

Early the following morning one of the men took off into the bush, never to be heard of again. The strain was telling. And that day Teleki, who would have followed the lake shore, listened instead to disastrous advice. Looming up ahead was Moite Mountain; to avoid the obviously rough going round its rocky base where it fell away into the lake, they were persuaded by their guides to go behind it, a detour that would take them a long way inland—away from the repellent but life-sustaining lake water.

On the night of the sixteenth they found a little water by digging in a riverbed. On the night of the seventeenth they found no water and so began the march of the eighteenth in very bad shape, starving, thirsty and exhausted, and without the all-important incentive of knowing that water was ahead. Teleki went on in front to try to shoot some meat. Luckily he killed an elephant and a rhino, which went a long way towards saving their lives, though the men by now had to be forced to eat. The rest of the caravan, on reaching a riverbed which proved waterless, gave up. Von Höhnel wrote: "The men were lying about staring vacantly before

them; loads and animals were in the most hopeless confusion; donkeys and sheep wandering aimlessly about, not an Askari or a donkey boy to be seen anywhere. All discipline was at an end and the men were utterly demoralized."

He must have thought they were finished. He had no way of knowing that Teleki, only two hours ahead, had found water by digging deeply at the base of a cliff in the sandy riverbed. Water to be sure, but as at Barsaloi, it seeped into their excavation so slowly that even the few men who had gone on ahead could not slake their thirst until long after dark. All through the night and into the morning of the nineteenth they sent back water to those who had collapsed. Gradually men straggled in. As the crowd around the water grew they began to fight over it and had to be subdued by force.

By morning most of the loads had been brought in. The caravan headed back towards the lake, having passed the range of hills running north from Moite. They made the shore in three hours but it was not until midday that Qualla came in with the stragglers and the news that four men had died in the night.

Alia, an El Molo settlement on Lake Rudolf

The place they had come to was Alia Bay, with people, and herds of elephant, zebra, buffalo, and antelope. Two tiny islands in the bay supported an El Molo settlement of about sixty huts. These people, who had never seen or heard of white men, thought they must be cannibals and were at first reluctant to meet them. The feminine-looking *kanzus* the Swahili porters wore puzzled them too, for they thought the caravan was of women. Today Alia Bay is deserted, with no trace of those El Molo settlements.

facing page:
Who was the master
engraver? Chipped images
found seven miles
inshore along an
old waterline hundreds
of feet above the
present lake shore.

following pages:
The Black Lake, with South
Island, "the isle of
no return"

Teleki and von Höhnel were ardent sportsmen, shooting indiscriminately at anything that moved. Though armed with the best rifles capable of propelling bullets clean through an elephant, they were appalling marksmen, and it was due only to sheer firepower that they ever killed anything. When hunting they would happily blast away all day until darkness forced a ceasefire or the survivors had limped out of range. Their elephant hunt in Alia Bay was typical. Teleki had killed three elephants and wounded many others in the bush behind Alia. Two of the wounded staggered off into the shallow lake where they stood belly deep, out of range. One animal escaped during the night and in the morning the Count sent Qualla with their canvas boat, laboriously carried from the coast, to finish off the survivor. Approaching the beast, Qualla fired a dozen shots from point-blank range without effect. Assuming, as sportsmen do, that the animal's stubborn vitality was due to the gun's feebleness rather than the gunman's, he returned for a heavier weapon. Once again he approached closer and closer, firing steadily, at which the elephant

suddenly charged with inconceivable fury, dashing the water around into foam. In the twinkling of an eye he was upon the fragile craft, which he first shoved before him for a little distance, and then seized with his trunk. He shook it, crushed it, tossed it about, and then contemptuously flung it aside. Finally without taking the slightest further notice of the men, or of the shots which Qualla continued to fire, he marched with slow and stately steps through the water, and disappeared behind a peninsula. This unexpected end of the struggle annoyed us very much, as we should probably greatly need our canvas boat in our further wanderings.

Thus the first boat launched on Lake Rudolf was also the first one sunk; as it happens, our own boat lies on the lakebed in Alia Bay, ironically close to the spot where Teleki's sank.

The caravan continued. Their objective now was the north end of the lake where dwelt the Reshiat, a large tribe, who, the guides assured them, could supply food in plenty. The increasing fertility of the country as they traveled on was encouraging, though they had no means of knowing how the Reshiat would receive them.

A wounded elephant destroys the boat Teleki laboriously transported all the way from Zanzibar within minutes of its first launching. We were later to lose our boat in almost the same spot at Alia Bay

Qualla

On April 4 they arrived at last in Reshiat and were welcomed fearlessly by an attractive people who readily bartered with them for food. Here they could pause and rest. The men could recover their strength and spirits, and Teleki and von Höhnel could once more plan the rest of the journey uncolored by the constant threat of starvation and thirst. And it did not take these men long to recover. In three weeks they were itching to be gone again, off into the wasteland to see what lay there. The Reshiat spoke of Basso Ebor, the white lake to the east, and inevitably the two men had to go there.

It proved an easy march of only a few days and on April 20, 1888, they had their first sight of the lake. It was much smaller than Rudolf, only seventy miles long by fourteen wide. This water too was brackish and had evidently been receding for some time. It contained many crocs and some hippo, and in the surrounding bush were elephant, rhino, and buffalo.

They called it Lake Stefanie, in honor of her Imperial Highness Archduchess Stefanie, widow of Crown Prince Rudolf, such being the fashion of the day. The lake has long since dried up, leaving only a patch of cracked mud that occasionally turns into a malodorous ooze.

It was here that the unfrolicsome Count Teleki gave way at last to jubilation over their discoveries. At no point in his book does von Höhnel take the liberty of commenting on the Count. He seldom even mentions his own feelings, apart from observing that things were going either well or badly with them. But their recuperation at Reshiat, topped off with another discovery, was too much for them, and safe from censorious eyes, they gave themselves up to revelry.

This day, on which we had achieved the last aim of our long expedition, was celebrated, to the best of our ability, by us and our people, with all the means at our disposal. We brewed ourselves a bowl of foaming liquor, made, it is true, of nothing but honey, water, tartaric acid, and doubly distilled carbonic acid, but which tasted delicious, and we emptied it with an enthusiastic "Hip, Hip, Hurrah!" in honour of the royal pair with those names it is our proud priviledge to associate all the geographical results of our arduous undertaking. Our people organized a fete in the afternoon . . . hoisted Count Teleki onto their shoulders and carried him to the accompaniment of much shouting and firing of guns.

Imagine this tiny band of people in one of the most remote spots on earth, hogsnarling drunk with triumph and carbonic acid, yelling and screaming into the impassive night. One moment they were there and the next they were gone; all around them the silent bush, unmoving and unmoved.

As Donaldson-Smith pointed out later, the normally meticulous von Höhnel fixed the position of Lake Stefanie some 20 miles east of its true location. One wonders at the actual contents of their "bowl of foaming liquor." At all events the party was a good one.

Having explored a little in the country to the north of Reshiat and accumulated a good stock of food, they set off on the return trip on May 14. Knowing the way now, they marched with confidence, making the southern end of the lake in sixteen days. They covered 235 miles in ninety marching hours, averaging fifteen miles a day. By comparison, their terrible journey north had taken twenty-eight days. Shortly after they left Reshiat they missed one of the men, who several days later was seen following the caravan. He had contracted smallpox and correctly guessing that he would not be allowed to accompany the caravan, decided to follow unseen at a distance. He was ordered to continue in the same way, living off food that was left behind. They never saw him again.

With their new-found hope and vigor they were able to pause awhile at the southern end of the lake to study its scarred terrain. Monstrous upheavals had torn up the stark land leaving a jumble of mountains, cliffs, deep gorges, and jagged boulders. Coal-black lava had been spewed out everywhere over the older red-brown rocks. By day the region was a sun-fired furnace through which howled a searing wind. At night the shadows and the cliffs were one, and the starlight sparkled off the waves of the lake below. All was desolation, lifeless and deserted.

Neumann passed through this part of Lake Rudolf eight years later. He wrote: "A violent gale blew unceasingly day and night. It seemed to come down like an avalanche from Mount Kulal rushing into the deep basin of the lake sometimes in terrific gusts. At times it was difficult even to stand, and cooking and eating were conducted under disadvantages. Nothing would stop on the table, the very tea was blown out of one's cup, while the black sand and small stones got into the food and filled one's bed at night."

It is like that to this day.

In these bleak surroundings are many ancient rock paintings, some of them exceedingly beautiful, created by Stone Age artists. Their like has disappeared completely, for the occasional nomads of today neither produce art nor have any notion of the paintings' origins. There is an elephant whose outline is exactly that of a mammoth; there are graceful giraffe, and greater kudu with fantastic spiraling horns; there are rhino, oryx and goats—a mystical exhibition in a tumbled gallery of fractured boulders.

Reshiat, 1888

El Molo, 1968

Turkana, 1888

preceding pages: Looking back, Teleki and von Höhnel could see Nabuyatom crater," the place of the Warhorns," at the south tip of the lake. Behind it belching fire and smoke, was Teleki's volcano, now dormant. Austin called this area "an abomination of desolation."

The only photograph we could find of Teleki during his Rudolf walk

At the lake's southern extremity, its base in the water, stands a symmetrical extinct volcano—Nabuyatom, "place of the war-horns," the Turkana call it. Halfway up the slopes of the great volcanic barrier behind Nabuyatom (which Austin later called "an abomination of desolation") Teleki's party came upon an active crater spewing out dense clouds of black smoke. They named it Teleki's Volcano. Within a few years it was dormant and Cavendish in 1898 thought it had destroyed itself. The Turkana, always ready with an explanation, told him that "six months ago the lake overflowed and as the water rushed towards the mountain there was a vast explosion, after which the water swept in where the volcano had been and put out the fire." But in fact it is still there, a small cluster of cinder cones difficult to make out from a distance. Though dormant now, the patches of boiling water that appear from time to time in the lake far below are evidence of the volcanic potential beneath it.

The expedition now turned north again, this time up the west side of the lake, heading for Turkanaland. Though they were the first white men ever to go there, the haughty Turkana were unimpressed, treating them as they treated all visitors—with exaggerated disdain. Severe famine made it almost impossible for them to get food, so that once again they were menaced with starvation. The Turkana medicine men concentrated on prodding Teleki into making rain, evidently considering this his only useful func-

tion. As a rainmaker he clearly had potential—why else would he be such a peculiar color? For his services they were willing to exchange large numbers of cattle. Teleki, desperately short of food, was keen to make a deal, but the old witch doctors proved crafty businessmen. They demanded, before any covenant, a few drops of Teleki's brand of rain. Since it seemed unlikely that it would ever rain again in the drought-stricken country around them, Teleki had to refuse, and no deal was made. From their first contact with Europeans, the Turkana found them falling short of expectations.

The expedition marched out of Turkanaland as soon as possible, glad to leave its vulgar people, and headed southeast for Baringo. They were soon in trouble. Every place they came to was famished and in a few days they too were starving. The entire caravan subsisted at

The lurking places of darkness....

one point on wild figs, berries, mushrooms and weeds. They even raided weaver birds' nests for the eggs and fledglings. Eventually they were at their wit's end. Von Höhnel was prostrate with fever, unable to walk. A third of the men were too weak to carry their loads. There was but one last resort, and they took it—piracy.

They were in Suk country, and scattered about were a number of *manyattas* with the cattle and goats they so desperately needed, but which the owners would not trade. They decided to plunder. Qualla attacked a manyatta at dawn with the forty strongest men, while the rest of the caravan tried to put as much distance as possible between them and any pursuers. The raid was successful—their superior numbers and the suddenness of the attack putting the Suk to flight. Such raiding is, however, in the hearts of all nomads, and before long a fight developed while the spoils were being driven away. The Suk were no match for Qualla, though, and soon conceded defeat. The caravan lost three men, but the booty enabled them to reach Baringo.

Once again they had made it against tremendous odds. At Baringo, Teleki weighed only 141 pounds, a considerable reduction from his 238 pounds recorded in Zanzibar. They were soon in sufficiently good spirits to calmly plan returning by way of Karamoja, thence south toward Narok, and back to the coast via Serengeti, for all the world like a package tourist excursion. But for various reasons they reluctantly gave up that plan and returned by a more

direct route, reaching Zanzibar on October 26, 1888. Their journey had lasted one year and nine months, during which they had walked nearly two thousand miles, and made many important geographical discoveries.

Although the lake we lived and worked on was still Teleki's lake, more or less, our presence marked the end of that era. For we came to Rudolf only because changes were being planned. In particular, the talk of a national park was depressing. Such sanctuaries seem to be made only in the wake of menacing expansion—apologies of paradise for the sins of human violence, aggression and selfishness. To see a park made where there is only wilderness would be infinitely sad, for it demonstrates a very real threat, a warning of man's imminent, merciless presence.

CHAPTER 3 THE TITANIC SAILS AT DAWN

*Maiden voyage of the Curse—strike uncharted obstacle and
founder—no signs of crocs—numbering the days of their lives—fabulous tradition—riverhorse snags a mugger—
numerous pack of hyena gorge upon our net—snares fouled by disagreeable lion—three
wizened enigmas—marauding tribesmen
massacre peaceful nomads—the elongated limb of the law—audacious
panther prowls our camp—a man taken by God—
shagged with horrors—the devil's mafia—cannibals—symbols of evil—
Lucifer's lieutenant the Great Lutembe—
ambiguous amphibians—Saurian City—the foundation
of New Crocodilopolis.*

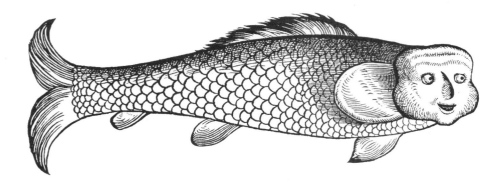

At three o'clock in the afternoon, having waited till then for the wind to drop, we were ready to leave on our first voyage across Lake Rudolf. The crew of four Turkana skinners made dismal farewells to their fellows, which I considered rather discouraging since we were due to return in a few weeks. There was no laughter or chatter; nothing but glum faces, and wistful looks at people and places previously taken for granted. A few coarse jokes from the ever-present swarms of children were our only sendoff; the silent adults clearly regarded the whole expedition as a mad circus led by a lunatic.

We headed out of the gulf onto a silky-surfaced lake heaving reminiscently of the windblown morning. Leaving Central Island to our right, we sailed for the east shore, visible twenty miles away as a line of jagged hills (the hills behind which Teleki's caravan nearly died of thirst). The smoothness of the passage had begun to soothe the suspicious Turkana when about halfway across the engine suddenly stopped. The crew stared at me while I stared at the engine. Nothing appeared to be wrong with it, and when I restarted it, it ran as if nothing had happened. Nobody spoke. They just sat looking miserably over the side, regretting bitterly their foolishness in agreeing to undertake the mission. We slept

that night on the shingly east shore, and in the cold morning followed the coastline south to Moite, where I planned to camp for a large portion of the survey.

This was the first time any of us aboard the Curse had been to the east shore of Rudolf, and we gazed curiously at our surroundings. The water was clean and clear compared to the west shore, where constant surf churned up a dirty suspension of sand and mud. Here, gray shingle beaches gave a refreshing look to the lake. But the nauseating taste of the brackish, soapy water was the same, and even after a year of drinking it we never got used to it.

In the morning sunlight the lake was a beautiful faded green that lightened towards the crest of each wave to pale yellow; this, in turn, in cloud-shadow or towards evening, softened to a dull, translucent brown, like yellow garnet or topaz. In the sunlight the wind tore off the wavetops, scattering them in a glittering golden spray under which the lake was a cold, green, ominous mass. As the wind freshened and the waves grew and the pace of the lake quickened, all the green would decay to brown, while the spray congealed into hot white masses of dissociated foam.

Even in the shelter of the shore the bow threw

Even in the shelter of the shore the bow threw up spray that was caught by the wind and hurled into our faces.

opposite:
On the eastern shore, waves retreating after a storm

up spray that the wind caught and hurled into our faces, the sodary water stinging our eyes so that they were soon red and swollen. About midmorning we reached Moite, where a long sandspit stretching out into the lake enclosed a bay at the base of the mountain, partly sheltered from the wind. We looked for a suitable place to camp and also for signs of crocodiles, of which none had been seen so far. The bay water was muddy and opaque, and we saw two hippos break the surface about a half mile away. As we neared the end of the spit there was a distinct thud, and the Curse shuddered hard. I thought we had collided with a hippo, but saw nothing in the wake and concluded that we must have hit something else, invisible in the dirty water. I was right. Soon the helm felt heavier and in a few minutes water began lapping over the floorboards. We were holed, and badly, and there was nothing to be done because the leak was at the bottom under a ton and a half of cargo. I turned and headed for shore with water washing around the faltering engine. It stopped a few yards offshore, and we had to drag the craft the last bit before it grounded. Breakers on the other side of the spit washed around, jolting the waterlogged Curse from side by side. Thus hindered in our frantic efforts to unload her, it seemed forever before we had her empty and could find the damage. I eventually located it, a mysterious neat and sizable, punched through the hull just off the centerline. I repaired it by bolting wood on either side, and towards evening we were able to continue, exhausted and discouraged.

This was the first day in what was to be over a year's work on the lake and already the boat had sunk and a lot of our equipment was damaged. I could not avoid a sense of foreboding.

No one had meddled with Lake Rudolf without paying for it one way or another, quite often with their lives.

That night we anchored in a tiny bay which seemed to be sheltered from the waves. But soon after midnight the wind started blowing, and before I woke it had rolled the Curse over and she sunk again. We righted and bailed her in the dark, but the next day the engine remained stubbornly lifeless with a waterlogged magneto. It stayed that way, and after various other mishaps and frustrations we rigged a crude sail and attempted the first crossing of Lake Rudolf under canvas. Even that very nearly failed, and we were ignominiously towed the last few miles to Kalokol by a highly amused McConnell.

Having repaired the boat and reassured the crew, we went back to Moite to try again. So far I had not even begun to think of my *purpose*, so preoccupied was I with the process of getting

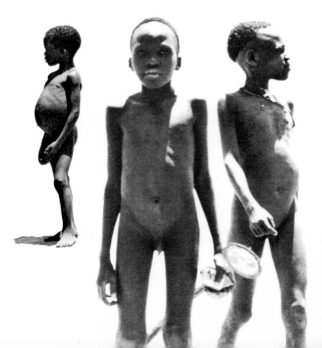

there. The object on this first trip to Moite was nothing more than to catch as many live crocs as we could, mark, measure, and weigh them, and put them back in the lake. During the survey I hoped to recapture some and thus obtain data on the rate of growth in the wild. A simple, harmless goal, I thought.

Growth rates were particularly important to the survey. In trying to grasp an overall picture of the life of a given species it is imperative to establish a set of criteria for estimating individual age. One must know the age at which breeding begins and ends in order to work out each female's reproductive ability. This in turn, combined with data on survival rates, allows one to assess the whole population's capacity to reproduce itself. One can then begin to judge how much mortality the population can withstand without declining. These are the basic data of population management, used to estimate

cropping (or hunting) rates, the species' ability to resist adversity, and so on. All this depends on being able to fix the age of each individual examined within a sample representative of the whole population, so that the whole population may be divided into relative age classes.

Estimating individual age is a roundabout procedure. Thomas Boreham, writing in 1794, aptly summed up the matter. "With regard to the length and shortness of life in animals, the information procurable is slender, observation slight, and tradition fabulous. Tame creatures are corrupted by a degenerate life; wild ones are intercepted by the inclemency of the weather. Neither do the things which may seem concomitant assist us much in the inquiry; as the bulk of the body, the period of gestation, the number of young, the time of growth, etc. These being complicated considerations sometimes concur, and sometimes not."

It is clearly impossible to fix the *absolute* age of any wild animal, and it gets more difficult as the individual animal gets older. Unless the birthday of an identifiable individual is on record, any attempt to age it is an estimate. What one does in practice is try to make various sources of evidence on age agree. Gradually, by a process of mutual corroboration, one deduces a method of estimating the *probable* age of individuals *relative to one another*. Finally one tries to make these *relative* ages correspond to *actual* years.

With the Rudolf crocodiles I began by making certain assumptions. First, that males grow faster than females. This assumption best accounted for the observed fact that the largest males were four feet longer and three and a half times as heavy as the largest females. It is reasonable to assume that in our random sample of

all the major zoos of the world for records of longevity in their captives.

The topic of longevity in reptiles has led to much "fabulous tradition." Reptiles *look* old to humans. Their gnarled skins, their lethargy and their bulk all imply age. These are subjective impressions based on human models. This is the basis of the simplistic mental association that tells us that because crocs are members of an ancient line (170 million years old) of the ancient family of reptiles, they are old. We do not notice our error in confusing the oldness of the species with the alleged oldness of the individual. It is a good example of the way in which our minds are influenced by symbolism. Primitiveness in crocs—a fact—symbolizes great age. We can barely resist thinking, therefore, that a big croc is very old. Schweinfurth in *The Heart of Africa* invalidated his otherwise reasonable conclusion in this way when he wrote, "When kept in confinement the crocodile makes scarcely any perceptible growth, and from the circumstances of the slow increase in its bulk the inference seems necessarily to follow that the creature lives to a great age." Hugh Cott in his study of crocodiles made the same mistake when he speculated, on the basis of a single specimen's growth, that large male crocs may be well into their second century. Such anthropomorphic fallacies are at the root of all the apocryphal veldt-belt statistics that so confuse men's appreciation of nature: the sort of drivel that a Mr. Green, for instance, serves up in his book *Secret Africa.* "A croc still living on a farm in the U.S. is reputed to be more than 800 years old. The age is determined (within a century or so) by the width of the snout, which broadens a quarter of an inch every 50 years. It is estimated that a croc takes 30 years to reach a length of three feet."

500 crocodiles the largest individuals of both sexes are not only representative of the largest in the population, but of the same age. Therefore if males are bigger than females they must be growing faster.

My second assumption was that the size of the animal was also a measure of its age—provided that crocs grow as long as they live. In animals with a fixed upper size limit, such as ourselves, size is a measure of age only during the growing years. But in many animals such as elephants, some fish, most reptiles, etc., growth can continue throughout life, so that the biggest are also the oldest. There is much circumstantial evidence to suggest that crocodiles go on growing as long as they live.

My third assumption, related to the second, was that there must be features apart from size that change with the age of a crocodile. I assumed that the number of bone layers in their jawbones (like the rings in a tree trunk) and also the weight of the eye lens were such features, and I used them (they have been successfully used in other species) to divide the sample into relative age groups.

Having made these three assumptions, I first divided the sample into relative age groups based on size. Then I tried to fit *actual* ages in years to each size of croc. I began by consulting

The greatest age recorded by any zoo for any species of crocodilian is actually less than 60 years. Two alligators in their 50's are on record, but in general crocodilians more than 40 years old are rare. In 1935 the zoologist Stanley Flower made a similar survey of recorded longevities with similar results.

I arbitrarily assumed, therefore, that the oldest and largest crocs on Rudolf were not more than 70 years old. To fill in likely ages for the intermediate size groups I then turned to the other sources of such data—recorded growth rates. In very young crocs growth rates have been recorded many times, the majority falling in the range of 1 to 1½ feet per year. But the observations get fewer as the study animals die off, or the observer's enthusiasm wanes, so that for crocs more than 5 years old there are hardly any growth records. Nevertheless, I estimated

Mr. Green, in
Secret Africa, tells us, "Age
is determined by the
width of the
snout, which broadens
a quarter of an inch every
50 years."

that in general it takes crocs an average of 8 years to reach sexual maturity. By this age the faster growth of males is apparent, as they attain 9 feet before maturing, compared to only 6 feet in females.

From about this age onwards growth in length slows down. This is because an animal's total "growth effort" is dispersed to all bodily aspects; a single morphological feature, such as skeletal length, changes less noticeably as the animal gets bigger. Thus, while old, large crocs gain enormously in weight each year, their length increments are very small. The difference in weight between a 15- and a 16-footer is about 280 pounds—total weight of a 9-footer. This changing weight-length relationship means that by the time they die large differences in age are expressed in only small differences in length. For all practical purposes this allows an "upper size limit" to be put to the individuals of the population in question. Of 278 females I examined during the survey the biggest were 9 animals 10 to 11 feet long; of 202 males the biggest were 11 animals 14 to 16 feet long.

From the outcome of the three original assumptions I was now able to draw a graph of size against age. There was enough data to start the growth curves for immature males and females. And I could fix likely end-points for the growth curves in very old animals. But between newly matured and old animals there was no data, so the slope of this portion of the curves had to be drawn in arbitrarily. Despite the paucity of data these curves were valid for the comparatively crude population analysis I was making of the Rudolf crocs.

It was chiefly in the hopes of acquiring the elusive growth data for medium-sized crocs that I planned the catching foray to Moite. To catch these crocs I brought a shark net. If it could subdue 500-pound sharks, I reasoned, it could do the same for crocs.

Just before dawn, while it was still dark, I gingerly swam about the entrance to a small Moite inlet setting a trap. The net floats were weighted to the bottom in such a way that they could be released from the shore, thus raising

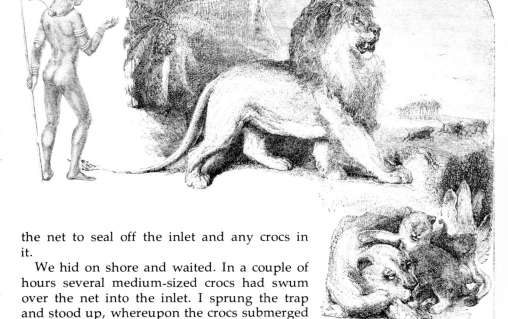

the net to seal off the inlet and any crocs in it.

We hid on shore and waited. In a couple of hours several medium-sized crocs had swum over the net into the inlet. I sprung the trap and stood up, whereupon the crocs submerged and made for the lake. Violent bobbings of the floats and swirls of mud convinced us of a big catch. Excitedly we hauled the net in—it proved to contain a couple of fish and many gaping holes, but not one croc. It might have been a spider's web for all the trouble these crocs had tearing their way loose.

In a week we netted a grand total of three 8-footers. Because they got wise to us, I tried setting the trap the evening before. During the night a hippo caught its foot in the net, dragged it all over the place, and while doing so caught me a croc—which drowned before I got to it.

On another occasion some hyenas, carried away by the seductive flesh-colored plastic floats, ate most of them in an apparent craze for low-calorie foods. I discarded the tatters of my net and tried snaring—setting rope nooses around a bait consisting of an oryx antelope shot two miles away and pulled with backbreaking effort over the rocky ground to the lake. But an itinerant lion, coming across the scent trail left when we dragged the oryx to the lake, followed it up, pulled the bait out and ate it; what

this page:
In the process of investigating age criteria, growth rates, etc., we concentrated on catching live crocs, using all the methods we knew.

THE ALIR.

following pages:
Camping at Moite under a
sombre sky

———

A few days
later a camel
patrol came in search of
the murderers

it left the now calorie-carefree hyenas polished off. I finally realized that my bag of three adult crocs (which I never saw again) was the local limit. What little time was left for this phase of the work I spent catching small crocs—up to five feet long—by hand, hoping at least to confirm that their growth rates were as expected.

The best technique was to dazzle them with a torch at night—then you could, if you were stealthy enough, wade up to them and with a quick lunge grab them by their necks. In this way we caught 150 crocs. Each animal was measured and weighed, then identified with a numbered plastic tag attached to the vertical scutes of its tail and returned to the lake. Later on I hoped to recover some of the marked animals and determine how much they had grown in the intervening time. Three, in fact, were recaptured nearly a year later; during this time none had grown as much as an inch longer, and two of them had actually decreased slightly in weight, leaving me with an enigma never fully solved.

Actually these three wizened crocs substantiated something I already knew—that crocs can be stunted under certain conditions. Several young crocs caught at the same time at Moite and kept in captivity grew over a foot a year as expected. Just why their wild fellows were apparently so stunted was an important question, which we will take up towards the end of this book.

The days at Moite had their own peculiar flavor. We camped among the huge red boulders strewn round the foot of Moite that were refuge as well to thousands of monotonously whistling rock hyrax. Our only shelter was a piece of canvas stretched over a metal frame. There were no trees nor shade of any sort, and, shielded from the wind, the place was a furnace by day. Every now and then the still air was disrupted by violently spinning whirlwinds which curled round

Recording a hatching croc's "chirrup" in order to attract other crocs for capture, marking, and release

opposite page:
A manifestation of Mingled Destinies

the shoulders of the mountain and tore through the camp like miniature tornadoes, scattering anything not weighted down with stones. Our first taste of these whirlwinds came early one morning as we got up. Suddenly a blast of air picked up my campbed and tossed it far out into the lake. I had to plunge into the cold morning water and swim out to retrieve it—an exercise that taught me to anchor it. Losing a bed, however, made the day for the Turkana.

Moite itself was a barren mass of rocks rising behind us fifteen hundred feet above the lake. About two hundred feet up a sharp change in the color of the rocks marked an old waterline, dating back a hundred thousand years or more, when the much larger lake was continuous with the Nile system. That was how crocs and hippo came to be in a lake that is today widely separated from all other inland waters.

Early one morning a man ran into our camp from the north. He came across the landslide of gigantic boulders at the foot of Moite, bounding from rock to rock with an air of great urgency. He arrived so breathless and excited that it was some time before he could speak. Since he was a Rendile who knew no Turkana or Swahili, we could understand little of his problem other than that calamity had befallen him "over there." Then came two children scuttling like hyrax over the boulders; one of them understood a little Swahili.

Learning to cope with the big ones

The old Moite waterline hundreds of feet high, where the lake level used to be thousands of years before human civilization

We learned that they were survivors of a sudden dawn raid on their encampment by marauding Borana. Armed with guns, the bandits were more than a match for the spears of the Rendile. They fled, except for two old men, past running, who were shot down. From our camp we could have witnessed the raid had we looked, but the wind, drowning all sound, kept us in ignorance. We had not even noticed the Rendile arriving the evening before to water their stock.

The man was anxious to go, for he planned to walk to North Horr, sixty miles west, to seek aid. We offered to look after the two children, a hindrance to him now, for which he was grateful. After speaking briefly with them, he left.

These two children were remarkable. About nine and seven, they were already almost past their childhood, taking catastrophe in their stride. Silently they watched the man go. As soon as he was out of sight they ran up the slopes of Moite and vanished among the boulders; we were not of their kind and they did not really trust us.

They hid in the rocks all day, showing themselves only when the Turkana held up some food and shouted to them to come and get it. The elder appeared from somewhere, took the food silently and returned to his hiding place.

Towards evening they came down, we thought to eat; but after accepting some food they walked out, wordlessly, following the man's footsteps, heedless of our warnings. Until they rejoined their own people they could not be happy, and so they went in search of the remnants of their family. In two hours it would be dark. That night at least would be spent out in the open, sleeping beneath a bush. We never heard what happened to them.

A few days later a camel patrol came in search of the raiders. In this roadless country camels were still the best transport, but they would never catch the raiders, free to move when and where they wanted. Looking themselves more like bandits than policemen, they stayed awhile to cajole tobacco and talk, the long, hopeful arm of the law.

Around camp the spaces between the boulders were filled with sand and pebbles. In these, one morning, I noticed the footprints of a lion. I followed them, my curiosity turning to gooseflesh

when I saw them lead to within a few feet of where we had slept. The lion's weight had made deep depressions in the pebbles, and I marveled at how so large an animal could approach so close and yet remain unnoticed. I had thought that nothing could get near without the clink of the iron-hard shingle. But there is a subtlety in a predator that defies description, a capacity to move without exciting attention, a wraithlike quality of unobtrusiveness.

The lion was apparently only inquisitive, but I did not trust it, for in northern Kenya maneaters are common. On the comfortable plains of Masailand, where food animals abound, the lions are good natured and leisurely, with time to grow luxuriant manes of long black hair. But in this arid, hard desertland they are fierce and unmerciful, for they must exploit any opportunity.

Although the lion never returned, we were often visited by a leopard. Unlike others of its kind this leopard did not come and go surreptitiously; on the contrary, it boldly announced itself with the harsh, grating cough that is the leopard's unique sound, an element of the African night seldom heard, and when it is, unforgettable. Ten to fifteen short, rasping grunts, ground out in close repetition. Out of the dark wilderness it comes, from no place. It is of the night; no other sound has such nocturnal qualities, so many implications of the invisible hunter, the sinuous master of darkness.

Our leopard was unusually bold and would prowl the boulders above us until he was within fifty yards of where we lay. Then, from atop a rock, he would cough aggressively, unafraid of the torchlight shone at him, asserting his domain, pushing us, urging us to leave, for this was not our place. Grudgingly, he left us unmolested, eventually climbing high up the mountain to complain mournfully to the stars of this encroachment upon his solitude.

It was interesting to watch the reaction of the Turkana to these beasts. In the part of Turkanaland they came from, near the lake, the wild animals had all been eaten or driven away long ago by the voracious people. None of the men had ever seen a lion, or even heard one roar, and they spent much time at Moite explaining to each other what none of them knew about animals. Then they would consult me, ostensibly for laughs but indirectly for information. How big was a lion? How strong? Could he, in one jump, leap from there to there (indicating a distance of a hundred yards)? Of course not, I would reply, nothing more than from here to there (indicating a distance of thirty feet). Instead of being amazed at the discrepancy, they would be indignant. How could I be so dumb not to know

that lions can jump farther than that? While they loved me to arbitrate their interminable arguments, they always hustled me as if I were a set of dice, to be shaken and prodded until the right answer came up.

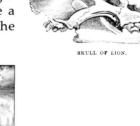

SKULL OF LION.

"Could he, in one jump, leap from there to there (indicating a distance of a hundred yards)?"

Of course, wild beasts figured prominently in the Turkana's mythology, and the men's naivety towards lion and leopard set me to thinking of the very potent symbolism crocodiles hold for mankind generally. This topic was very far from being a mere curiosity. In the symbolism of crocodiles, I believed, was to be found the key to their relationship with man the exterminator, as well as man the preserver. To understand what crocodiles evoke in men's minds is to understand crocodile destiny insofar as that is a function of man's destiny.

What came immediately to mind was a story told by the famine campers of Kalokol, a tale full of the stuff that both Turkana and crocs are made of. A certain man (nobody recalls just who) gave unforgivable offence (no one remembers quite what he did) to another man, who engaged a witch doctor to fix him. After throwing his bones and so forth, the soothsayer announced that the first man, a bad one, was to be taken by God. It came to pass that the accused was sitting one night on the prow of a canoe in the gulf when suddenly there was a mighty commotion and he disappeared off the prow. Immediately a storm developed and a whirlpool formed round the man, still visible in the water. Gradually he was sucked down, and as he vanished the sound was heard of many baboons in great agitation. God had taken him.

Three days later he reappeared near shore, and rose, Christlike, above the surface bleating like a sheep—terrifying and fascinating all who saw him. But he was embarrassed, they reasoned, and returned to the water. Eventually he washed up on the shore, with all his soft parts eaten off by turtles, and was buried under some doum palms on the spit. God was returning his body, but keeping his spirit.

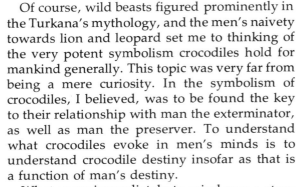

The actual circumstances, the material core of the legend, probably went something like this: a man out fishing fell off his canoe and in the darkness his frantic screaming and thrashing about in the water greatly alarmed his companions. The sudden onset of the night wind, which blew particularly hard that night, coincided with the drowning. Later, his body, stiff with rigor mortis, was seen from the shore apparently moving of its own accord (though in reality it was only wave action—and turtles—that moved it).

To his former companions the circumstances of the man's death and subsequent reappearance were so peculiar as to be explicable only as a supernatural event. Clearly he must have been a bad man to have met such a fate. In all probability it was a crocodile that caused the "accident"—the man was getting his just deserts.

The Turkana, it must be remembered, are at the cultural phase of animism. Physical events and wild beasts are imbued with essentially human characteristics so as to explain their otherwise inscrutable activities. The Turkana's God corresponds in cultural time to Job's God—an impetuous deity as vindictive as benevolent; possessed of power, yes, but irresponsible and tyrannical. Such a God was indistinguishable from the devil; all imponderables were basically the handiwork of the same spirit, who was devilish or compassionate according to his whim.

The crocodile eulogy in the Book of Job is a recognition of God's power—but at the same time a reprimand of *misused* power. "Upon earth there is not his like who is made without fear

SUNDAY SCHOOL ADVOCATE

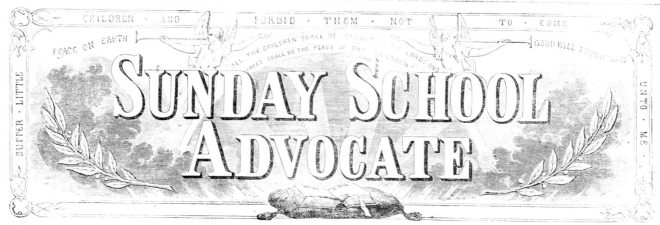

VOLUME XVII.—NUMBER 5.   JANUARY 22, 1888.   WHOLE NUMBER 380.

For the Sunday School Advocate.

THE CROCODILE.

This hideous monster has several names. It is called the Alligator, the Crocodile, and the Cayman. But, give it what name you please, it is an ugly creature—a huge river dragon, whose "room is much to be preferred to its company."

That poor little boy is in the mouth of one of these monsters, and feels himself rather uncomfortably situated. But yonder is his mother running to his rescue. Poor woman! Her motherly heart is deeply moved, and alarm is written on her face and in her actions. But what can she do, all unarmed as she is, with such a mighty monster? Can she pierce his iron scales with her fingers? Can she wrench open his fearful jaws? Is she stronger than this river dragon? No! she can do none of these things. Yet she knows how to conquer the reptile. She will plunge her fingers into its eyes. That act will make it feel an agony so painful as to cause it to forget its hunger, drop the child, and slink back to its home in the river. Then she will lift her bleeding boy to her breast, soothe his anguish, bind up his wounds, and watch over him until he is well again. Should he recover, he will be likely to keep out of the alligator's path hereafter.

I read the other day of a young girl "who, by singular presence of mind, saved herself from the jaws of a crocodile. When she felt herself seized, she sought the eyes of the animal, and plunged her fingers into them with such violence, that the pain forced the crocodile to let go his hold; but not until after having bitten off the lower part of her left arm. The girl, notwithstanding the enormous quantity of blood she had lost, swam ashore with the hand that still remained to her. 'I knew,' said she coolly, 'that the cayman [that is, crocodile] lets go his hold if you push your fingers into his eyes.'"

In these northerly regions this monster is unknown. It loves warm weather. Hence it is found in hot climates only. A species of it is found in the southern states; it abounds in the rivers of all tropical climates.

But though this scaly monster does not haunt the rivers of the North, yet there is another great dragon ever prowling about our streets and watching our homes, seeking whom it may devour. It is more terrible than the alligator. Its jaws are mighty to crush and destroy all its captives.

The name of this monster is SIN! Children, beware of it; keep out of its way, and you will be safe.

W.

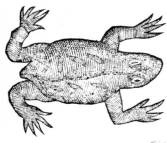

. . . he is a king over all the children of pride." The Turkana say essentially the same thing, that the children of pride, bad people, will meet their reward at the hands of something too strong for mortal man, an evil thing, such as a crocodile or a devil.

This is the explanation for the apparently nonchalant way they wade about the "crocodile infested" waters of the gulf, sometimes in sight of interested crocodiles floating farther out. Ask them about it and you get a straightforward answer: "My conscience is clear, therefore I am in no danger." Theirs is not the contempt of familiarity, nor the apathy of resignation. It is the supreme confidence of an intact ego. To a man who has no doubts about himself an attack from a scaly, evil crocodile *must* be bad magic.

The Turkana's contempt for crocodiles is not peculiar to them—it is universal. Among more civilized people this contempt is intensified into loathing. Crocodiles epitomize reptiles—and reptile means "that which creeps, a worm." Robinson, in his survey of poets and their sentiments towards animals, deplored their irrational hatred of reptiles but nevertheless conceded that "a reptile is not perhaps an amiable thing." He noted that for the poet "the necessities of speech require a word that shall compendiously express the idea of the contemptible and crawling, and at the same time potentially hurtful. And reptile fulfills this obnoxious duty. . . . Their toads are loathsome, their frogs obscene. Their chameleons are turncoats, and their scorpions traitors. Their snakes are utterly abominable."

He cites many examples. James Beattie called a servile poet "the reptile muse, swoln from the sty, and rankling from the stews." "Thomson," remarks Robinson, "was as usual, 'shagged with horrors' " when referring to the "reptile throng." Coleridge asked: "What if one reptile sting another reptile? Where is the crime? The goodly face of nature hath one disfeaturing stain the less upon it." Eliza Cook wrote:

> *Why, why does heaven bequeath such gifts*
> *To fascinate all eyes, that mark*
> *With magnet charm, till something lifts*
> *The mask, and shows how foully dark*
> *The dazzling reptile is within*
> *Beneath the painted shining skin?*

Nineteenth-century African travelers wrote in like vein. A typical example is from Reginald Maugham's *Wild Game in Zambesia:*

We now come to what I think is impossible to refrain from regarding as the loathsome, abhorrent, and repulsive among the inhabitants of Africa—those revolting forms which nature would seem to have created in some regrettable moment of boundless vin-

dictiveness, for the express purpose of surrounding the beautiful and useful members of the animal creation with the ever-present risk of a ghastly death by constriction, venom or drowning. Were there traceable in this incomprehensible dispensation any beneficial or indeed intelligible purpose . . . the horrible mission of the reptiles might be understood. But there is none whatsoever . . . one fails hopelessly to comprehend their inclusion in the scheme of nature. . . . Take for example that hideous blot upon the creation, the crocodile.

Even the early game preservers in East Africa loathed crocodiles. Charles Pitman, Uganda's first Game Warden, who was charged with the preservation of game in that country for twenty-four years, waged a seventeen-year campaign to exterminate crocodiles in Uganda, poisoning, shooting, trapping, offering bounties for eggs, and so on. Pitman once said: "My own summing up of the crocodile's character is that this foul beast is a typical bully and a great coward."

The Turkana's rationalization of the essential unpredictability of a croc attack goes to the root of croc's symbolism, for primitive and civilized people alike. For all of us, crocs symbolize evil. They are the sentinels of evil—the devil's mafia—who carry out assaults, murders, intimidations, acts of vengeance, and other unspeakable crimes. Above all they stand for violence (often sexual violence). Huge ravening predators, armed with massive, teeth-studded jaws; strong, unrestrainable, indestructible and destructive.

How do crocodiles fulfill their symbolic role? What is it about them that strikes the human unconscious as evil? In the immediate, everyday sense it is simply because they *are* violent. Every year a few Turkana are killed by crocs on Rudolf; those are the facts. (This aspect we go into in more detail in Chapter 8.) But there are other far more destructive predators in Africa (for instance, lions) that are not as feared or as "evil" as crocs. What we want to identify here are the other sources of their "evil."

By far the most potent is the fact of *eating.* Medieval bestiaries depicted crocs as "hell-mouths," the portals of irrevocable, despicable bestiality. (There is also a sexual element in this image, the ghastly cavern beset with biting, savage teeth.) A crocodile is a consuming, ravenous, *raging* beast. A passage from Solinus goes: "The Egyptians . . . account a crocodile a savage, and cruel murdering beast, as may appear by their hieroglyphics, for when they will decipher a mad man, they picture a crocodile, who being put from his desired prey by forcible resistance, he presently rageth against himself . . ."

It might seem that to be eaten is in itself nothing to be ashamed of. If someone is killed by a crocodile, why is it worse if he is then eaten?

"Will he make many supplications unto thee? Will he speak soft words unto thee?"

The answer is simple enough. One of civilization's imperative taboos is against cannibalism; little else arouses such fear or loathing. And we do not easily distinguish, emotionally, between a human eating a human and an animal eating a human. Or even between a human eating an animal if this is done in an unritualized or otherwise "barbaric" (e.g. uncooked) way. The fear of being eaten by an animal is much greater than the fear of merely being killed by it. The fear of the unconscious wish to be cannibal is greater still. Such fears generate volcanoes of rage and

Lutembe

terror. Nor should we be so culturally arrogant as to suppose ourselves too far removed from cannibalism. Given the conditions of physical and mental anarchy that accompany war, for example, or other cataclysms, cannibalism soon reappears.

It was almost inevitable that crocodiles should have such notions of purely *human* evil projected onto them. They are too well placed, too inviting, and altogether too guilty to evade such typecasting in what humans call "nature's plan."

It is around the matter of cannibalism that the symbolism of crocodiles twists and writhes. To be eaten by a croc is to be consumed forever *by evil*. One forfeits all hope of immortality. One's soul is irrevocably Satan's, one's body is dung.

Now, to be enveloped by evil, in the nursery logic of our unconscious, is to *be* evil, for all practical purposes. We see this in the Turkana's view of croc attacks. They appear to be quite callous about victims of attacks. But in fact they are not being cruel or cynical. They are simply taking it for granted that the victim was an evil person—why else would a croc have attacked

Hesamut, the Egyptian hippo goddess, carrying champsa

Sebek, the Egyptian crocodile god

him? At the very least he has been *touched* by evil, the devil's thumbprint.

After all, a crocodile is a serpent—the fundamental symbol of the dynamism of evil, a projection of the very substance and energy of which evil is composed, both sexual and destructive. In the Garden of Eden it was the serpent which through Eve induced Adam to *eat* of the tree of knowledge and thereby forfeit his innocence. To eat of and be eaten by evil—to know it—is really a monstrous proposition.

Another croc story illustrates the linking of an evil beast with an evil man—a sort of mutual recognition. It concerns the celebrated Lutembe, a semi-tame croc that lived near Entebbe in Lake Victoria in the 1920's and 30's. Lutembe was a sacred crocodile that would come when called for offerings of fish. But as befits an ambivalent deity, there was also "ordeal by Lutembe." In this, accused but protesting thieves were dragged before Lutembe and (no doubt with the aid of a judicial prod or two from behind) watched closely while the crocodile gave judgment. If guilty, the man was bitten or even eaten; if innocent, he was ignored. The unequivocal justice was apparent to all. Once eaten the man *had* to be guilty. (And the system neatly sidestepped that often irritating aspect of the judicial process—the accused's version of the crime.)

Lutembe, as Lucifer's lieutenant, was possessed of astonishing symbolic intensity. It is told of Lutembe that a Catholic missionary, enraged beyond measure by the crocodile's popularity with the flock, cast aside his bible, picked up his gun, and swore everlasting damnation upon the pagan reptile. Singing, it is said, "Onward Christian Soldiers," the avenger marched to the lake shore and opened fire upon Lutembe. But his bullet merely glanced off the crocodile ("slingstones are turned with him into

stubble . . . he laugheth at the shaking of a spear . . .") as Lutembe disappeared into the lake.

This amphibiousness of crocodiles is a most influential component of their symbolism. To be amphibious is to be ambiguous; neither one thing nor the other, unpredictable, obscure, and therefore dangerous. Such ambivalence has Jekyll/Hyde qualities—the calm, peaceful exterior concealing a vicious, raging other self; it equals treachery, a crocodile "characteristic" typically invoked to rationalize the dreadful humiliation of being attacked unawares. (This aspect is taken up again in Chapter 8.)

When man is menaced by something, like a crocodile, operating outside his normal sphere

of comprehension, he soothes himself—calms his fears—in several ways. An agressive man may resort to threats, or arm himself and prepare to fight if molested. A confident man, like a Turkana, may consult his ego and assume that since crocodiles are beyond him they are supernatural. As a believer in the sheer power of his own thoughts, which assign evil, supernatural phenomena to evil men, he will protect himself with that most potent of all defenses—a clear conscience. But a more intellectual man, also converted to the omniscience of thought but impatient with mere intuition, might employ his cunning—a human weakness that has undermined culture from the dawn of civilization. Of the many devices of the cunning, the most striking—and fundamental—is to do the opposite of the obvious. If crocodiles (in men's minds, at least) threaten one, why not placate the malevolent spirits be being nice to them? Instead of hating crocs and trying to destroy them, why not love and preserve them? Make friends, make obeisance, adore and protect them—surely then all will be well? We have already mentioned Lutembe, a contemporary example of the sacred crocodile. There are many others. The Bakwena of southern Africa were known as the crocodile people, and had a crocodile as their totem; crocodile carvings have been found at Zimbabwe; crocodile face-masks are common in West Africa and New Guinea.

But the most famous instances of crocodile worship come from ancient Egypt. There is a myth, full of basic symbols, that translates the origin of such hate turned adulation. Once upon a time Menes, first King of all the Egyptians, was set upon by his own dogs while out hunting. In his flight he came to Lake Moeris, where lay a large croc baking in the sun. The croc, rapidly sizing up the situation, offered to ferry the desperate king across the lake. With all saurian ceremony Menes was sculled over to found the city of Crocodilopolis, about 3000 years B.P. Its people revered all crocodiles, and worshipped a crocodile god, Sebek. This crocodile cult spread to other cities. At Ombos, mothers of children eaten by crocodiles felt privileged to have provided something for Sebek's delectation.

The myth of Menes neatly sums up the story of how the early Egyptians, hounded by evil (dogs are potent symbols of violence and evil), wished to free themselves of its tyranny. Since their cultures were water-based, the evil in reality was often crocodilian in origin. By a deft mythological ruse the ambiguous, amphibious croc, the real villain, crossed the wicked waters, taking with it the bedeviled ancestor. Lo and behold, on the opposite side (always greener) they were friends. The classic

religious shift of invoking an original debt to be paid off forever in installments of obeisance and self-humiliation then comes into operation. The evil crocodile was ordained sacred; what ordinary folk construed as acts of enmity the enlightened now knew to be inscrutably benevolent.

We may shrug off the story of Crocodilopolis as a historical curiosity—but it is no such thing. The current adoration of lions, leopards, wolves, bears, wilddogs, etc., by civilized people whose recent ancestors tried to exterminate the same beasts as evil vermin is practically the same phenomenon, culturally. Love of animals is not often a spontaneous affection—it usually arises in the aftermath of violence and hatred. For the Crocodilopolitans, the evil they wished to placate was part of their external world, the very real and everpresent evil that lurked in the life-sustaining waters they depended on. For the more civilized man of today the evil represented by the animals he tends to love is no longer external but *internal*. It is the evil that stems from his knowledge of his own capacity for destruction and hatred.

It seemed to me that Lake Rudolf could do without another Crocodilopolis, though mankind was rapidly putting all wildlife into that category, there and elsewhere. Whether man exterminated Rudolf's crocs out of fear or hatred, or saved them in a guilty inversion of that same antipathy, seemed equally barbaric. They were neither evil beasts nor wonderful manifestations of nature's ineffable plan. They were simply crocodiles.

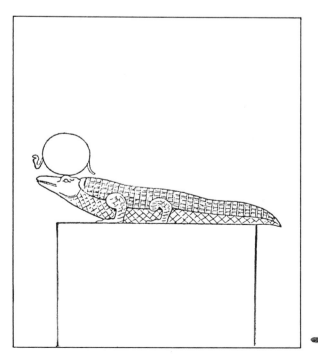

CHAPTER 4 THE FLAT EARTHISTS

*Gulliver's travels through Turkanaland—unruly
dispositions of these people—palsied gesticulations, shrieking voices, scornful indifference—assumed
contempt of aviation—last of the flat earthists—predilection for tobacco—
superabundance of magical mystery men—paradox of the
fully-dressed naked man—plastic fantastic champions—El Greco the Wildman—
Tukoi flips his lid—spartan life at variance with their gluttony—reputedly devour dogs—Manifest
Destiny comes to Turkanaland.*

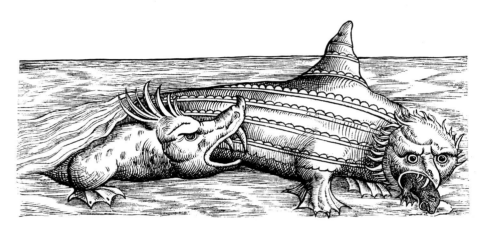

"A Turkana is the centre of a field of direct interpersonal, enduring relations based on agnatic, maternal and affinal kinship, with a residual category of quasi-kinship, *viz.* bond-friendship. This field comprises the network of social relations specific to that man, and is not entirely coincident with that of any other individual." That is how a sociologist, P. H. Gulliver, summed up the Turkana in 1948 after an eighteen-month study.

Actually the Turkana are a striking people who make a strong impression on anyone who sees them. It is impossible to mistake them for another tribe. Traditionally they are nomadic pastoralists herding cattle and goats, camels and donkeys, in the semi-desert of northwestern Kenya. As a cultural mode nomadic pastoralism is an ancient, specialized offshoot of the mainstream of human evolution, which is towards a settled, communal life. Nomadism produces one particularly impressive cultural quality: equilibrium. Hunters and pastoralists share it—harmony, stability and contentment, qualities that urban man finds increasingly elusive. A Turkana is above all happy; one hears more laughter in the hard, harsh land of the Turkana than anywhere I know.

Several prominent character traits go to make up the Turkana's peculiar brand of contentment. One that has struck visitors to their land from the very beginning is their fantastic bombast. Von Höhnel's first meeting with the Turkana describes it well.

Three warriors came dashing towards us down the hill. They stopped at a distance of some fifty paces, and with ear-splitting shrieks and menacing gestures, flung themselves and their weapons about, evidently expecting to overawe us, but their apelike proceedings only provoked shouts of laughter from our side, though we could not help admiring the pluck with which they faced a party of strangers so far outnumbering themselves.

Soon after we had pitched our tents, however, the camp was filled with Turkana of every age, and these people being the very noisiest we ever met with, the wood soon echoed with their shouts, whilst the way in which a dozen warriors advanced to greet us resembled the charge of an enemy rather than the peaceful welcome we knew it to be meant for. With uplifted spears and shields and apelike gestures they sprang towards us, hiding behind every bit of cover they came to, to dash out again the next minute. If a baboon had been carried off by a leopard or some other wild beast, his comrades might have come to his rescue something in this style. After these preliminary contortions, however, the warriors squatted quietly down and waited for a present.

"Three Turkana warriors came dashing towards us down the hill. They stopped at a distance of some 50 paces, and with ear-splitting shrieks and menacing gestures flung themselves and their weapons about, evidently expecting to overawe us."

Famine campers at Kalokol. Doum palm trees in the lugger are individually owned.

The abrupt switch from aggression to indifference is typical. There are no half measures in the Turkana demeanor; indecision and feebleness are rarely seen. Whatever the emotion of the moment, it is given all they have. What appears to us a simple observation is delivered as a furious tirade. They are a people still capable of swift, certain decision uncorroded by self-consciousness or second thoughts.

Von Höhnel found their manner of speaking "rough, harsh and repellent. A short, eager reiterated *Hé!* occurs at every turn, and appears to express alike, joy, surprise, anger and scorn." He went on: "Turkana songs are noisy and unmelodious, and the dances are grotesque, consisting of wild ungainly jumping about, accompanied by obscene gestures and a long-drawn-out howl of *hu, hu-hu!* Timid people would be anything but comfortable in Turkana. Fortunately we were not troubled with nerves, and therefore the wild goings on in camp did not affect us much. Now some warrior would dash down upon us as if to make a hostile charge; and then there would be no end of noise and confusion over the purchase of some goats, the loud *Hé! Hé!* of the tribesmen resounding over the camp as if a fight were imminent."

The expostulation *Hé!* that von Hönnel referred to is one of their more obvious peculiarities, and as he remarks, it denotes the whole gamut of expression, from mild surprise to incredulity, depending on its delivery. To imitate this sound say "hay" as quickly and loudly as you can, at the same time superimposing a vigorous hiccup as if you had been kicked in the stomach. Turkana conversation includes endless gesticulation, and the language is guttural, rapid, and deafening; there is seldom any languor in their speech. Where other men talk, they shout; where other men shout, they shriek. Their heads and arms jerk about as if spring-loaded.

As soon as he can walk the Turkana cultivates the arts of insolence and arrogance. The first step is to master the posture of one who has just been grievously insulted. The vehemence with which this pose is struck denotes the degree of emotion to be expressed. The posture consists of the subject's suddenly turning sideways and staring into the distance in order to detach himself from the astonishing, indeed incredible, words he has just heard. At the same time he shifts his weight onto one leg, and, with one arm akimbo, sticks the other leg forward. With

an entire homestead under cover of darkness in order to avoid him.

Von Höhnel made another observation typical of Turkana indifference. In the arid country of Africa are many sandy watercourses in which it is often possible to find water by digging. Teleki was astonished to see Turkana cattle digging water for themselves instead of drinking out of man-made holes as is done elsewhere. Had he come to know the Turkana better, however, he probably would not have been so amazed, for one can almost hear them saying, with their look of feigned surprise, "If the cattle want water, they can dig it themselves." Arthur Neumann, who visited Rudolf eight years later, independently made the same observation. He had bought some Turkana donkeys which amazed him by digging their own water.

The Turkana indifference is legendary. When a poor man is unable to muster a respectable funeral, it is not uncommon for the deceased to be left where he dies. For a pauper it is no further dishonor; the Turkana see no point in struggling against circumstances. In other parts of Kenya you will often hear it said that among the Turkana it is the custom to drape the dead in trees rather than to bury them. The Turkana

"Hé, Hé."

his free arm he then gesticulates and exaggerates as wildly as he can.

Most Africans spit as a means of punctuating and emphasizing conversation, but none so violently as a Turkana. He doesn't merely spit—he ejects a slug of saliva that hits the ground with a thud that makes one instinctively dodge and sends up a puff of dust as if a bullet had struck.

The visitor to Turkanaland is likely to be received with either hostility or indifference. Gulliver experienced both during his sociological studies. Whereas the Jie, a closely related tribe to the west of Turkanaland, were friendly and helpful to a man, and altogether ideal subjects for research, he found the Turkana hostile and frankly interested only in gifts of tobacco. The one subject he could interest them in was war; about everything else they were evasive, going so far on one occasion as to pack up and move

A Turkana maiden observed by Teleki and von Höhnel, and Lokwar, the skinner, with scars earned for killing women

Landing on Ferguson's spit in the twilight, after a month's work at Moite

deny this, saying that the legend goes back to a terrible famine many years ago: Starvation was affecting the animals as much as the men, and packs of savage dogs roamed, attacking and eating those too weak to fight them off. To avoid the dogs, people dying from hunger climbed trees, where they then expired. In certain places the trees came to be festooned with dead and dying, giving rise to the bizarre legend. It is the sort of story the Turkana delight in—it appeals to their sense of the dramatic and absurd.

The three intrepid warriors who descended on Teleki and von Höhnel, for all their antics and bombast, would unhesitatingly have fought him had Teleki reacted aggressively instead of with amusement. But since Teleki wouldn't fight, the Turkana simply shrugged their shoulders and went to the opposite extreme —indifference. It was amusing for a while to hold a market with these white-skinned curiosities from the south, an opportunity for much shouting and frivolity. But when Teleki moved to another place he found the novelty wearing off and got a more typical reception: "[Were] we not downright fools, not to know that good manners required us to exchange assurances of friendship with them before we began trading? And how dared we take water from their river without permission? In a word, who had asked us to come at all?"

Having seen Teleki and von Höhnel, and

therefore as many white men as they ever wanted to see, the Turkana thereafter greeted all strangers in the aggravatingly offhand way they love to affect. They make you feel not just insignificant, but downright redundant. Your trappings, your philosophy, and your curiosity are treated as coldly as brass by a magnet. One of the early visitors to Turkanaland, Martin Johnson, felt this keenly. Johnson was an American, and predictably he arrived with a formidable array of gimmicks which, he figured, were bound to impress the natives, and thereby provide fascinating material for the great pictures he hoped to make. His prize contraptions were two planes, the first to fly to Lake Rudolf, and being amphibians, they could land on the lake.

So it was that one day Johnson, his wife Osa, and Vern, his pilot, landed on Ferguson's Gulf at Kalokol. They waited with interest to see the reactions of these people, who had never seen an "aero" before. The Turkana reacted with shrieks of laughter—directed not at the flying machine but at the funny Americans. Such comical fellows! They virtually ignored the aircraft.

Piqued, Johnson thought perhaps they hadn't fully comprehended the nature of his beast. Accordingly he asked Vern to fly the plane off the water and put it down again, this time on the land, a maneuver that would surely confound them. But as the craft circled above them, "they only smiled as if to humor me . . ." This time the plane, having rolled to a stop, did attract attention. The Turkana noticed that the wings made a tempting band of shade over the scorching sand, in which an exasperating crowd promptly settled.

They had one more try. Vern took one of the men for a flip, but on their return he stepped out as if nothing whatsoever had happened and sat down again to enjoy the shade of the wings. Before leaving, Johnson asked an old man if he would like to possess a plane of his own. No, the old man replied, he certainly would not; whoever heard of a Turkana making a fool of himself in a flying machine?

One thing about the Turkana endeared them to us forever. On a clear starry night near the beginning of the survey we all lay wrapped in our blankets gazing at the sky. The men, a little distance from me, were arguing and eventually appealed to me to arbitrate. Three of them contended that our journey across the lake from Kalokol, a distance of twenty-four miles, had brought us significantly closer to the edge of the earth, while the fourth maintained that it was still a long way off. It took me a moment or two to grasp the significance of this. But there was no doubt about it. They were flat earthists, not by persuasion but by inner conviction. A few questions established the fact beyond doubt. The earth was as flat as water, as everyone knew, and would I please settle their dispute?

I marveled at the sensation of distance our twenty-four-mile voyage had given them. Here were men who could walk forty miles in a day and arrive at their destination fooling about like children arriving at a birthday party. But crossing the lake, which none of them had done before, left them feeling that there couldn't be much farther left to go.

Later on I put it to them that the earth was round. They thought that a funny idea, but when I persisted they simply found me tedious. On a similar evening I saw a satellite arcing across the sky. Since to them all the stars were on the same plane, they found the satellite exciting, as it was obviously bound to collide with another star sooner or later. With their flair for rationalization they exclaimed at each near miss, and when it vanished intact they looked forward eagerly for the next one to appear. I tried to explain that the satellite was in fact circling the earth, which was round. This raised a laugh or two. Really, this white man could be quite entertaining.

Then I said that the satellite was not a star, but an object thrown up there by Americans or Russians, peculiar people who lived far away,

An elderly flat earthist

near the edge of the earth, and that it contained either a man or a dog. They considered that an excellent form of punishment, but were curious about people who found it necessary to punish a dog so elaborately. I told them that the dog was not being chastised, but was being used to test the machine before a man used it. Apart

from the dubious validity of using a dog to test a man's reactions, they felt that if in fact my far-fetched story were true, the dog or man was obviously being punished, for having disappeared from sight had he not gone over the edge of the earth, to be banished forever?

The Turkana believe utterly in the omniscience of thought. Anything inexplicable in everyday terms is reckoned supernatural and explained according to the interpreter's fancy. Thus Teleki found that one or two rockets sent up after dark ensured cordial relations with the Turkana. To a Turkana, invoking some magical intervention when the rains fail or the fish refuse to hurl themselves into your net conveniently rationalizes the incomprehensible or bothersome. There is nothing like a little magic, properly concocted, for whiling away the long hours of a famine or a flood.

Consequently there is a constant traffic in spells in Turkanaland. An aggrieved party, who for some reason decides against settling the matter by goats, or by beating up the offender, will resort to casting a spell. Medicine men and diviners abound, for the dream of obtaining power and riches by taming the supernatural has captured the fancy of many a bold warrior. A little imagination and legerdemain, an eye for a bargain, and lo and behold, you are a magical mystery man, retailing to the gullible consumer what you got wholesale from God.

The Turkana are supreme egoists. They deal with their hard, unrelenting lives by taking scrupulous care of their egos. Spiritual enigmas are dumped in the lap of a vague god who doubles as devil according to his mood. But he is not an almighty god: rather he is respected for his mystique and because he has the free run of the supernatural. In day-to-day affairs, on the other hand, a Turkana has utter self-confidence, asking advice, permission, or opinion of neither man nor god.

Every Turkana man knows himself to be a stunningly glamorous fellow. A great deal of his time is spent on his person, mainly his head. He may wear leather sandals and a cape that flutters behind him as he walks, but otherwise he is naked—perhaps a bracelet or two and a goat's hoof lucky charm (like a rabbit's foot, an ironic symbol of luck when one considers the fortunes of the original owner), but seldom more than that. From his chin up, however, the story is different. Frequently his lower lip is pierced and a clumsy metal rod inserted like a proboscis. Some fancy rings in the nose, like a bull. But the soul of his beauty resides in his hair, he believes. It is teased and fluffed to form a chignon a foot or more long which is plastered with colored mud. Real dandies stick a long thin rod

into the end of this, and whenever possible ostrich feathers are stuck in the top. A Turkana man with a newly done coiffure has a tremendous swagger to him. The world is his, he is invincible. The women, for the most part too busy for groovy hairdos, content themselves with maintenance-free ornaments, such as enormous piles of necklaces, and massive rings around their wrists and ankles. Their hair is simply teased out into wringlets that fall evenly around the head. They wear leather aprons fore and aft, embroidered with beads.

The Turkana have a most refined concept of nudity. A newcomer to the land is struck by the way the men, stark bollack naked, strut about as if clothed in the very finest raiment, such that all must glory in the sight of them. If you were to ask such a man how he wanders about nude without embarrassment to himself or others, he would be annoyed, for improper nakedness is frowned upon by the Turkana. He would condescendingly explain to you that if you looked you would see that he was uncircumcised, and therefore fully clothed. If for some reason the normally concealed part of his penis were to emerge, he would, as it were, be disrobing; and this, except under the appropriate circumstances, is considered most unseemly.

The women, unadorned with such natural garbs, are required to clothe themselves. Infants go entirely naked, but the girls must dress themselves from an early age. There can be few races to have preserved such an untrammeled sense of decorum.

But the Turkana are renowned not only for their nakedness, their voracity, their arrogance, and their toughness, but above all for their men's genitalia. For sheer size they can have few equals. Surrounded by such giganticism, the Turkana not surprisingly revere size, and a man exceptionally blessed enjoys a certain prestige. This peculiarity of the Turkana is singularly fitting, for it underlines, as nothing else could, their talent for exaggeration. Anything not larger than life is somehow made to seem so; life for them is all or nothing.

The Turkana are intensely proud of their reputation as fearless fighters. They were the last tribe in Kenya to accede to the British insistence on peace, and they only did so grudgingly and with a lasting bitterness. By denying the Turkana the right to initiate fights with their enemies (that is, any other tribe) the Government itself became, symbolically, the enemy. To this day the older men refer sarcastically to the Government as "the enemy." To a Turkana man war is the sole purpose of life. Much of his apparent indolence has nothing to do with laziness; it is merely a concomitant of peace—anything less than

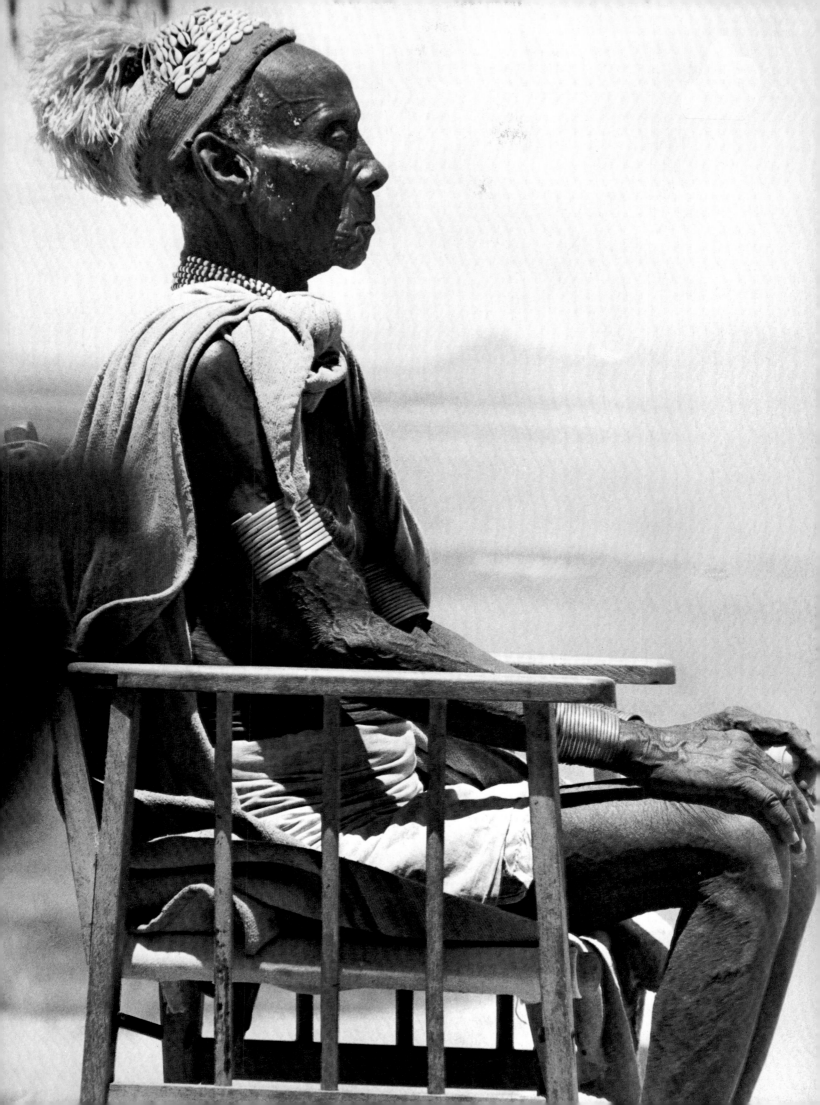

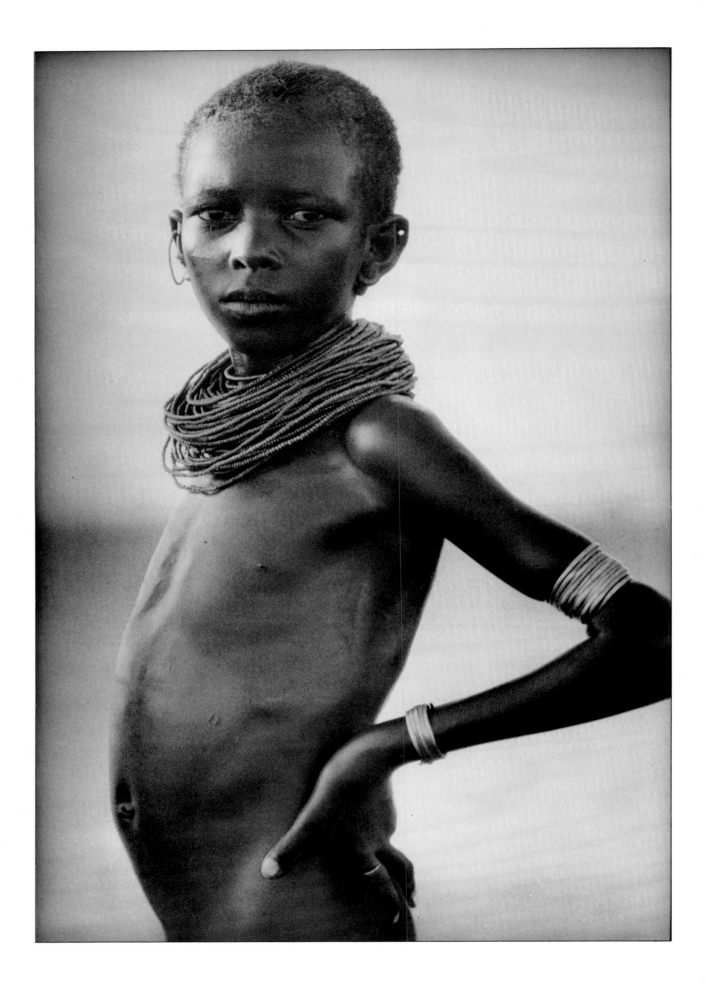

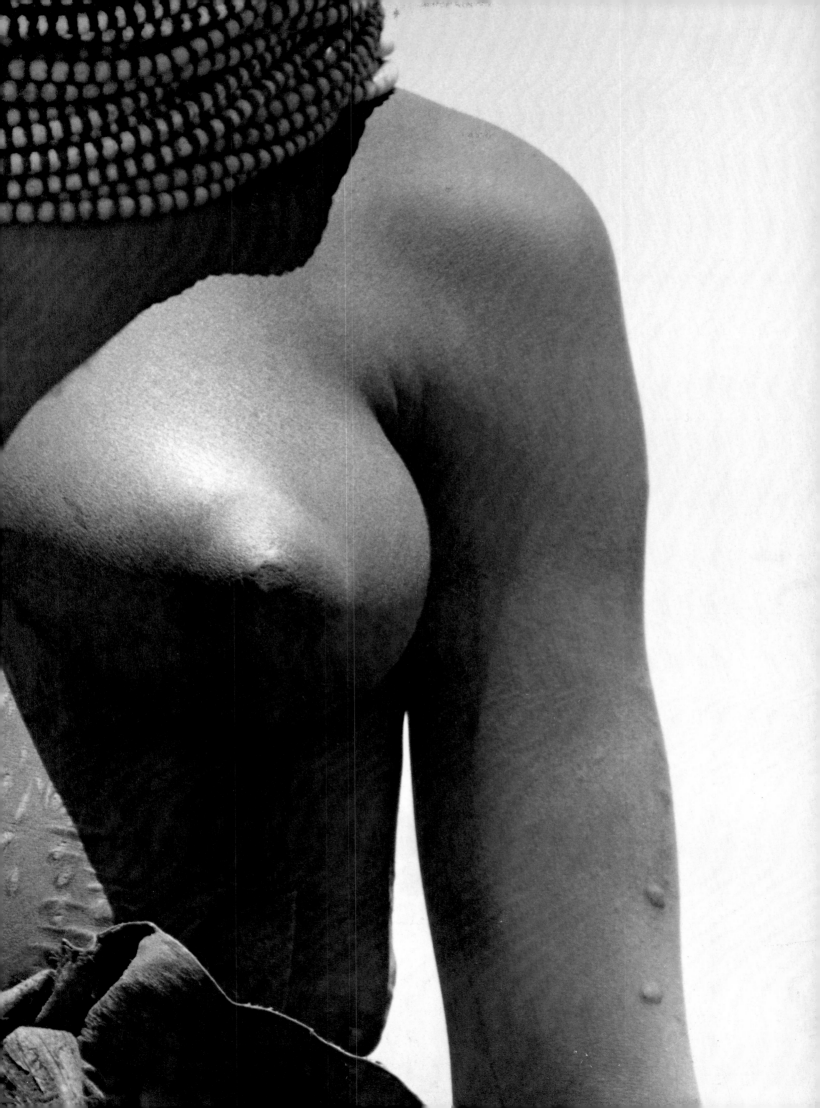

life as a warrior is beneath him. Whenever they can the Turkana still carry out ferocious raids on their neighbors, ostensibly to steal cattle, but really to fight. Unlike the effete Masai, whose pathetic efforts to keep up the image of a fighting nation too long after they have ceased to be one has led only to decadence, the Turkana still are a tough people. The environment is partly responsible; only a Turkana could endure Turkanaland.

One thing the Turkana do is at first sight strangely at variance with their otherwise contemptuous manners: they beg. Wherever you go in Turkanaland people of all ages and ranks tug at you, cajoling or demanding whatever takes their fancy. Their main interest is tobacco—to a Turkana there is no greater prize—and both sexes chew it or sniff snuff. The most insolent warrior or the most dignified elder will drop all pretense to beg tobacco. Teleki's first encounter with them began with an aggressive demonstration that ended almost as soon as it had begun with the warriors waiting expectantly for gifts of tobacco.

These endless demands are extremely annoying at first, at least until one comprehends the basis of this seemingly anomalous trait. The westerner dislikes handing over his possessions and resents attempts to make him do so. But among pastoralists such as the Turkana a different outlook prevails. Turkana families are completely autonomous units; there is no community as such. They are brought up as individuals acting primarily in their own interests. Indeed if they did not, they would not survive. Within the family the father is the head, and he reckons his wealth in terms of his domestic stock, his camels, cattle and goats.

The ambition of every Turkana man is to acquire as many cattle and goats as he can, for not only is his status judged by his wealth, but the more goats he gets, the more wives he can buy. And the more wives he has, the more goats he can raise, and so on.

In cultivating his fortune, however, a number of factors work against him. First of all, to buy wives he must part with goats. Secondly, when his sons leave his family and take wives of their own, the father is expected to pay the first bride price on behalf of each of his sons. Thirdly, all disputes are settled by payment in goats. Fourthly, the wealthier a man gets the more his relatives and friends sponge off him, for the poor always feel their poverty is owed something by the wealth of the rich. In all these transactions the owner of the goats sees his fortune being whittled away, and he fights against it as hard as he can. But to maintain harmonious relations with other families he must conform to custom.

A few rounds of Ngalisio at Alia

Thus the son must demand of his father the goats to pay for his wife. But his father has a formidable array of excuses acquired over a lifetime's haggling—so the son learns to demand that which is his by customary right, but which will never be given him until he demands it.

And so it is throughout their affairs. That which you want you must demand, and likewise that which is expected of you must be given. In order to win you must learn to demand more

Mr. McConnell

Our flying
machine after a month of
particularly scaly
landings

El Greco the
Wildman with the flakes of
Leviathan's flesh

than you expect to get—what you lose on the wives you try to win back on the daughters.

Thus it is possible to put their outstretched palms in context, and even more, to find that they themselves are generous by nature towards people and demands of which they approve. Their society has a rare harmony, and the Turkana, for all his wild and independent spirit, is proud to say that he is the friend of all other Turkana.

In the Turkana language there is no word for "yes." The affirmative is taken for granted. This seems strange to us in a society where affirmation is sufficiently striking as to require a special word. Deep within his soul the Turkana affirms everything. His relationships with his fellow men are positive with a natural exchange of things understood. There is a fundamental communion of the spirit where affirmation needs no verbal recognition, and yet an immense individual liberty is retained.

In the hot lazy afternoons the Turkana of Kalokol gather in little groups beneath the rustling palms where deep pools of black shadow absorb them. There men sleep for a while, or talk. When the subjects of sex, politics, and business have for the moment been dealt with, they often begin a game called "Ngalisio," a game that springs from the very substance of their characters. It is a true game, uncontrived and intuitive. It is a simple game that can be played anywhere, any time, by varying numbers of players. Two rows of shallow holes are scooped out of the ground in which a number of small stones are placed. The players squat around in the dust, and, one at a time, move stones in various combinations from hole to hole.

The game in various forms is played all over Africa, but nowhere more avidly than in Turkanaland. It has an air of great mystery to nonplayers like the westerner, for it seems to them fantastically complex. Some think it has esoteric, even mystical, qualities, that only an African could fathom. The onlooker trying to unravel

the play sees only endless inconsistencies: the number of holes varies; so do the number of stones and the number of players; there is apparently no clear pattern in the manner of moving stones from hole to hole.

When the observer asks for an explanation the answer he gets, like as not, is a laugh. He presses for details and gets only a vague description of moves, never an outline of the form of the game. Finally he asks what has to be done to win, and with much laughter is told that hardly anybody ever wins. It is not surprising therefore that the game should be considered esoteric. But the game is really very simple. The object is not so much to win as to play. The aim is to acquire as many stones as possible, perhaps all. Yet it is impossible to get all the stones, and each player knows that sooner or later another player will take his stones from him. Nevertheless he always dreams of one day acquiring all the stones, and so he plays a perpetual game that is interrupted each time he has to leave, but never ended.

Dawn in Turkanaland

The game reflects his life. Always there is the dream of one day acquiring everything; but the society is so structured that the dream is impossible. A man simply goes on living and striving until one day he dies, and the game is continued by the survivors.

And so the Turkana will laugh when you ask about his game, not because he wishes to conceal it from you, but because he is unable to explain it to you. A man learns to play simply by playing. Each move is learned by testing it against the other player's approval or disapproval. Thus he does not know how he learned to play any more than he knows how he learned to live. And the greatest thing about the Turkana is that he knows for certain that life is merely living. He knows fulfillment, and asks nothing extra of any

man, nor of fate.

When I was about ready to leave on the first journey to the other side of the lake, it was announced that four men were needed to skin crocs and generally assist. There was no direct response, but several men intimated to Bob McConnell that they might be interested. Then, after some direct discussions with me, four men said they would accept my money and accompany me to the other side. They never actually agreed to become my employees, obedient to my orders. Rather, they went as far as their dignity permitted, while making it quite clear that they considered my intentions both ill conceived and pointless. I was made to feel that in some way it was an honor to pay them.

Volunteers were then sought for the post of chef. This astonished them. However, one man, Atikukeni, who had traveled outside Turkanaland, announced that for an additional fee he would run the kitchen. His cooking, it turned out, consisted of dropping slabs of catfish, some fat, and plenty of sand into a pan and heating it for an indeterminate period. The result was then dumped, wordlessly, before us. There was, to be sure, nothing to say.

Though the crew were all Turkana, they came from the famine camp at Kalokol. As such they

"The Turkana are by no means dainty about dirt; they eat everything, even their dogs."
(Von Höhnel)

Ebei takes forty on a tent mallet

Elata using community toothbrush

Our men daily consumed vast quantities of croc meat, and their fire with a huge bowl of simmering flesh, often complete with scales, presented an awesome sight.

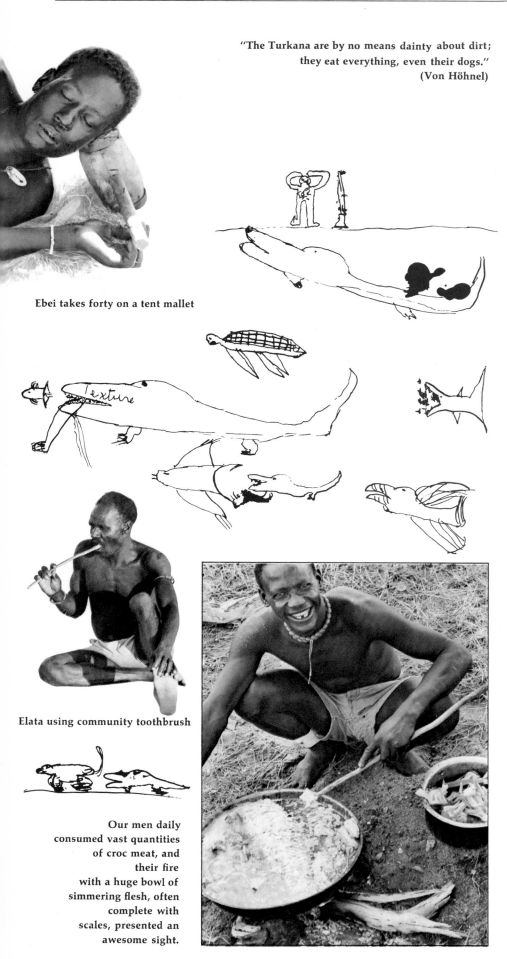

were, of necessity, subsistence fishermen rather than the nomadic herders and warriors they dreamt of being. They were ashamed of their poverty and—to them—dishonorable livelihood, and placed an exaggerated value on their dignity. This, inevitably, robbed them of their capacity for spontaneity and enthusiasm, leaving them, for their kind, unusually introspective and petty.

Atikukeni, as well as being cook, was the company grumbler, and his groans were heard monotonously throughout the survey. Tukoi was taciturn and direct. He was the only one who had any idea of getting the work done and we always gave orders through him. Goaded by Atikukeni, Tukoi represented the others in their numerous disputes with us, and was a stubborn negotiator. Ebei was dumb and affable. He saw himself as a wag and soon became the camp jester. When we were not around he entertained the others at our expense, very wittily, apparently. Elata, tall and rugged, was the oldest at about fifty. He was unusually shy for a race of opinionated extroverts, which gave him an engaging quality.

Elata and I once had a bitter quarrel at Kalokol over some trivial matter of principle at the end of which he snarled his resignation and stalked off across the sand spitting like a steam engine. But at the start of the next trip he appeared and announced laughingly that he was back on the payroll. When I said that we were getting along fine without him, he looked so genuinely puzzled that I took him back. Apart from this, the crew stayed with us until the end of our time at the lake. They were loyal, and in their own, often inexplicable, way took their responsibilities seriously. I often found them irritating, timid, and thoughtless. They always found me irritating, foolhardy, and incomprehensible. They would do so much and no more. Mutinies were fairly frequent, but short-lived. On the east shore we had the upper hand, for they depended on us for transportation home. After some particularly humiliating experience, such as my telling them that they were nothing but famine-camp flower children, good only for smoking *bhangi* and dancing, they would send Tukoi to announce that I was to return them immediately to the other side. I would answer that a couple of hundred miles walk around the lake shore should be nothing to such rugged fellows—they were free to go. But within a few hours the matter would be forgotten.

They worked for money and did not confuse anybody with false sentiments. Our purpose was of absolutely no interest to them. They would do what we asked so long as it did not involve any risk that to them seemed unreasonable. What we saw as timidity was to them common sense. Courage and initiative, after all, subserve selfish motives, and in his own interests the Turkana is bold and fierce. Naturally we found their detachment from our aspirations intensely aggravating on occasion. When extra work was needed to rectify some mishap they saw only misery, and would set up a woebegone chorus of whines.

Halfway through the survey a fifth man joined the crew who was quite different from the rest. We called him El Greco the Wildman, for his knock-kneed physique made him look like something out of an El Greco painting. He was a real Turkana from the bush, an adventurer who joined us purely for the hell of it. He had none of the reserve and plaintiveness of the others; for him the gusto of the moment was all that mattered. Swashbuckling, enthusiastic, and always cheerful, he never objected to a special task, and despite our lack of a common language we had no trouble communicating, for he was intelligent and quick. The Wildman spoke no language but his own. English sounded comic to him and Swahili he scorned as beneath his dignity. But we could address him in any language and he would laugh uproariously, not in mockery, but out of enthusiasm, and go off content to discover the meaning of the message later. He had that particular mixture of affirmation and independence that is the true Turkana character.

The Wildman's stomach was a mass of jagged scars. We asked him why, and he told us that he once had a bad belly ache which a sorcerer had offered to cure by slashing open his belly to release the malevolent spirits obviously lurking within. We asked if the treatment had worked, and with a great shout of laughter he said: "No!" He was at once delighted with the medicine and indifferent to its uselessness.

Later, when I brought a plane to the lake to replace the feeble Curse, the men tried hard to treat it with the indifference they thought proper, as their ancestors had treated Martin Johnson's years before. They all succeeded except Elata, for whom the first few trips were

just too much. He could not bring himself to look out of the windows and sat as still as he could, staring at his lap. The others teased him about this, and he chuckled, but remained steadfast. At length he was ready to look outside, and he did so gravely, almost politely, and without comment. The others asked him then what he saw. But he only smiled—was he to explain to a lot of grinning hyenas what the world looked like from a plane? *Hé!* such foolery.

The Turkana's studied indifference to flight did not fool me—in reality they were very dubious about the whole thing. Men simply were not made to fly. One day I was flying across the lake a few feet above the water when Tukoi, who was sitting in the co-pilot's seat, suddenly let out a blood-curdling scream and started flailing about. For a pilot there is always a slight worry that a nervous passenger might panic and seize the controls. I wondered how I was going to subdue him once he got free of his seat belt. Then he subsided a bit and I saw him reaching behind his back trying to get at something. Still whooping and wriggling, he found it—a much flattened but still mean-looking yellow scorpion. It must have really hurt, for it had stung him in the small of his back where his belt prevented him from getting at it. Thereafter we kept a sharp lookout for stowaways when loading the plane.

Elata, despite his shyness towards strangers, was always on the lookout for a chance to play crude Turkana practical jokes on the others. He had a peculiar way of laughing—it began within, his old face remaining impassive until after he started to laugh; suddenly it would craze into a thousand wrinkles, like a windscreen hit by a stone. He would sit, whooping and cackling so loudly that the Egyptian geese would take fright and circle around camp, honking fretfully.

He was childishly mischievous and would provoke the others into laughter for no reason at all except to spend half an hour laughing. At night his gritty voice switched to a rasping snore, hilarious to the others, who would wake him just to tell him how funny he sounded; and of course, that would simply make him vomit up great gouts of laughter himself. And so it would go on.

following pages:
Turkana man wears sandals and a cape that flutters behind him as he walks; otherwise he goes naked.
A west coast Leviathan is divided, and one foreleg heads straight for the Sunday roast.

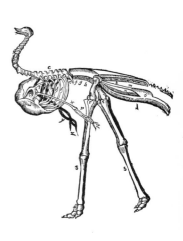

The Turkana are an economical people. Theirs is a merciless country devoid of luxury, from which even the wild animals have long since disappeared. They are tough, hard people accustomed to the bare essentials of life only. One might suppose that this would produce a spartan reserve; but no. At the slightest chance they give way to frolic and vanity, to gluttony and indulgence. And their appetites are voracious. When Teleki entered Turkanaland there was a severe famine from which his own party very nearly died. Yet the Turkana would gaily barter a dozen goats for a pinch of snuff—at once attaching great value to minute quantities and displaying a careless disregard for the morrow.

The Turkana have a reputation for exceptional voracity. Von Höhnel wrote: "The Turkana are by no means dainty about diet; they eat everything, even their dogs." Nowadays, sophisticated Turkana claim more discerning palates, tending to rank the order of edibility of things. Thus croc meat is good if there is nothing else; but they pretend that it is only under relatively trying conditions that they eat it. On the east shore the men daily consumed vast quantities of croc meat, and their fire, with a huge bowl of flesh, often complete with scales, was an awesome sight.

To convince us and remind themselves that they weren't the indiscriminate feeders people said they were, the men invented a particularly irritating habit. It was a rule that the croc carcasses were not to be butchered until my investigations were complete. More than once a particularly valuable piece of material had been found broiling merrily on the fire, useless to science. Thus when there were several crocs to be examined at once, the carcasses would end up all together in a line. While skinning them, the men would debate which ones were fit for human consumption. Invariably at least one would be condemned. Sometimes when there was only one croc they would even condemn that, and then grumble that they had no meat to eat and wanted to go home.

When asked what was the matter with the "bad" croc, they would reply:

"It's abnormal."

"What's abnormal?"

"Can't you see, it's thin and deformed—quite disgusting in fact."

They would shrug their shoulders and wander off, making it clear that it was pointless trying to edify such a steelbrain.

There was of course no difference between the carcasses, but if I scoffed at them they would go off in a huff and wash their knives. I longed to switch the rejected carcass while their backs were turned for one they had said they would

eat, and actually succeeded in doing so three times. But it remained a private joke, for they would have been offended to think that I thought I could hoodwink them so easily. Later, while they were eating the erstwhile reject, I would stroll over to their fire and ask how it tasted. Huge grins and chomping jaws proved how delectable it was. I asked if anybody would notice if somehow the carcasses got mixed up. "Of course," they chorused, "we Turkana are very particular about what we eat."

The Turkana, as a people, are tough, wild and aggressive. At the same time they are peaceful in a way that only contented people can be. Turkana warriors will fight fiercely to the death, and cherish their fighter's vocation above all else; yet they are devoid of viciousness or hatred. They are in equilibrium with their environment. Fighting, famine, and disease regulate their numbers and those of their livestock. There pastoralism is an ancient, stable cultural mode. But like the ancient, unchanging crocodile, it is a stagnant mode in the evolutionary sense. Its very harmony casts its own dark shadow because it *cannot* change, or meet change.

The tranquility of the Lake Rudolf wilderness will be disturbed, because urban, industrial, "successful" man needs the land and its resources. Therefore he will civilize it. The famine campers of Kalokol barely ripple Ferguson's Gulf for their subsistence. But the seething cities and towns must feed off the country; the fish of Rudolf are needed to feed those who will never see the lake. The spears and necklaces of the Turkana will be exported to satisfy the atavistic curiosity of tourists on their travels through the curio shops of Africa. The windy distances of Lake Rudolf will be shortened and obscured by roads and planes and hotels and sightseers and fishermen and game wardens and scientists and town planners and all the other conquistadores of the superior civilization of today and tomorrow.

Like the American Indian a century ago, the Turkana have met an intruder which neither their bravest warriors nor their strongest magic can deal with; they have come upon their Manifest Destiny. The Turkana, the crocodiles, the lake and the land—all are about to be rubbed out and repopulated with development, obedience, and progress. The Sioux and Cheyenne and the Turkana would have understood each other perfectly. The warriors would have fought each other and there would have been glory in the land. Glory and peace, the peace of human beings living in harmony with their own natures and with the world around them.

CHAPTER 5 THIS IS REPTILE COUNTRY

*Moite days—Curse yields up the ghost—replace
with heavier-than-air flying machine—mysterious nocturnal intruder—Elata astonished by Leviathan's
tail—Guy Pool slain by bandits—inclement weather spawns violent tempest—
Providence delivers us from watery grave—Nimrod's
nomenclature—tallyho of the all-time world record—Phobosuchus, King over all the Children
of Pride—phantoms of genesis—mode of hunting the sly saurian—thieving lions feast on our specimens—
miraculous escape—Turkana fear supernatural intervention.*

After strenuous weeks spent in abortive efforts at catching live crocs, the main work could begin—a year of collecting forty to fifty crocs every month for study. Except for a brief spell on North Island (Chapter 6), the collections alternated between Moite and Alia Bay; but these two places were so different in character that the trips stick in my mind as one collective journey to each.

Peter joined me at this stage and shared the tedious hours of day and night hunting, not to mention dragging the crocs back to camp for processing. His devil-may-care manner was a tonic for the rest of us, though he clearly confirmed the Turkana crew's suspicion that all white men were completely crazy.

Just before he came, the wretched Curse gave up the ghost. I was on my way, alone, to Kalokol on a windy day following a hard blow that had left a heavy swell. The nineteen miles to Central Island were uneventful, but once there the underwater base of the volcano piled up the swells much higher and steeper, and I needed all the helm I had to keep course through the turbulent water. Because the Curse's engine was unreliable, I had rigged an outboard engine over the side as an auxiliary. Shortly after passing the island a pintle sheared, and the rudder—overworked in the heavy sea—carried away. It was a fairly tricky situation. Kalokol was eight miles away, and though I was past the violent water around the island, the sea was still rough, with a strong wind blowing. Quickly starting the outboard, I began to steer the craft by varying the revolutions from each engine according to the bias needed. The following sea tended to turn the boat beam on, requiring constant juggling of the two throttles. What's more,

Hunting was arduous without a boat

Vital parts

it was impossible to reach both throttles from one position, so I was scrambling madly to and fro all the way to the gulf—nearly two hours away.

As a result of this episode and the fact that the Curse needed many other repairs, it was decided to lay her up forever before she drowned the lot of us. The idea was to replace her with a plane. I hoped to borrow enough for the right sort of machine and then resell it after the survey for about as much. The great advantage of a plane was in saving time—the most limiting factor in the survey. Flat desert country around Lake Rudolf meant the plane could land pretty well anywhere. The ideal machine would have been a Cessna 180, but as none was available at the time, I settled for an old nosewheel Cessna 182, which had a reasonable performance and could lift half a ton. It served us faithfully to the end, and without it the work could never have been finished.

One of our first Moite trips was to a small rocky inlet ten miles south of the mountain. It was a desolate spot with long wide beaches that were difficult to hunt because of the lack of cover.

One morning Peter and I awoke as usual in the first light of dawn and went over to the men's fire to sit for a few minutes and watch the sun come up. Suddenly one of them called

out at a distance, very agitated, and demanded that we come and look at something. He led us to a spot about fifty yards from where we slept and pointed to the ground. There, clearly visible in the dust, were the tracks of a man, only a few hours old. The tracks were distinguished from our own by the light camelskin sandals the owner had been wearing; none of us possessed such shoes. The man had crept up in the dark, stood and watched us for a while, and then left as silently as he had come. Why? Who was he? We had seen no sign of the Rendile or El Molo herdsmen who sometimes watered their stock in the lake; these people would in any case have come openly during the daytime. We followed the tracks but soon lost them on

hard ground; nor did we ever discover who made them. It was an unnerving incident, for it meant that bandits might be in the area. We often remembered them in the cold dark nights when the wind howled and the solitude pressed hard upon us.

Hunting was arduous without a boat, for we had to walk many miles each night to find enough crocs. Eventually it became impossible to get a sufficient number of specimens simply operating from camp, so we decided to hunt a small swamp six miles to the north in which there were good numbers of crocs. Unfortunately there was nowhere near it to land the plane, so we had to walk.

Setting off two hours before sunset we would arrive as it was getting dark. We would hunt until midnight, tie the night's catch of crocs to a submerged tree, then walk back to camp and sleep until dawn. We could have slept in the swamp, but after the ominous night visitor I did not want to leave the plane unattended for longer than absolutely necessary. In the morning we would return, measure and skin the crocs, collect the bits and pieces, and carry the skins back to camp. In all, this meant walking nearly thirty miles a day with only a few hours sleep, and it was a relief to give up the swamp after four days, when it no longer yielded enough adults.

About two o'clock one afternoon a big croc came out about four hundred yards below camp. I stalked it from the dunes behind the beach and got easily to within seventy-five yards, and sliding the gun through a tussock of spike grass, killed it. It turned out to be a large male nearly thirteen feet long. Such a big croc would be a valuable source of really fresh material for the various organ collections, so I was anxious to skin it as quickly as possible.

For an hour or so after death a croc's body writhes and twitches in reflex response to any irritation such as a knife point, and is difficult to skin as a result. This particular beast, only a few minutes dead, was particularly mobile. But

the value of such fresh material made me determined to get inside immediately; so we held on to the bucking, heaving croc and got to work.

Topsell, in his splendid medieval bestiary, *The Natural History of Serpents*, gives among many tips and warnings the advice that "the tayle of a crocodile is his strongest part," and that when attacking "they strike him down and astonish him with their tailles." However that may be, it happened that Elata was squatting alongside the animal sharpening his knife when someone jabbed the base of its tail, causing it to take a mighty swipe. The huge three-hundred pound hunk of armored meat caught Elata square across his ribs with a sickening thud, bowling him down the beach. He sat up, truly astonished, and there ensued that delicate moment while he debated whether he was the victim of labor mistreatment or the butt of a huge joke. Happily, the Turkana reacted typically—and the sand being soft and the laughter loud, Elata gave way to his own peculiar mirth. He began shaking like a scratching Labrador while deeply buried chuckles rumbled around inside, escaping occasionally as wild hoots. Afterwards sporadic reminiscent guffaws would set off new bouts of laughter. Elata was a tough old man and apart from a large bruise suffered nothing from his astonishment.

Eventually, having exhausted all crocodile sources within walking distance of camp, we had to look still farther afield. As we had a little extra fuel for the plane, we planned to fly south about fifteen miles to a small bay partly sheltered from the wind with lots of good crocs in it. Taking two men, blankets, a torch and the rifle, we took off just before sunset, somewhat delayed by a croc we had shot late in the afternoon.

We arrived as it was getting dark, and with only a few minutes in which to look for a suitable landing place I circled the area a couple of times. With the light failing rapidly I saw what looked like a good spot, made one low pass to inspect it, and without thinking what such a smooth

"They strike him down and astonish him with their tailles."

stretch of ground might be, I landed. Touching down on target, I shut the throttle and waited for the plane to slow down. As it lost speed and the weight settled on the wheels it suddenly felt as if the brakes had been applied full force, and realizing in the same instant what was wrong, I jammed the throttle open in a doomed attempt to take off again. But it was too late. Even at full power the craft simply slewed to a halt. I shut off and sat there cursing my stupidity; in my haste I had failed to realize that the inviting stretch of smooth ground was the sandy bed of a dry watercourse—the very last place to land a plane.

We dispiritedly shot three good crocs that night, wondering if they were going to be of any use, for we anticipated many weary hours manhandling the aircraft out of its dismal sand-pit. The organ collections would be ruined and probably the skins too. What if the plane couldn't be moved? To leave the machine where it was,

The most we ever asked of the plane was an incredible load of 12 good crocs in addition to Peter and the Wildman, plus our bedding and equipment.

Refueling at Alia

following pages:
The sculptured volcanic moonscape called Central Island, where we often found ourselves marooned in afternoon storms

wide open to destruction by bandits, was too much to contemplate, for the insurance was unequivocally "invalid if damaged by war or acts of terrorism and violence." We would simply have to dig like ant-bears.

We began work well before dawn to get as much done as possible before the sun started baking up the area. It was soul-destroying labor scooping the abrasive sand away with our hands from in front of the wheels, making a roadbed of sticks, and then laying our blankets down as a final surface. The distance to hard ground was only about seventy yards, but the path we made was so uneven that it was impossible to manhandle the plane, which weighed three-quarters of a ton, over it. I had to start the engine over and over; each time the plane moved forwards a few feet and then sank again into the sand. The laboriousness was more enervating than the actual physical effort, and we wondered how long the battery would keep starting the engine. The seventy yards seemed an impossible distance, and the wind, inevitably, chose this

day not to blow, so that within a few hours the sand felt as if it were on fire. By ten o'clock we were only half way, and were compelled to go and rest.

At this point I recalled a game warden friend who once got his truck hopelessly bogged down in the middle of a river. Seething with frustration and rage, he resolved to punish the machine for what was obviously a deliberate attempt to obstruct him. Suppressing his anger, he calmly ordered his men to go and cut themselves a stick apiece, six feet long and two inches thick, and to cut him one too. Puzzled by this strange order, the men went off, and when they returned he stationed them around the offending vehicle. Then, roaring like an elephant, he threw himself upon the machine and beat it with his stick, ordering the startled men to do likewise. He accompanied this with a stream of vile oaths, of which he had a fine collection, and they belabored the truck thus until their rods were shattered and their anger spent.

At about twelve o'clock, having got to firmer sand, we thought of a way to cover the last fifteen yards in one go. The reason the plane dug itself in so easily was that its nosewheel was forward of the center of gravity and was pushed underground, so to speak, by the weight of the machine behind it. We figured that if we could suspend enough weight from the tail to counterbalance the craft, perhaps we could keep the nosewheel from digging in. First we tied on a large rock, but this proved insufficient. Then we got Ebei to hang like a fruitbat from the same point. This was a most unpleasant job, for when I revved the engine he was given a violent sandblasting. He stuck it out, though, and the idea worked until the last moment, when the nosewheel, striking a particularly soft patch, plunged in bringing the propellor hard down onto the ground—a shower of sand and gravel attesting to the force of the impact. My heart sank, and on inspecting the damage I found both propellor tips badly bent. They had to be straightened before we could fly. Using two hard chunks of lava, one as a backing and the other as a hammer, we straightened the blades, to our satisfaction at least, though I was not sure how this was going to be explained to the engineers back in Nairobi.

Now, having extricated the plane, we still had to get airborne. All around was rocky eroded ground—most unsuitable for any sort of flying operation. After much casting about, we located an area 130 yards long without major obstruction which would have to be the runway. There was a sharp bend a third of the way along and the surface was extremely rough. The hot, still air left no margin for error; nor would there be a

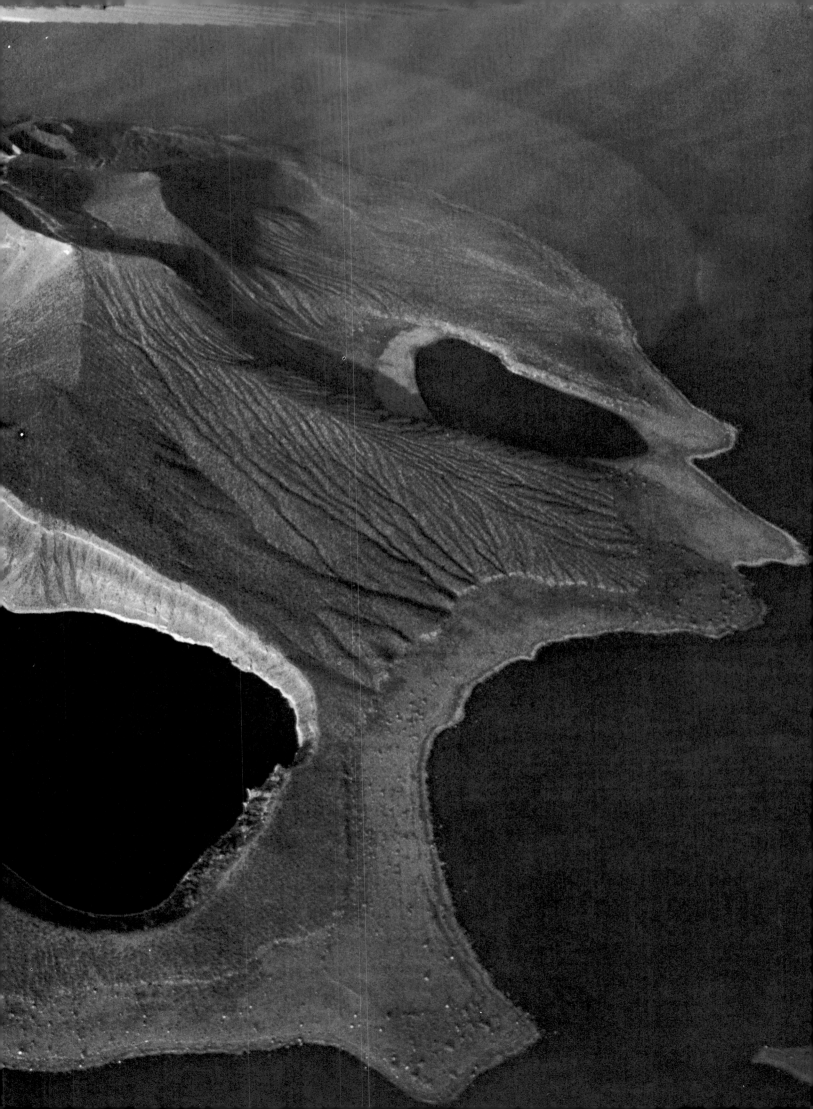

second try, for the strip ended at a gully. Using the entire available distance, I took off. Landing nearby on more suitable ground, we loaded up and returned to camp, unsure whether the expedition represented a gain or a loss.

Near the southeast corner of the lake are some fresh water springs called Loingalani. Teleki camped there on his way to Lake Stefanie, and El Molo and Samburu herdsmen water their stock there. It is a peaceful spot in the barren, lava-strewn desert that surrounds the lake, an oasis surrounded by a grove of doum palms that shelter the traveler from the hot vicious wind and relieve his gaze from a glaring wasteland.

Predictably, one of man's first organized intrusions on Lake Rudolf was at this place, and the inevitable "hotel" was built over the spring. It was made of palm logs and thatched walls from which visitors could sally forth to get seasick on the lake in quest of fish. Most of them, thinking how sick they had been on the flight from Nairobi, stayed by the bar congratulating each other on having found Lake Rudolf (invisible from the bar), and would return with glowing

reports of the fantastic place they had been to. Anyway, they were happy and had good memories, for they had been hospitably entertained by the manager, Guy Pool. But you can no longer spend a careless weekend at Loingalani, for the hotel has closed.

About eight P.M. on the night of November 19, 1965, while we were farther north, near Moite, six bandits armed with rifles attacked the hotel. There was only one guest there that night, a Catholic priest, who was sitting with Guy Pool in the hotel lounge, talking and sharing a drink. It was a quiet evening, the whole place as usual standing completely open and unprotected. So far as anyone knew there was nothing to be afraid of, although the vast region of Kenya to the north and east was subject to sporadic attacks from Somali *shifta*.

The first sign of trouble came with the firing of shots at the main building. Alarmed and no doubt frightened, Guy leapt to his feet, and shouting for his keys, ran to his bedroom for his gun. He never found the keys, and instead of fleeing as the servants had, he hid under his bed. The bandits found him and dragged him to the lounge, where they tied him to a chair.

A striped hyena that became tangled in ropes securing a collection of night crocs twenty yards offshore and underwater

The priest, who never left the lounge, they bound back down on the table. What took place between the bandits and their captives will never be known; all that can be said for certain is that the two men were shot dead and left where they were bound.

Before leaving, the bandits shot up the radio telephone, power generator, and two of the three vehicles there. In the meantime they had captured a third man, an Italian driver named Tony who was also working at the hotel. Forcing Tony to drive, they used the undamaged vehicle as a getaway car, making forty miles before running out of fuel near a place called Gus. Abandoning the car, they disappeared into the bush, taking Tony with them. Rumor has it that after killing him they skinned him, and members of the gang were reputed to wear pieces of his skin. Whatever his fate, he was never seen again.

So bloodshed and sudden death shattered the peacefulness of Loingalani. On the one side the quiet green waters of the lake, on the other the harsh unpredictable desert, both inscrutable, both as cruel as they are beautiful.

We did not know of the incident until several days later, when we returned to Kalokol. A possibility had hardened into a grim fact, and from then on the lake always seemed different; more distant, a little colder, with yet another secret to be guarded. The northern frontier was subsequently closed to visitors until 1971.

Not long after I brought the plane to the lake, a friend lent us an aluminum dinghy that he had dredged up from the bottom of another lake where it had sunk and been abandoned years before. Though old and only twelve feet long, it proved invaluable, allowing us to work further from camp and save precious time. At the beginning of each new trip to Moite or Alia we would transport all the equipment across from Kalokol in five or six loads in the plane, finally leaving it at Kalokol for safety and making the last trip to the east shore in the dinghy. It was a faster boat than the Curse, usually crossing in three or four hours depending on the weather. But the voyages were always somewhat anxious, for the tiny craft was incapable of weathering the open lake when the wind blew, so that there was always the risk of being caught halfway across. That was exactly what happened to us once, very nearly putting an end to all our activities.

For a week past there had been a succession of still spells alternating with periods of drizzle and wind. It was the season of uncertain weather when storms blew and the lake received its annual pittance of rain. Often Moite would be hidden in dark foreboding clouds. Strange tides would surge into normally sheltered inlets, and

even the crocs became unsettled, so that we would find them basking on usually deserted sandbars. These storms, generated up towards Ethiopia, swept down the lake, hustling the water into long fast rollers that were especially ill-tempered because they had to ram against the lingering swell from the south.

We left Moite, on a still, quiet afternoon. The north sky was black and blotchy like the back of an old croc—the aftermath of a storm we'd just had. Instead of clearing, though, it swirled and glowered, and we knew that another blow might be boiling up. But there were even chances that it would die down, and time, as always, goaded us on. To complete the work meant using every day to the full; many times better judgment had to give way, and we fell back on luck.

Today was one such day. Central Island, bearing in mind our speed on a none-too-calm lake, was about three hours away. For an hour the going was good, with no wind and only an uneasy swell. Then, like an ominous whisper, we felt a puff of cold new wind from the north. The sky was darkening and the first gust was soon followed by more, so that within a quarter of an hour it was blowing steadily. The breeze rapidly freshened, inciting the waves that up to now had been milling about, to concentrate in one direction. We had to force our way straight through them, the steep slopes and sharp crests making heavy going.

All the time we had to keep reducing speed.

It was not long before we were really worried, for the waves kept growing and our speed diminishing. At any time a wave could pile up and break into the boat, swamping us in an instant. The spray was icy cold, and the sodary water in our eyes left us half blind so that steering became increasingly difficult. The boat was pounding so hard against the ever-growing waves that we expected a seam to open at any time. Our objective was the lee of the island, now only a mile or two away. The wind kept freshening, reducing our speed and building the sea. There came a time when it was touch and go, the engine driving us towards the island, now tantalizingly close, and the storm smashing us back into the lake. Without the shelter of the island we would have been swamped; but the old volcano saved us and we struggled to shore. Had we gone down with such a north wind we might well have been blown the entire hundred miles to the southern end of the lake, assuming we did not drown.

With enormous relief we pulled the boat up on the beach and prepared to see the storm out on the island. It lasted the whole night and most of the next day, and it wasn't until late the following afternoon that it was calm enough for us to

Leviathan is taken

leave. When we came to launch the boat we found it completely buried in sand, for the storm, the most violent I ever saw, had moved the entire beach back fifteen yards, nearly taking the boat with it. This, combined with the pounding of the day before, had strained several seams, and when we put the boat in the water it leaked so badly that water came in faster than we could bail it out. As we had nothing with which to repair the seams, it looked as if we were stranded on the island. Then I saw that most of the leaks were well forward, on the part of the hull that stuck out of the water when the boat planed. Kalokol was nine miles away, a journey of forty minutes at full power. Provided we planed the whole way, thus keeping the bow clear of the water, we reckoned we could just make it. If the engine faltered, or if the sea roughened, we would sink. But the plan worked, and bailing hard and breathing even harder, we arrived at Kalokol.

It turned out that in our limited time getting forty crocs a month was the major problem. So, whether we liked it or not, hunting became for us the dominant activity in the day's work; we had to *be* hunters. We had to learn all the tricks of a croc hunter's trade and naturally adopted many of their ways. Though I needed a random sample and therefore shot any adult available, the bigger ones—being older and smarter—were relatively scarce and therefore more interesting. While hunting we got the habit of referring to our quarry by the names used by croc hunters, who also prize the bigger ones for their bigger hides. Any less than 6 feet long (the length at which most females mature), being relatively worthless, were given derogatory names. Five- and 6-footers were "lizards"; 4- and 5-footers, "watchstraps"; and any smaller, "geckos." Crocs 6 to 8 feet long were "good muggers," and the majority of our specimens were of this size. Those in the range of 8 to 10 feet were "bonus gators"; 10- to 13-footers were "magnums," while anything bigger than that, a rare beast, was a "monster pebbleworm." (Fourth-Dynasty Egyptians, who used to mummify crocs, including 15-footers, likewise had a professional eye for a big croc and called anything bigger than 10 feet a "great" croc.)

This classification, of course, bore no relation to a crocodile's status from a biological point of view. Nevertheless it relieved us of the need to be objective, as did another evergreen pastime of all croc hunters—speculations on how big crocs get. There is something intriguing about the dimensions of large animals, particularly mysterious, highly symbolic ones like crocodiles. The temptation to exaggerate is apparently very

strong and many a fabulous monster lurks—unmeasured—in the jungles of Africa. "At any rate I have seen several longer than the little A.I.A. and she measures 42 feet . . . twenty five yards away lay the biggest crocodile I had yet seen. Comparing him with the A.I.A. . . . I reckoned him to be quite 50 feet long." This bit of bushwhack, from *A Visit to Stanley's Rearguard*, by a Mr. Werner, is typical of "big croc" stories.

The biggest croc is a mythical beast, but it should be possible to determine at least the "record" croc, the biggest ever convincingly measured. But even this will always be doubtful, for between reading the tape and recording the result the odd foot or two has a sly way of creeping in. Anderson, in his *Zoology of Egypt* (1898), reports that despite a meticulous search of the literature he could find no authentic measurement of a croc as long as 17 feet, though 14- and 15-footers were common. The biggest we shot on Rudolf, which was as big as any we saw, was 15 feet 9 inches long. Of 30,000 crocs the Bousfields claim to have shot on Lake Rukwa, the longest was 17 feet 4½ inches. During Charles Pitman's 17-year campaign to exterminate crocs in Uganda, the biggest he measured was 18 feet. (That this was the only one exceeding 15 feet emphasizes their rarity.) Hugh Cott in 1961 made a search of the published records of big crocs. The biggest he turned up were one 17 feet 5 inches killed by the naturalist Hubbard on the Kafue River in 1927, and one 18 feet 4 inches claimed by the croc hunter Eric von Hippel on the Semliki River in 1954. But the record Nile croc is one shot by an unknown hunter on the Semliki in 1952: the skin was bought by

A firewood expedition in our overused (and overturned) boat

Watchstrap

Gecko

Lizard

facing page:
A one-time all-night
pistol record for perch,
98 lbs. Alia Bay,
May 28, 1966

———

A cracked
cranium and a bleeding leg

the Marketing Corporation of Uganda (which handled tens of thousands of croc skins in its time) and measured 19 feet 6 inches long.

While a 20-foot Nile croc is probably a fabulous beast, the world-record croc is actually bigger than that. It was an estuarine crocodile, *Crocodylus porosus*, reckoned to yield the biggest individuals of any living species. The trophy

La Gironière was so impressed with his prize that he carefully prepared the skull and sent it to the Agassiz Museum at Harvard. Nearly a century later, in 1924, Thomas Barbour, the herpetologist, searched the Agassiz Museum for La Gironière's croc. Sure enough, he found an enormous skull, unfortunately unlabeled, but of an estuarine croc and with a palate injury corresponding to La Gironière's musket shot. It is highly likely that this is the one from Luzon; but if it is, then La Gironière's tale (written 29 years after killing the croc) is tainted a little with fabulous tradition, for the skull measures a fraction less than 36 inches. Since the length of a croc's head is not more than one-seventh of its total length, it is easy to calculate that the croc was only 21 feet long, not 27. Nevertheless, this is still the "all-time world-record" croc. The difficulty the hunters had rolling it out of the river is not surprising, for a 21-footer would weigh 1¼ tons.

following pages:
After our boat blew away,
hunting meant wading
all night
and then walking miles
back to camp dragging the
crocs behind us.

———

Rolling up a 1250-pounder

———

A new all-night
record, 15 feet 4 inches

———

Collecting "the
Wormes of his teeth," in
this case leeches,
much as the fabled tooth-
thrush is said to do

———

A blanket
of desert predators smother
the post-mortem

belonged to a Frenchman, Paul de la Gironière, who lived near Luzon in the Philippines. In 1825 he was greatly annoyed by a crocodile that killed and ate one of his horses. Assembling a posse of spearmen, he led a chaotic tallyho after the croc, which because of its bulk and the smallness of the river, was unable to escape. Nevertheless, six hours and uncounted spear thrusts later it was still alive. La Gironière had fired several musket shots from close range, once into the reptile's mouth, seemingly without effect. In fact he later found that his musket caused scarcely any injury. Then a resourceful hunter drove a lance into the animal's back with a hammer and by a fluke found the spinal cord and killed the croc.

The beast was so heavy it took all forty hunters to roll it ashore. "When at last we had got him completely out of the water we stood stupefied with astonishment. From the extremity of his nostrils to the tip of his tail, he was found to be 27 feet long, and his circumference was 11 feet, measured under the armpits. His belly was much more voluminous, but we thought it unnecessary to measure him there, judging that the horse which he had breakfasted must considerably have increased his bulk. . . ."

Despite what we consider the awesome size of present-day Nile crocodiles, they are dwarfs compared to the crocodiles of former times. The family is an ancient one, tracing its lineage back 170 million years. Since then the house of crocodile has changed remarkably little compared to most other animal types—a tribute to the success and vigor of an evolutionary form that saw the rise and fall of uncounted orders of other animals. But the real monsters are long dead—even the massive estuarine crocs are mere pebbleworms compared to some of their ancient relatives. For some of them, like *Dinosuchus neivensis*, the Terrible Crocodile, a 30-footer that sculled the swamps of Colombia 100 million years ago, a Nile croc would have been no more than a handy snack. But the biggest of them all was *Phobosuchus*, the Fearsome Crocodile, an almost unimaginable 45 feet of pure croc. Just picture a croc 45 feet long (tipping the scales at 15 tons) lying asleep on a sandbar with its jaws agape.

There is a skull of Phobosuchus in the American Museum of Natural History 6 feet long by 3½ feet across. Some of the teeth are 6 inches long and 2 inches thick. The Fearsome Croc must have been one of the very few animals that swapped hunting yarns with *Tyrannosaurus rex*, the gigantic reptile that was the greatest terrestrial predator of all time, for the two were much of a size. Today these magnificent animals are but phantoms of genesis, scraps of fossilized bone from which we are hard-pressed to deduce even their shapes, let alone reconstruct their lives.

Since it was impossible to shoot all the crocs we needed during the day, we had to hunt them at night as well. We had hoped to do this from

a boat, but the wind ruled that out. Then we found that because the lake was shallow a long way out, most of the crocs were out of range of a hunter walking along the water's edge. So we had to go in after them. Our technique was for one of us to walk in front with a torch, followed closely by a rifleman. Behind him came one of the men to tow our kills along. This was necessary because if we left them on shore they were quickly stolen by the lions or hyenas that followed us when we were hunting at night.

The torch bearer would cast around for crocs, whose eyes shine red in torchlight. Finding a suitable one, we would try to approach without alarming the wary animal, which more often than not would silently submerge and disappear. Once down, a croc can last up to an hour without breathing. Although the light dazzled the crocs, many things worked against us to warn them of danger. It was essential to keep downwind, for their sense of smell is extremely good. Their hearing is keen too, and this was our greatest problem, for the ground underfoot was seldom easy to traverse soundlessly. Mostly it was a vile ooze studded with sharp chunks of lava and rocks ("sharp stones are under him: he spreadeth sharp pointed things upon the mire"). Every now and then someone would plunge into a soft patch, for it was a constant struggle to keep upright. Many were the crocs lost at the last moment as somebody subsided noisily into the lake. Scattered about were hippo footprints, deep holes in which the lava chunks clutched at you like gin traps. A shoe torn off deep beneath the mud was almost impossible to retrieve without alarming a croc floating a few feet away.

The extensive weed beds the crocs liked were worse than the open water, for the weed contained sharp spicules that lacerated your legs. And in it dwelt a fiendish beast in the form of a small water bug with a bite like a beesting. It was strange how often their attacks coincided with the critical moment when the gunman was about to squeeze the trigger, causing him to give an involuntary, disastrous twitch.

Early evening before the wind got up was the worst time, for one had to be particularly quiet in the still air. But the major problem was lake flies. These tiny insects swarmed in thousands around the light, constantly flying into our eyes and under our clothing. Sometimes the swarms were so dense that they reflected enough light back from the torch to expose us to the crocs. Or they would collect in the pool of light reflected off the water where the croc was, bothering it as they did us, so that it would submerge to avoid them. When the wind got up hunting was easier, for it masked our noise and dispersed

the lake flies. But then the waves jostled us, making shooting more difficult, and late at night, after one had fallen over or waded into deep water, it was bitterly cold. Often we would startle six-foot Nile perch that swam off with vigor enough to knock us off our feet. Their heads were hard as iron when they collided with your shins.

Floating crocs presented small targets, for only their eyes and the tops of their heads were above water. To guarantee a hit each time we found we had to get within fifteen yards. To shoot at greater distances meant occasional misses, and we found that in the long run we got better results by patiently getting really close.

facing page:
A 148-pound head

We check our equipment before begining the night's hunting

Emissaries from Technolopolis under cover of night

Having fired at a croc it would invariably disappear beneath the muddy water, whether it was wounded, dead or alive. If hit it was often not far under, and a foot would break the surface as it slowly rolled over and over. Usually, though, the bullet caused a sudden wriggle of its tail that drove it rapidly several yards even if it was dead. Thus by the time we stumbled to the spot where the croc had been shot there was seldom any sign of it, nor any means of telling whether it was dead or alive. So we would search for it by treading about until our toes bumped into it, at which point the success or otherwise of the shot would become apparent. As the dead ones give reflex movements long after death, the process of recovery was always full of scaly surprises.

The water was usually two or three feet deep, so once we located the croc we had to raise it to the surface, still unsure if it was alive. A stunned croc tends to lie motionless until disturbed, whereupon it abruptly regains consciousness. Once after "treading up" an 8-footer we took for dead, Peter began to tie a rope around its neck. Without warning the beast reared up with a violent thrashing. Its head struck Peter square in the middle of his chest with a noise like a mallet driving in a tent peg. The heavy bone of a croc's skull is covered only by a paper-thin layer of skin, and apparently it felt like being hit by a car. Luckily it did not crack his sternum, but the bruise lasted for weeks.

Of all the distasteful tasks we expected the Turkana to perform, night hunting was the most hated. To go into the water in the dark and deliberately provoke crocodiles was to them ridiculous. It was only by appealing to their pride that I got them to do it at all. When Peter was not there I had to rely on one of the men to wield the torch, which meant standing in front of me, i.e., between me and the croc, while I shot. It was all I could do to aim, so hard did they shiver; and our respective ideas of what constituted close range differed widely.

My biggest difficulty was persuading them to hold their ground whenever the situation looked menacing. Once, while hunting with Tukoi in very shallow water, a magnum croc surfaced about six feet away. We had not known it was there and the abruptness of its appearance was alarming. Although a large croc so close looks

fearsome, it is easy to kill at that range, and whipping round, I raised the gun to fire. But Tukoi took off like a reedbuck, his feet in the shallow water sounding like the skittering of a duck as it flies off water. The light went with him, of course, and just then the croc lunged past for deeper water, actually brushing my legs as it did so. There is at such times an awful moment of apprehension as one waits in the dark to find out whether the animal is attacking or fleeing.

On another occasion I was hunting in a patch of swamp where a lot of *msuaki* bushes had been drowned by the lake. Going along the water's edge on dry land, we approached a croc near the shore. I fired, but it was a bad shot, and the croc, wounded, made straight for us. Just as I was about to fire again, having let the croc get really close, my torch bearer fled. I never discovered if the croc was simply confused by its wound or attacking me, but in this case I think the latter. As the light disappeared I leapt aside and the croc stormed past me in the dark. Moments later a violent commotion began in the bush behind me, where the croc was thrashing around and roaring. I shouted, not very politely, for the torch, and then saw what had happened. The croc's momentum had driven it firmly beneath the twisted stem of a fallen *msuaki* bush, where it wriggled helplessly, pinned to the ground.

Holding the torch was bad enough, but what the Turkana flatly refused to do was "tread up" the dead bodies. We did not blame them and accepted that as our duty. It was a lot easier on the nerves with a pistol in one hand. But in this as in other matters the Wildman was an exception, and far from having to encourage him, we had to restrain him.

The Wildman's night shooting debut was typical. He had been told by the others what to do and followed quietly behind us as we approached a croc. I shot at it, and we started looking for the body. After several minutes of fruitless search I realized it was probably only wounded. The Wildman meanwhile had been searching with us, and suddenly with a triumphant whoop he reached down into the water and came up clutching an enraged and wriggling croc. Scorning the beast's snapping jaws and whipping tail he staggered towards us to show his find. I gestured to him to let go of it, a command he found rather puzzling, and very reluctantly he dropped it into the lake, where I could finish it off.

We got the others to explain to him about wounded crocs and he agreed to be more circumspect in the future, though it in no way dampened his spirits. It seemed that he looked upon

El Greco dragged this Nile perch about 5 miles to be weighed (185 lbs)

night shooting simply as a very fine way to spend an evening.

We got a taste of what could happen with a wounded croc midway through the survey, and the scare of that night was a sharp reminder to shoot accurately. Peter and I were hunting in Moite Bay, along a rocky shore with deep water only a few yards out. The slippery stones underfoot made the going extremely difficult. The air was still and cold, with everything around us black as Egypt's night. Behind loomed the mountain, brooding over the bay, the haunt of many large crocs. Altogether it was an eerie place that we seldom hunted. That night we saw a good croc about nine feet long, and approaching successfully, I fired. It seemed a perfectly good shot, and wading up we were surprised when the croc, still very much alive, started thrashing about on the surface, snapping its jaws viciously. I saw that the wound was too far forward, leaving the brain undamaged.

I tried to kill it with my pistol but succeeded only in exciting it further. It began to attack us every time it surfaced, though the wound had dazed it enough for us to dodge each time. Suddenly it disappeared, and thinking that one of my pistol shots had taken effect, we looked for the carcass. The ferocity it had just displayed made us somewhat reluctant, though.

I soon found it. Stumbling around, I bumped into a scaly flank, felt it whip around, and next moment its jaws closed on my leg. I let out a great howl and wrenched my leg clear. Luckily it could not bite with more than a fraction of its normal strength or I would have been unable to free myself so easily; a croc that size is quite capable of killing a man.

Making a last feeble attempt to find the croc, we easily convinced ourselves that it had gone, and went ashore, glad to leave the place. Examining my leg, we found that I had escaped literally from the dragon's mouth, with nothing worse than deep gashes. They bled a lot but eventually healed without trouble.

The Turkana were aghast at our story. Why, they demanded, did I leave the croc alive after it had bitten me? How could I be so incompetent? Was it not a blatant messenger from God bent on mischief? The fact that I had been bitten and then escaped might mean it was a case of mistaken identity—probably the croc was after them, only realizing its error on tasting the wrong leg. This incident upset them much more than it did us, and they never forgot to remind me of my blunder at the start of each new trip to Moite. Somewhere out there in Moite Bay a vengeful crocodile was waiting for someone with a bad conscience.

CHAPTER 6 SNAKE ISLAND

After the catching fiasco at Moite, I made a brief journey to North Island before settling into the routine collection of specimens. An isolated protrusion in the northern half of the lake, North Island consists of an old volcano from which a newer volcano erupted and died not long ago. Dull black lava flows run down into the water, leaving only two small beaches on exposed parts of the old volcano. I arranged for Van Someron to take me and two men there. Van was a Kitale farmer who kept a boat at Kalokol, sometimes driving up to the lake to take people out fishing. He was to return after two weeks, during which time we would have no contact with the outside world. It was not until Van's boat disappeared over the horizon that I really began to feel the island's solitude. The stillness and silence were so pervasive that one came to listen carefully to everything: the birds and the waves, and the wind. The island itself seemed to creak and groan a little now and then. But if one stopped and listened again one never heard anything.

Close up the island looked like a huge pile of lava and ashes, smelling strongly of sulphur. It had a crude texture, a look of rawness, for real soil had yet to form. The lava mantles radiated such intense heat by day that one automatically avoided them. In any case they were quite unnegotiable, for the brittle crust would collapse unexpectedly, dropping one into what seemed like a pit of broken glass. The soft material of the older volcano crumbled and slid away at the slightest touch, so that the only place a man could walk was over the compacted dust in the hot deep gullies criss-crossing the island. A few green bushes grew at our campsite on the east beaches but elsewhere only sparse wiry bushes, spike grass and a few twisted, stunted trees. Tangles of succulent creepers grew in the ravines. In several places fumaroles of hot gas told of the island's origins.

The first thing to be noticed was the extraordinary abundance of snakes. Everywhere I looked were old shed skins, and across every patch of dust went their sinuous tracks. These snakes were mostly puffadders, a particularly poisonous species of viper. I also found cobra skins, and skins of several harmless types, including pythons. Their ancestors had presumably floated to the island on flotsam from the Omo River delta, fifty miles to the north. Their economy was based on the even larger hordes of rats that found refuge in the labyrinth of tunnels and crevices in the tumbled lava. In the extreme heat of the day the snakes took shelter, so that I seldom saw any. But at night the island came alive with foraging serpents rustling and slithering about—a frightful place to walk over. And in the twilight, as if to further emphasize the creepiness, gusts of bats would erupt from their lava hideouts . . .

The long dim shadows of surrounding trees
The flapping bat, the night-song of the breeze.

After three days and nights on the island, I had one of the most frightening experiences of my life. While the two men and I were following a gully that let us cross from one side of the island to the other, I trod on a snake. It almost had to happen on that island, however vigilant one was. In the instant before my foot touched its back I saw it, and was therefore able to take the action that probably saved my life. As the frightened snake reared up to defend itself I kicked out wildly, can-can style; though it bit me, its fangs pierced my skin for only a fraction of a second before my flailing leg flung it aside.

As the snake made off I saw that it was a large, copper-red animal, identical in appearance with a variety of spitting cobra common at low elevations in Kenya, and I have no doubt that that is what it was. An effective bite from this species can kill a man very rapidly, depending on circumstances, perhaps within half an hour. Examining the bite, I saw two fang marks about a centimeter apart, from each of which ran a trickle of blood—evidence of how deep the fangs

went. The wound smarted, like a thorn prick.

It took me a few seconds to fully comprehend what had just happened. I had been bitten by a potentially lethal snake. Feeling cold and very afraid, I began walking slowly back to camp. It was a twenty-minute walk, and though that was suddenly a very long time I did not hurry, for raising my pulse and blood pressure by steeplechasing back would only hasten absorption of the poison. I told the two men at camp that I might need assistance; but they only laughed, for they did not share my view of the matter. If one of them had been bitten there would have been no end of a commotion, but since I was already mad, a snakebite wasn't going to make much difference.

Even back at camp I still felt nothing more than a sting. I waited another hour and still felt nothing. Gradually I realized that somehow I had escaped being poisoned. There could be only one explanation—in kicking out with my foot I had thrown off the snake before it injected any poison; a split-second later and the story might have been very different.

My purpose in coming to North Island had been to eliminate all the crocs there in order to observe the rate at which they recolonized it. This would give some idea of how much they moved across wide expanses of open water. Before beginning the survey I had flown over the island and seen many crocs there; but that had been during the breeding season, and now I found very few. To some extent this already answered my question, though I now needed actual figures to support the observation that

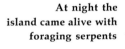

At night the island came alive with foraging serpents

crocodiles move freely over many miles of open water. Perhaps, like marine turtles, crocs travel to specific places like islands to breed.

While on North Island I had occasion to ponder the topic of crocodile breeding—an aspect of their lives that needs to be known in some detail if their efficient management is to be contemplated. That crocodiles breed seasonally has been known since ancient times. According to Plutarch, not only was the nesting of crocs a sign to the Egyptians that the floods were near, but also the location of the nests marked the height the water would rise to. But it was not until recently that the relation between water level and breeding was quantified. In 1961 Hugh Cott published his monograph that parted the Nile cabbage, so to speak, and clarified many aspects of crocodile natural history. Cott noted that crocs in all localities nested one to three months before the time of lowest water levels. Hatching thus takes place after the onset of the rains, and the hatchlings therefore start life when the habitat is expanding, as the floods invade the surrounding vegetation. This gives them shelter and brings them into contact with small food animals ("so soon as the young ones are hatched they fall instantly into the water, but if they meet with a frog, snail, or any other such thing fit for their meat, they do presently tear it to pieces").

Since Lake Rudolf has no (surface) outlet, the level falls a few feet each year during the dry season, rising again in April and May when it rains on the catchments of the seasonal rivers emptying into the lake. In most years less than five inches of rain falls in the vicinity of the lake itself. The absence of an outlet also accounts for the lake's salinity—the salts added by the rivers remaining while the water evaporates.

This concentration of breeding at a specific season has many other consequences on crocodile biology. It precludes, for instance, the evolution of a predator specializing on young crocs at a vulnerable age, a factor that may have influenced crocodile fortunes. A more important consequence is one long known in bushlore but objectively confirmed only by Hugh Cott and later by Mulji Modha—namely, territorial fighting. As the dry season progresses many African lakes and rivers dry up, first to pools, later sometimes completely. This concentrates the crocodiles, often to the point of overcrowding. Under such conditions animals generally exhibit territorial behavior that functions to space individuals and thus prevent essential activities—such as mating—from being frustrated by sheer numbers.

After nearly a year's continence it is to be expected that something of an orgy should

A Narrow Escape from a Snake.

herald the open season for sex. So far as scaly reptiles are capable of orgies, that is what they have. The fiesta months on Rudolf are October and November. Mulji Modha, a Game Department biologist, spent some months studying crocodile nesting behavior on Central Island while we were on the east shore. He observed the big males to claim certain stretches of shore, swimming up and down in ceaseless patrol, like the submarines of human nations. No other mature male is tolerated in these territories. Should one trespass, innocently or in challenge, it must fight the croc-in-charge. Such a fight between two 15-foot, half-ton leviathans is spectacular. Huge old jaws, pitted and scored like corroded chunks of cast iron, studded with long sharp teeth, are wielded by bulging neck mus-

"He maketh the deep to boil like a pot; he maketh the sea a pot of ointment."

cles. Massive tails plated with heavy, pointed scutes lash from side to side, exploding the water. Ancient rituals, fought out with savage bites and bone-cracking blows. Gleaming chips of broken teeth sink to the bottom through blood-clouded water. Birds swerve crazily about; there is tension in the air. Eventually the vanquished will submerge and flee, surfacing again in neutral water, there to float bleeding and frustrated, while the victor sculls slowly along the shore again, eyes aglint with victory and excitement.

Mulji Modha was the first biologist to describe these fights. The museum-based authorities who write natural history books deny their taking place at all, despite the fact that alligators have long been known to do the same. One of the newest bestiaries, Wilfred Neill's *Last of the Ruling Reptiles*, ridicules the matter of crocodile fighting: "Today, even the most scholarly works on crocodiles assert that . . . male crocodiles fight one another in the breeding season! The assertions . . . trace back . . . to Elizabethan fancies. . . ." Actually, the endless claims and counter-claims made in natural histories are themselves a sort of territorial battle of knowledgeability, as fiercely fought over as crocodiles beaches.

Female crocs swimming into these courtship areas instead of being attacked with intent to harm are, so to speak, raped, just as happens among humans in times of strife. All these goings-on have (since Elizabethan times) fired the fancies of hunters and travelers, people very prone to long, tall tales of nature, often dispensed as "authentic, eyewitness" accounts. For example: "Suddenly one horrid head rose vertically out of the water, the gular pouch working frantically, as its owner most unmelodiously yodelled its love song. Almost simultaneously the other head rose perpendicularly, also in full throaty song. The heads steadily approached each other until chins, jaws and throats were practically touching, and there they were poised for nearly half a minute during which time mating was evidently taking place. The weird croaking crooning continued throughout."

Mulji Modha's accounts of mating, as befits a biologist, are minus these embellishments. Nor did he see anything to suggest that crocodiles, among the most solitary of animals, form any sort of permanent association between individuals. But legend has it otherwise: Topsell tells us:

The males of this kinde do love their females above all measure, yea even to jealousie, as may appear by this history of Peter Matyr. There were certain mariners which saw two crocodiles together in carnal copulation upon the sands neer the river . . . the greedy mariners foresook their ship . . . and with great shouting, hollowing and crying, made towards them in a very couragious manner: the male at the first assault fell amazed, and greatly terrified ran away as fast as he could into the water, leaving the female lying upon her back (for when they engender, the male turneth her upon her back, for by reason of the shortnesse of her legs, she cannot do it herself). So the mariners finding her upon her back and not able to turn over herself, they easily slew her, and took her away with them. Soon after the male returned to the place to seek his female, but not finding her, and perceiving bloud upon the sand, conjectured truly that she was slain, wherefore he presently cast himself into the river of Nilus again, and in his rage swam stoutly against the stream until he overtook the ship . . . would certainly have entered the same, had not the mariners . . . battered his head . . . and so with great sighing and sobbing departed from them. By which reaction it is most clear what natural affection they bear one to another, and how they choose out their fellows, as it were fit wives and husbands for procreation.

The American alligator has an impressive roar with which to accompany its sexual escapades. William Bartram, the eighteenth-century explorer, gives us an unforgettably exaggerated description:

It most resembles very heavy, distant thunder, not only shaking the air and waters, but causing the earth to tremble; and when hundreds and thousands are roaring at the same time, you can scarcely be persuaded, but that the whole globe is violently and dangerously agitated.

Though Nile crocs do occasionally roar, they are for the most part quite silent and wary, so that great patience and sharp eyes are needed to observe their behavior.

A month after mating the female is ready to lay her eggs. Coming ashore at night she finds a spot soft enough in which to dig a slanting hole. At the end of this, a foot or two beneath the surface, she hollows out a chamber for the eggs. The nest ready, she turns round and lays her eggs, which roll down to collect in the terminal chamber. She then fills in the hole with the earth or sand dug out, and in a few days there is little trace of the nest. Sometimes the nest is made in a concealed position under a bush or in grass; more often it is made in an open sandbank.

I found that the number of eggs laid bears a close relationship to the size of the mother. A newly matured female of 6 feet lays about 15 eggs. As she grows the number of eggs laid increases in proportion to her body weight. The largest clutch recorded is 95 eggs, corresponding to a body length of 12 feet. There is thus no such thing as an "average" crocodile clutch size, for it varies with the age structure of the female population from place to place. On Lake Rudolf the low average clutch size—33, in contrast to localities in Uganda and Zambia with averages in the 50's and 60's, is probably a reflection of stunting.

On Rudolf female crocs begin maturing when they reach 5 feet or so in length. An increasing proportion of mature animals occurs with increasing body size (and age); three-quarters or more of the females more than 8½ feet long are sexually mature. This contrasts sharply with crocs elsewhere. Hugh Cott in Uganda found no mature females less than 7¾ feet long. But despite this marked discrepancy in size there is actually little difference in age of maturation—another indication of stunting in the Rudolf population.

Very old female crocs stop breeding altogether, though they keep on growing. Five per cent of the mature females I examined on Rudolf, all over 10 feet long, had regressed ovaries, implying that they no longer bred. Normally growing crocodiles could therefore have a breeding life of about 25 years, producing (if they bred every year) about 1400 eggs. The overall hatching success of 69 per cent of eggs laid means one female would produce 966 young crocs. In practice the average will be lower, depending on the life expectancy of the average female, and other factors.

Having laid her eggs, the female then keeps a long vigil. For the three months of incubation she will remain in the vicinity of the nest,

for her presence at the time of hatching is crucial. If undisturbed she will spend much of that time lying ashore on or near the nest; if intruded upon she will disappear and no sign of the mother or her nest will be visible. (The Turkana find croc eggs to eat by prodding likely places with their spears until the tip comes up wet.) Nevertheless she is somewhere around, for she will unerringly reappear at the right time to unearth her young. Unless she did so they would probably perish, for during incubation the earth above the eggs compacts, making it difficult or impossible for the young crocs to burrow out unaided.

Several times while working on the east shore Peter and I found ourselves walking, and once practically camping, on nests that we didn't know were there until we heard the ready-to-hatch crocodiles "chirruping." A chorus of underground chirrups, audible fifteen or twenty paces away, is often given by crocs shortly before and for some time after hatching—perhaps to guide the mother to them. (I would love to know how the crocs in their eggshells, sealed off from the air, achieve such vocalization.) Basking hippo, livestock or wild animals watering, storms and other disturbances often transform the local topography extensively during incubation, making the already inconspicuous nest even more difficult to relocate. Such a homing beacon should at least facilitate unearthing the nest. The nests we discovered in this way would within a few days be opened up by an adult croc (by the mother, probably, or perhaps any female) at night. Once I slept by a nest to watch it being opened, but in the dark could see little of the female's activities when she came. Trying for a closer look I alarmed her and she disappeared. When she failed to return in the next few days I finished the job for her, getting repeatedly bitten by the impressively fierce little crocs for my pains. It was worth it, though, for according to Wilfred Neill's natural history (written, like its medieval antecedents, at a considerable distance in all senses from its subjects) "not even the most unreliable of the legend-mongers claims actually to have seen liberation of the young by the female. . . ."

A large Lake
Rudolf croc hatchery

following pages:
"So soon as the young
ones are hatched they fall
instantly into
the water, but if they
meet with a
frog, snail or any
other such thing fit for
their meat, they
do presently tear it to
pieces." (Boreham)

portable croc bed

They espy a booty

48% of our croc stomachs were empty. This exception contained five different species of fish.

In fact these observations were most important to crocodile management. They tended to strengthen my suspicion that by far the most critical phase in the life history of the Nile crocodile is hatching. Unless the females are able to unearth their young, recruitment will suffer severely. And it may be that females, if harassed, abandon their nests.

Once out, the young crocs scramble to the water, where they remain close to one another for several days as they become accustomed to their new environment. Gradually they disperse, and by the time they are a few weeks old each is an autonomous individual that will live alone for the rest of its life.

Of course, most of these facts of crocodile reproduction, (enlarging upon those already described by such men as Hugh Cott, or Tony Pooley in Zululand) were gleaned by Mulji Modha and myself in the course of our respective projects on the lake, so that while on North Island I limited myself mostly to conjecture. One day an unusual hunting episode introduced another train of thought on croc biology.

It happened that from my bed I had a clear view down the beach, a fact I attached no importance to when making camp. One day I awoke as usual as it was getting light, on a blustery morning with a heavy surf pounding the beach. For a few minutes I lay on my back watching the clouds scudding untidily overhead, each one catching a dull red glint of the rising sun. I then rolled over and glanced idly down the beach, where to my astonishment I saw what was surely a monster pebbleworm. It was still dark and I had to peer down the rifle scope before I could be certain. But there it was, about eighty yards away, a huge croc

awash with the waves breaking over it. Certain that it would take flight at any moment, for I was in full view, I decided to shoot from where I lay. Wriggling around, I finally got the rifle settled, squeezed off a shot, and killed it.

This was the only croc I ever shot from my bed (what in hunting parlance could be called the "sack-shot"), and it proved to be the second biggest of the survey, measuring 15½ feet, and weighing just under half a ton. It was remarkable, though, in another respect, for its stomach contained the remnants of a large mammal it certainly had not found on the island (there are none)—material proof that crocs readily swim long distances, for the closest point on the mainland was nine miles away. This one had probably just swum over, which would account for its ignorance of our presence and unusual lack of vigilance. There was of course no reason why crocs should not move all over the lake—what seems a forbidding stretch of water to a man is probably nothing to a croc.

CROCODILES ATTACKING NATIVES.

To find out what and how much crocs eat was one of the goals of the survey. And in this lay one of the most puzzling things about Rudolf crocs. Forty-eight per cent of the crocs we shot had empty stomachs—a quite different observation from Hugh Cott's for the large numbers of crocs he examined in Uganda and Zambia, most of which contained food of one sort or another, as would be expected. Of 591 crocs examined by Cott in Zambia, 14 per cent had empty stomachs. Of 587 examined by the hunter Eric von Hippel, 24 per cent had empty stomachs. Though no other comparable data exist, the high incidence of empty stomachs on Rudolf seemed a definite and unusual phenomenon. The obvious implication was

that in a given time Rudolf crocs ate less frequently, and therefore less altogether than crocs elsewhere. Other things being equal, this would inevitably slow the growth rate—a conclusion for which I found much circumstantial evidence during the survey.

My efforts to explain why Rudolf crocs ate so seldom were largely fruitless. I began by observing how crocs caught their staple food—fish. Topsell, in his *Natural History of Serpents*, supposed crocs to be adept and cunning predators. "When they desire fishes they put their heads out of the water as it were to sleep, and then suddenly when they espy a booty, they leap into the water upon them, and take them." But in reality they do not take booty as often as that, or in quite the fashion he describes. If you watch a croc fishing the first thing you notice is the large number of "bosh shots." Its technique is to float quietly in the shallows, feet touching the bottom, jaws open and eyes just at the surface (the yellow lining of the mouth, which contrasts so sharply with the otherwise cryptic colors, perhaps serving to lure fish closer?). This animated fish trap either waits motionless for fish to swim by, or moves slowly about until within range. Then, like a striking snake it lunges forwards, or swipes sideways, thirty-six sharp teeth on each jaw meshing as the mouth snaps shut. But usually the fish dodges, and many bites are made before anything is caught.

Some young crocs I kept in captivity for growth studies occasionally displayed a fish-catching technique that Topsell would surely have taken as evidence of cunning. Swimming very quietly to the "shores" of their tank where they had seen a small "shoal" of fish, they would run their chins alongside the fish. Then, very slowly, they would bend their bodies round until the tip of the tail, like the chin, was aground, thus trapping the fish in the half-circle of their bodies. Then they would swipe at the fish in the usual way, whose only escape was to jump over the crocodilian enclosure.

Another common method on the lake was used when a hunting croc startled a shoal of fish in shallow water. For a second or two the fish, if disoriented, would jump and skitter about. Then the croc would very often give a tremendous wriggle of its tail that propelled it right out of the water to land among the confused fish, greatly increasing its chances of catching one.

Once in possession of "booty," the croc lifts its head clear of the water and, rather like a dog with a large hunk of meat, bites the catch and turns it round to swallow it headfirst. One night a 9-foot croc I was watching from the shore caught a large and spiny catfish. It then swam straight to where I stood (dazzled by the light, it couldn't see me), came halfway ashore and began to pound the wriggling fish on the ground. It then swallowed the limp and helpless prey. I had read of this behavior and was pleased to confirm it, though how often crocs do it is hard to say.

I could see nothing in their feeding behavior to suggest why they ate so little. Perhaps, though, there was something about the feeding conditions on Rudolf that made it difficult for the crocs. We did notice that after storms some of the crocs had unusually large stomach fills—one nine-footer contained just over 400 small tilapia, for instance. Why the aftermath of rough weather made it easier for crocs to catch fish I can't say. All the observation showed was that crocs *can* eat a lot more than they normally do. A possible explanation for any feeding difficulty is the wind. Crocs find it increasingly difficult to catch fish as the water roughens, and the extreme windiness of Lake Rudolf may well prevent a normal rate of food intake.

I routinely examined the stomach contents of all the crocs collected. This led to the discovery that Rudolf crocs were less well fed than others, and also to a possible hint of why. Of those crocs that had food in their stomachs, 91 per cent had eaten fish. Moreover, 87 per cent of these crocs had eaten only one kind of fish—tilapia. There are many species of tilapia in Africa and generally they are the most prized food fish among humans, for they are palatable and abundant. Tilapia are medium-sized, bream-like fish, living in

Crocs begin life very small compared to the size they ultimately reach

facing page:
Ode to Bacon
(digging a croc
blind and simultaneously
uncovering clutches
of chirruping champsae)

following pages:
Central Island

Sir Richard Burton said
catfish "tasted like
animated mire."

Ebei stuck
his entire head into this
perch, but we had run
out of film.

The in-transit croc
shot from my
gonking-mat on North
Island

shoals. That they should form such a high proportion of crocodile diet on Rudolf was remarkable in several ways. Firstly, though they are common in the shallows (where crocodiles do their fishing), so are other species, like the large, seemingly easier-to-catch catfish. It was particularly surprising to find tilapia so much eaten in view of the fact that elsewhere crocodiles seldom have such an unvaried diet. Hugh Cott records many kinds of animals in crocodile stomachs—they eat anything they can get, in fact. (Recently a hunter friend of mine found a fully grown porcupine inside a croc!) We found occasional turtles, birds, insects, and other crocs in the stomachs of Rudolf crocs, but very few. This was obviously a consequence of the extreme scarcity of other animal life along the lakeshore. But the predilection for tilapia was still obscure. Hugh Cott also recorded another significant fact: in one area (Mweru Marsh, in Zambia) he found crocs eating a high proportion of one fish type, in this instance catfish. And this locality also had the highest incidence of empty stomachs (though not as high as on Rudolf). It seemed, therefore, that where crocs ate only one kind of food animal, they got less food. Just why this should be so is a puzzle. Perhaps a sort of physiological apathy sets in if there is only one food animal to stimulate hunting.

But I don't think so. My captive crocs (from Moite) were fed on live fish of one species only, and they grew as fast as any crocs for which there are records. My suspicion—and it can be only a suspicion—is that the crocs on Rudolf are overcrowded, and this in some way depresses their appetites.

Though these data and speculations justified the hundreds of stomach examinations I made, actually making them was most unpleasant. An earlier writer on African travel aptly remarked that "after paunching a croc a nauseating stench hangs like a persistent fog about the carcass." Possibly the only good service the wind ever performed for us was to disperse these fetid miasmas.

Not everybody considers the inside of a croc repellent. Pliny, for instance (who obviously never paunched a croc himself), passes on these handy tips:

It [the croc] lives on land amongst the most odoriferous of flowers; hence it is that its intestines are so greatly in request, being filled as they are with a mass of agreeable perfumes. This substance is called *crocodilea*, and is looked upon as extremely beneficial for diseases of the eyes, and for the treatment of films and cataract, being applied with leek-juice in the form of an ointment. Applied with oil of cypress it removes blemishes growing upon the face; and employed with water, it is a cure for all those diseases the nature of which is to spread upon the face, while at the same time it restores the natural tints of the skin; an application of it makes freckles disappear as well as all kinds of spots and pimples.

The cosmetic industry it seems has overlooked a mass of possibilities. Nor is that all, for Pliny was unaware of yet another crocodile elixir mentioned in medieval bestiaries: "Crocodile dung is made into an ointment, with which wrinkled old women of pleasure anoint their faces and become beautiful again, till the sweat flowing down washes it off."

What crocodiles eat has excited more popular attention than any other aspect of their biology. One of the finest examples of admirable curiosity gone astray is an ingenious explanation of the brown liquid in a croc's stomach that is the end-product of the digestive process. Eric von Hippel contends that "However empty (the stomach) may seem . . . there are always pints upon pints of . . . plankton concentrate in it."

But such discursions take us away from the real reason for men's curiosity about crocodile diet. Eating is a highly evocative subject to humans, full of sexual and above all cannibalistic symbolism. In the associative processes of our unconscious thinking little distinction is drawn between a man eating a man and an animal eating a man: they both connote cannibalism. Opening up a croc always raises the possibility of finding human remains inside—something bound to excite any

Man without a dog
Jffr. Baron. 1972 (145)

human. This lends a juicy, macabre air to poking around inside a croc's gut. And from time to time the inquisitive have indeed found "anklets, wristlets and other lugubrious objects" inside crocodiles. Ever since the time of that great liar, the mythical Sir John Mandeville, it has been considered obligatory for writers of African memoirs to have personally found "lugubrious" relics of human meals in the crocs they shot. Not to do so, they felt, would be to risk being spurned by their readers. And many are the yarns of voracity that years of gin and solitary safari have nurtured. Such as this *bundu* classic gleaned from Robert Foran's *A Breath of the Wilds*:

This croc, which measured 12 feet from tip of tail to tip of snout, must have had a catholic taste in its form of diet. On opening up the stomach we found a strange assortment of articles—sticks, about a dozen round and smooth pebbles, an African woman's foot, an African man's hand, some coloured beads, wire bangles and anklets, a waterbuck's hoof, the claws of a cheetah, a shinbone of a reedbuck, the shell plates of a large river turtle, the horns of a goat, the hoof of a calf, and a variety of other strange objects. I felt delighted at having been its executioner.

One thing nearly always found in croc stomachs has stimulated a curiosity both idle and scientific out of all proportion to its significance—namely, stones. Crocs of all sizes have sand, gravel, stones or other hard objects in their stomachs. This debris seems to absorb all the disappointment of not finding human remains; at least there seems no other plausible explanation for the extraordinary attention given them. De la Gironière, in his story of slaying the world record croc, relates how a priest begged him to paunch it:

The worthy priest demanded that the stomach should be opened in order to ascertain how many Christians the monster had devoured. Every time, he said, that a cayman eats a Christian he swallows a large pebble. . . . Then we opened the stomach and took out of it, by fragments, the horse . . . and about 150 pounds weight of pebbles, varying from the size of a fist to that of a walnut. When the priest saw this great quantity of stones he was appalled: "It is a mere tale," he could not help saying. "It is impossible that the animal should have devoured so great a number of Christians."

This admirable skepticism would do well for most other accountings of stomach stones. They have been reputed to cure stuttering, a belief that may stem from an ancient treatment of carrying a mouthful of small stones that rattled against the teeth of the patient so painfully when he stammered that he soon learned not to. Demosthenes is said to have cured

himself in this way though he did not use croc stones.

Someone, convinced like Gironière's priest of stomach stones' esoteric significance, hit on the trick of bestowing on them a technical name—gastroliths. From then on they *had* to be important. Hugh Cott supposed the gastroliths to act as ballast, but could adduce no evidence for his hypothesis. If stomach stones have a function, it seems to be unknown; the chances are they are merely incidental debris.

228 Christians

North Island is one of three large volcanic islands in the lake. The other two, Central and South islands are bigger, though just as bleak and raw-looking. South Island has a sharp-edged profile of cones and cubes, broken by scooped-out cavities and curves. The bare rock is dull red, like burnt brick, splotched with sulfurous yellow, and faded, weathered brown. Shrouds of glinting black lava from not-so-old volcanic upwellings lie hotly over the bedrock. The whole structure looks unfinished, like an interrupted explosion.

The flatter parts of Central Island have patches of bush and South Island even has a few thorn trees, but otherwise they are as bare as North Island. The Turkana, desert warriors, do not much like the islands or the lake, a wariness that is echoed in their disdain to give them names. All the islands are disparagingly called "that island," and the lake "that water."

The Turkana's suspicions of the islands are not wholly unjustified, for they have been the scene of many strange and some disastrous happenings. Once while preparing to move our camp over to Alia Bay, we heard that two Turkana had been lost on the lake. They had been fishing from their flimsy raft made of three waterlogged doum palm logs lashed together when an unusual offshore wind blew them out into the lake. On the last flight across to Alia, it happened that Ebei was on board. As we passed Central Island he turned to look back, as if recollecting something. Several nights ago, he casually remarked, he'd seen a fire on the island. He'd meant to tell us, but it had slipped his mind. Did we think it might be the lost fishermen? We were struck by his offhandedness—had we not flown within sight of the island the chances are he never would have remembered the fire. As it was, he dropped the subject without even asking if we were going to fly over and look.

We did go back and look. There was nobody on the main island, nor did we really expect to see anything. The Turkana often

A valuable goat
stolen from mysterious
South Island

think they see lights there, for it is a mysterious place to them, the subject of much magic and fantasy. Occasional eruptions of volcanic fire and smoke still occur to catalyze the mystique.

Just south of the main island are two rocks, the peaks of submerged volcano. Before abandoning the search we had a quick look at these, and sure enough, standing forlornly on one of them were two men. A desultory wave or two and they sat down as if the whole thing were too boring for words.

After we left for Alia, Bob McConnell sailed over and rescued the lost fishermen. When they were blown away, he learned, they spent one night clinging to their raft before it washed up against the rock. Then they forgot to secure the craft, which drifted away and left them unable to get to the more hospitable main island a mile to the north. The bedraggled castaways found themselves on a bare, dome-shaped rock with no animal life on it but itinerant cormorants that clambered about during the day, drying their feathers. A fissure sheltered them from the worst of the sun, and a few bushes with edible roots growing in the cracks of the lava kept them alive for the next nine days. But that was all. They had lit a fire by spinning a shaft of wood on another piece of wood, but it soon burned all the fuel there was and went out. This was the tiny fire that had been seen on the mainland eight miles away by a sharp-eyed observer. Or was it? There are many fires seen on Central Island, but few lit. It is the sort of quirk one expects of the lake—to have a fire set but not seen, a fire seen, yet never lit. Somehow I feel that the castaways were rescued by just such a coincidence of fantasy and fact that combined to tell the truth though not made up of it.

When they stepped aboard Bob's boat they made certain to bring a tiny bundle of roots they had dug up but not yet eaten. Of their ordeal they had little to say. Asked what they had planned to do if not rescued, they replied ''Nothing.'' It was obvious that God was about to take them, and they had not presumed to contest his whim. It now appeared that God was not ready for them, in which case the matter could be dropped.

South Island, of about thirty square miles, is the biggest island on the lake. In many ways it is also the most mysterious, for it has several secrets, two of which in particular will never be revealed. Although uninhabited, there are more than 500 feral goats on it—a living reminder of a past habitation by men. These goats were first seen in 1934 by Sir

Fuchs found human
bones and pottery
shards

Vivian Fuchs' expedition, the first recorded visitors to the island. Fuchs found human bones and pottery shards, as well as the goats. Nobody knows who these people were or how they got to the island, or when. A band of aventurers of long ago, bent on discovery and new lives, perhaps.

Before Fuchs set off on his expedition he spoke of his plans to visit South Island to Ludwig von Höhnel, after whom the island was originally named. Von Höhnel, then seventy-seven, had not forgotten his terrible journey with Teleki in 1888. He considered Fuchs' plans madness, and said so:

I fear that I have not warned you seriously enough that you must be very careful and not underrate the risk of the enterprise. If the weather conditions are anything like they were at our time then you would be senseless to try the venture. I do not think the lake at any time of the year is so calm as to be navigated with a small collapsible boat to justify any attempt to reach the island.

On July 28, 1934, Fuchs left two members of his expedition, Martin and Dyson, on South Island to survey it. They were to return not later than August 13. But they never did return, nor were they ever seen again. An aerial search of the island and neighboring mainland revealed nothing. Attempts by Fuchs to reach the island in another boat were frustrated by bad weather. Two oars, two tins,

and Dyson's hat were eventually found washed up on the west shore seventy miles north of the island.

While the circumstances of their death can only be surmised, there is one plausible explanation. Firstly, the objects washed ashore suggest that they were afloat at the time of the disaster, probably making their way back to the mainland. There had been no storms, and their boat was a seaworthy type with two four-gallon buoyancy tanks, which were never found. Had they simply holed the craft on an underwater object they could have done so only very close to the island, for a short distance offshore on all sides is deep, clear water. Such an accident would have left them within easy swimming distance of land. Had their engine stopped, or the vessel sprung a leak on the way back, they could, at the worst, have drifted to shore by clinging to the buoyancy tanks. There can be little doubt that they met a much more violent end.

There are two ways in which their boat and its tanks could have been destroyed and its occupants killed—attacks from either a hippo or a croc. Big male crocs in territorial mood will attack canoes as they would other crocs. Just how ferocious and destructive a big one can be was made frighteningly clear to two other scientists in 1962. They were sounding Lake Chishi in Zambia from a small rubber dinghy when, without warning, they were set upon by a crocodile. In its first assault it tore open the front compartment of the

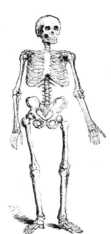

dinghy, collapsing it, and then began threshing about with the boat draped over its back. While the men were trying to shove themselves clear of the beast, one of them was seized by his foot. He managed to free himself, after which the croc renewed its demolition of the boat, clambering over the side, biting savagely at everything and rapidly shredding the rubber hull. It ignored their efforts to beat it off with an oar, and soon only the rear compartment remained intact. Since the croc was obviously committed to their total destruction, the two men took to the water, a desperate but as it happened, wise move. In the rough water they somehow managed to swim away unmolested. They saw no further

Many a boat ride has ended in the jaws of hippos

The El Molo love
to tell the story of the
bold Turkana hunter
who years ago
visited El Molo island
and resolved to kill a hippo
for himself....

———

opposite:
On these flimsy
rafts of doum palm logs
Turkana and El Molo
fishermen
nonchalantly sailed
the waters of Lake Rudolf

———

following pages:
Nguya, an El
Molo on safari in Alia Bay,
with a 201-pounder
he had stalked
and speared at midday

———

Nguya's inspiration
down south in Loingalani,
a 60-mile walk

———

An El Molo mother

———

An ancient
"mole" in her lair

157

sign of the croc (or their boat) and had to swim for two hours before they made land. Had they stayed with their boat the croc would undoubtedly have killed them.

P. B. M. Jackson, a biologist, records six attacks from as many crocs while he was in a boat on Mweru Marsh, near Lake Chishi. All were consistent with the territorial aggression described by Hugh Cott and Mulji Modha. Such attacks are most common in places where crocs are unharassed and therefore unafraid of man.

August is the beginning of the breeding season on Rudolf. It is highly probable that Martin and Dyson, ignorant and trusting of crocs, were attacked by an old black-backed male as they unwittingly infringed its territorial waters on their way back to the mainland. A half-ton croc could have crunched up their small canvas boat like a biscuit, leaving the explorers at its mercy in the lake.

An even more formidable aggressor would have been a hippo. They are actually more notorious than crocs for attacking boats (also for territorial reasons), and since a large male hippo weighs two or three tons the ease with which it can pulverize a small boat is obvious. A sudden, furious attack on the unsuspecting scientists and it would have been all over in a few minutes, with nothing surviving but a hat and a few pieces of debris. Von Höhnel's foreboding proved well grounded.

Not far from Loingalani, near the mainland opposite South Island, are two small islands, the headquarters of a tiny tribe, the El Molo. They are poor people subsisting mainly by hunting and fishing, for they possess few cattle and goats. In Teleki's day they were more prosperous, with sections of the tribe living at Alia Bay and Reshiat; but now they are mostly confined to the vicinity of Loingalani, numbering only a few hundred persons, living in unbelievably small hemispherical huts dotted aimlessly about like molehills on the lava. Many of them suffer from a disease which bows their legs, sometimes grotesquely—a deformity that, combined with their low numbers, makes them seem like a dying race.

But under the mantle of wretchedness you will find a friendly, pleasant people with occasional women of unexpected beauty. Unlike the Turkana they are perfectly at home in and on the lake; indeed, it is their refuge from marauders and their means of livelihood. Even in Teleki's day they were netting fish, and they are exceptionally skilled hunters and fishers. Some have canoes, but mostly they travel about the lake on the precarious doum log rafts that the Turkana also use. These rafts actually ride

More soup

opposite:
The volcanic rock looks unfinished, like an interrupted explosion

underwater when loaded with nets and one or two men, so poor is their buoyancy.

The El Molo technique of hunting hippo is startling in its audacity and bears a striking similarity to the old way of whaling. During the day a hippo finds a patch of quiet water just deep enough for it to lie on its side submerged yet reach the surface to breathe. Often its flank remains exposed. Finding such a hippo comfortably set up for the day, a band of hunters send in a lone harpooner who makes his way swimming and crawling up to the drowsy beast. To do this without alarming the hippo is an extraordinary feat of stealth, not to mention courage. His harpoon is attached to a long line which he gathers into coils tied around his waist with a slip knot, so as to leave his hands free. When close enough, he thrusts the harpoon deep into the hippo, whose reaction is either to kill the hunter or to make for deep water and concealment, towing the hunter behind. But the effects of the wound and the water that is forced into its body when it dives soon causes the hippo to make for shore. The rest of the hunters, anticipating where the hippo will come out, wait in ambush. When the animal reaches shallow water they all attack and kill it with spears.

The El Molo love to tell the story of the bold Turkana warrior who many years ago visited their islands. When he heard how the El Molo hunted hippo he resolved to kill one himself before returning to Turkanaland. Already familiar with the art of spearing, he was easily instructed in what to do, and endowed with courage and skill in stalking, he successfully approached and harpooned a hippo. But in his eagerness he had missed a crucial detail of the instructions. Instead of tying his line to his waist with a slip knot, he used a fixed one. When the hippo made for deep water he found himself pulled along by a very short rope, and unable to control his progress, was drowned.

CHAPTER 7 THOU BRAKEST THE HEADS OF LEVIATHAN

Tales from the bay of Alia—an Asian-type picnic—
Shingle Island—Ebei Piscator—colossal Nyle perca fish—noisome flesh of crocodile relished by Turkana—
grisly carnival of the night-hags—Desolation Row—geese of Egypt—
hindrances and vicissitudes of the chase—
Nile's poys'ny pirates lie baking them in the sun—the wormes of their teeth—
the Sad-eyed Lady of the Lowlands—
stagnant pools and quaking bogs—an all-night record— tubing
the crocodile—marooned.

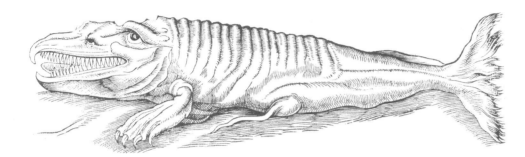

Most of our time on Lake Rudolf was spent at Alia Bay, midway along the east shore. We had planned to divide our collections equally between Moite and Alia, but towards the survey's end the scarcity of crocs at Moite forced us to concentrate on Alia and the coast to the north.

Moite, for all its bleakness, gained a certain peacefulness from its sheltering mountain; there were even a few thorn trees and some stunted palms. But Alia is just a windswept stretch of lava that in times past was the lakebed, with no vegetation or shelter of any sort. Our camps, of necessity simply stuck on the water's edge, were exposed to the hot, abrasive wind that blew unendingly from the east. In my diary there is an entry for November 16, 1965, that reads: "Today there is just a breeze, gusting 10 mph, glorious respite after 5 days of continuous wind, with no break at all, day or night." There is something intensely aggravating about the inescapable buffeting of uninterrupted wind. It has a claustrophobic effect because it deafens you to all but nearby sounds. On a clear calm day you see much farther because you hear more, and from a greater distance.

Sometimes we camped on a small island half a mile offshore at the southern end of Alia Bay. It was nothing more than a sandbank four hundred yards long by one hundred wide, but the spike grass on it made it seem less forbidding

than the mainland with its hot black lava. On the island we felt safe from sudden attack by *shifta* bandits, a possibility that always lurked in our minds in those last few moments before sleep. For the same reason it was a favorite campsite of the only other people who ever came to this part of the lake. These were the wild Merrille hunters who from time to time made daring sorties down the east shore of Rudolf all the way from their native Ethiopia, a hundred miles to the north. If necessary they can live afloat, cooking on fires in the bilges of their canoes, even taking their women and children with them. If you fly low over them in a plane they dive out of their canoes like frogs and disappear in the reeds.

About three-quarters of a mile farther out into the lake was another, smaller sandbank. We called it Shingle Island, and it would figure prominently in our recollections of the lake. During the day, particulary the early morning and evening, large crocs were often to be found sprawled over its beaches, for it was much used as a resting place by the bigger ones that could swim out to it from the mainland. It yielded us many good specimens over the months.

Because all our equipment came over from Kalokol in the plane, which economy forced us to use as little as possible, we cut everything down to the bare essentials. Our only shelter

Merille hunters can live entirely out of their canoes, cooking over fires in the bilges.

Andy Warhol

BREAD and BUTTER & HELLMANN'S
PICKLES   REAL
                     MAYONAISE

RITZ CRAKERS

Andy Warhol 20

was a piece of canvas stretched over a frame—a tent would have been too heavy, too wind-resistant, and in any case unbearably hot inside. The crocodile skins, which had to be kept shaded and wet all the time, were housed in a small tent that the wind gradually shredded into ruin.

For food we relied on fish, supplemented by Ritz crackers and Hellmann's mayonnaise, bread-and-butter pickles, condensed milk, and a few treasured tins of grapefruit. We made soup from grand-sounding packets like Egg-drop, Turtle, Mushroom, and Chicken Noodle. But the vile sodary water polluted every flavor. We treated the water with citric acid and tried to kid ourselves that this made it taste better. Like the Wildman's bellyache, it was enough that we sought a remedy; that it made no difference was unimportant.

Our shelter was the only shade, so it doubled as dissection room. As a result it soon looked like the aftermath of a really successful Asian picnic through which various insects content-edly picked their way. Headstrong flies became hopelessly bogged down in anything liquid the moment your back was turned, and what they didn't plunder, the ants did. Over everything blew the sand. All our food crunched with sand. The rifle actions jammed with it. Our blankets were like emery cloth. The microscope grated with sand. We firmly believed towards the end of the survey that even an unopened jar of pickles already contained special gray Rudolf sand.

The fish we caught in a number of ways. The better-tasting tilapia and perch took special fish-ing that we seldom had time for, so we relied on the greasy black catfish that sculled about the shallows, scavenging. The men caught these on crude lines baited with croc meat. When a catfish bit they would land it by sprinting ashore before it shook the hook loose from its leathery mouth. Ebei devised a technique of creeping up to the fish in the shallows next to the leftover carcasses and killing them with a *panga,* the long knife used for chopping wood. The catfish were real delicacies until Atikukeni had abused them in his frying pan . . . plenty of grease, skin, salt, and sand, but there was seldom anything else.

Occasionally giant Nile perch swam into shal-low water under cover of darkness, and we shot several of these with a pistol as they lolled in the shallows. The all-night pistol record perch weighed a fraction under 100 pounds. On rod and line we caught bigger ones, our two best weighing 149 and 180 pounds. In the Nile they apparently grow much bigger, up to 400 pounds, but we never heard of one that big on Lake Rudolf.

We tried other ways of varying the menu. The beautiful spotted Nile turtles—the Tyrse of the Egyptians—that the men often caught while fishing were good eating, but we had to be quick to get any before the Turkana had them tucked inside. We sampled croc's eggs, which the men considered a great delicacy, and found them disgusting. Livingstone had the audacity to write that "crocodile's eggs taste like hen's eggs, with perhaps a smack of custard," which goes to show what havoc years of *tabu* safari can play with one's palate. Croc meat is even worse. I have eaten nearly every kind of wild animal meat and found all of it good with the single exception of croc. It has an oily, pungent flavor however cooked, cut-up, or disguised.

If there is one thing the Turkana cannot do, it is ignore something edible. They may not extend themselves anticipating a future hunger, but they are incapable of discarding food already before them. Despite their huge appetites they obviously could not eat all the croc meat we had (though they tried); at the same time they could not bear to throw it away. So they dried it to eat later. Now, fresh croc meat is repellent enough, but it is fragrance compared to dried croc meat—I know of nothing with quite the same flatulent odor. Our camps were always festooned with strips of drying meat. I pleaded with them to desist. I threatened them. I said it would poison them, that they would grow webs between their fingers at the new moon. But they had long since learned to ignore me.

On each return to Kalokol they would blithely expect me to transport this gunge in my plane. These were the subjects of our bitterest arguments. I would flatly refuse to have the stuff near me—and their bedrolls would mysteriously triple in size, reeking like garbage dumps. They would resign. I would fire them. But inevitably I would be conned into it, to find myself flying across the lake buried in a mound of feculent flesh with a stench so acrid that I swear it singed the nostrils.

When we had finished with the croc carcasses they were dragged a short way from camp and abandoned. In that harsh country where survival meant exploiting every opportunity, our dead crocs were a scavenger's bonanza. All day long a squabbling throng of vultures and marabou storks bickered and fought over the remains. Small hooded vultures, dingy and craven, scuttled hysterically about. The bigger white-backed and griffon vultures stumbled around, bullying the smaller ones and cheating each other. Innocent-looking sacred ibis hung about like pickpockets. And on the outskirts skipped dapper, shiny ravens, droll and jaunty, "on their way to the carnival (tonight) on desolation row."

Amongst this jostling mob strode tall, skinny marabou storks, sneering down at the rabble, and snatching scraps from the vultures. Clouds of dust rose, dirty feathers drifted about, as these

Ebei in our kitchen perched on the skull of a 16-footer speared by Merille "poachers"

Somehow Peter managed an invitation to join the Merille

Fishing Turkana style

We camped this way for over a year

The shade tent for salted skins

birds kicked and clawed, hissing and rattling over the bones, the daily carnival of the offal-eaters.

From a distance the marabou looks like a neat and well-groomed undertaker, with grave posture and dandy gray feathers edged in white. But if you should see it close up it appears altogether different. Like Dorian Gray's portrait the bird has become debauched and revolting. Its feathers are spotted, its white front stained with festering ooze from the carcasses; its beak is unspeakable. A pimply red complexion with long unkempt hairs, the gross, pendulous bag of skin that dangles from its neck like an old woman's breast—all this confers upon it an air of irredeemable depravity.

At night a cackling howl of hyenas took over, dragging the skeletons about and crunching up the bones with their massive jaws. In the moonlight we could see their ghostly forms, the big spotted ones and the smaller striped hyenas, loping about, chuckling over this and that. It was a macabre scene set in the deserted lava stage, the insane, windblown laughter and crackling jaws of the night-hags sounding like some demoniacal convocation of witches that had one alternately laughing and shivering. And over it all, monotonously, like some weird metronome, came the eerie yelps of the jackals.

One night two lions prowling about our camp surprised a large croc about eleven feet long asleep on the shore. After a considerable struggle they killed and ate it. We heard the noise of the fight, for it was only a short distance from where we slept, and in the morning found the remains and tell-tale signs of the encounter.

That evening we saw the two lions, bellies full and swinging, as they moved off to less crowded parts, having lain up during the day in a patch of long grass by the water. Lions are common along the shores of Rudolf; we heard them roar on most nights when the wind was calm enough for their voices to reach us. Once, at half-past nine in the morning, a lone lion walked along the water's edge, roaring across the bay. It did not see us, for we were on our island. We watched, the Turkana awed into silence, as it paced slowly along, stopping at intervals to exult. The black lava and red rocks behind, the heat shimmer around, gave peculiar emphasis to the lean yellow lion, maneless and sinewy, calling to the sea and the sand and the sun.

There were always some Egyptian geese around camp. In my first few weeks at the lake I shot a goose occasionally to avoid the yellow slabs of catfish that made one's tongue curl up like a millipede. But I soon gave up these attempts to vary the menu. The stringy goose

drumsticks looked and tasted like oily rubber bands wound round a stick, so that one was almost happy to go back to fish. Then too, as the days wore on and we came to know the geese round camp individually, we found ourselves too sentimental to shoot them.

Altogether we viewed the geese with mixed feelings. When we first arrived they avoided us, but soon they would edge up to camp like nervous old ladies forever apprehensive of imaginary perils. But their curiosity and love of company drew them on, sidling about pretending not to look, stiff and awkward, unable to relax. At every alarm, imagined or real, they would take flight, hissing and honking about the camp with a proprietary air.

If they had a nest nearby they were insufferable, for an expectant mother goose cannot sit still for long. In the middle of a broiling afternoon when the only moving things are the delirious lava beetles and a mad scientist laboriously stalking a sleepy croc, a broody goose will abruptly launch into flight—and the alerted quarry slips into the lake. More than once a busybody goose collected a bullet through an outstretched wing from an enraged hunter, a cloud of feathers erupting like a burst of flak. But the geese were comforting at night, for the chances of bandits getting past them were small.

Much worse than the geese were the spurwing plovers, for being smaller and sneakier, they could remain unseen until the last moment, and then fly off screeching their high-pitched alarm. Many a long stalk over needle-sharp spike grass or searing hot pebbles was sabotaged by a plover, squatting small and prissy in a slight depression near a sleeping croc, invisible until too late.

The coming ashore of crocodiles, apart from its interest to hunters, has excited men's curiosity since ancient times, presumably because of its hint of ambiguity, the transition from an aquatic to a terrestrial mode. Pliny wrote that "all the daytime the crocodile keepeth the land but he passeth the night in the water," a fair approximation. The night is mostly spent in the water, but the day is spent partly ashore, partly afloat, the pattern of movements being fairly constant for a given locality, varying somewhat between localities. In general, a large proportion of a given crocodile population—up to ninety per cent—comes ashore in the early morning and late evening. The middle half of the day finds a much smaller proportion ashore at any given moment.

Biologists trying to explain this behavior have dogmatically asserted that it is to bask in the sun, assuming quite arbitrarily that a crocodile depends on the direct absorption of solar radia-

Ebei executes his
latest style of catfishing

tion for its good health and happiness. Hunters put it colloquially, saying that they bask to "recharge their batteries." But the proponents of the "battery charging" hypothesis have no evidence for it. The observations of Hugh Cott, Mulji Modha, and others suggest that crocs actually avoid the sun, as they come ashore in their greatest numbers at the cooler times of day. They also come ashore at night, particularly late at night, or when the water is rough—obviously not to bask. When disturbed by man crocs need not come ashore at all. That crocs deliberately bask in the sun is, in the present state of the evidence, "a mere tale."

A much simpler explanation is that crocs come ashore by day merely to rest, since (for reasons unknown) most of their fishing activity is at night.

Equally fabulous are the speculations as to why, when ashore, crocs gape. The traditional interpetations are aptly summed up in this verse:

The Wren, who seeing (prest with sleep's desire)
Nile's poys'ny pirate press the slimy shoar,
Suddenly coms, and, hopping him before,
Into his mouth he skips, his teeth he pickles,
clenseth his palate, and his throat so tickles,
That, charm'd with pleasure, the dull Serpent gapes,
Wider and wider, with his ugly chaps:
Then, like a shaft, th'Ichneumon instantly
Into the Tyrant's greedy gorge doth fly,
And feeds upon that glutton for whose Riot,
All Nile's fat margents scarce could furnish diet.

The myths of the crocodile bird and the ichneumon have been earnestly repeated for a long time. Both depend on the sensation of unguardedness that the gaping mouth conveys. The symbolism of a bird taking advantage of the inviting, open cavity to penetrate and peck is no less plain than that of the mongoose darting in. The whole topic is a tangled maze of classic sexual symbols.

"...freede from the wormes of his teeth...he is constrayned to remain agape."

The legend of the crocodile bird is particularly widespread.

As we sayled further we saw great numbers of crocodiles upon the banks of the ilands in the midst of Nilus lye baking them in the Sunne with theyr jawes wide open, whereinto certaine little birds about the bigness of a thrush, entering, came flying forth againe presently after. The occasion whereof was told me to be this: the crocodiles by reason of theyr continuall devouring beasts and fishes have certain pieces of flesh sticking fast between theyr forked teeth, which flesh being putrified, breedeth a kind of worme, wherewith they are cruelly tormented; wherefore the said birds flying about, and seeing the wormes, enter into the Crocodile's jawes to satisfie theyr hunger thereon, but the crocodile perceiving himselfe freede from the wormes of his teeth, offereth to shut his mouth, and to devour the little bird that did him so good a turne, but being hindered from his ungrateful attempt by a pricke which groweth upon the bird's head, he is constrayned to remain agape.

The bird described in this passage of Giovani Leone's sounds like one of the many species of plover (sometimes called crocodile birds) that often consort with "basking" crocs. Around the turn of the century two eminent herpetologists, Anderson and Flower, went to great lengths to determine whether or not birds habitually freed crocs of the "wormes of their teeth." Neither their observations, nor those published by others, yielded any evidence for it: a delightful, but fabulous tradition. Recently, however, a reliable observer, Rob Glen, told me that he saw a bird pecking at the mouth of a croc. No doubt from time to time such occasional observations have boosted the myth's credibility.

The incomparable Topsell enlarges on the dan-

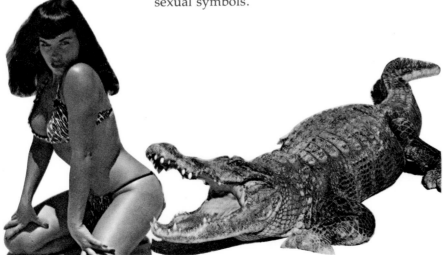

gers (to crocodiles) of a vulnerable orifice when mongooses are at large.

The Ichneumon or Pharaoh's Mouse . . . watches the crocodile asleepe, and finding theyr mouths open against the beames of the sunne, suddenly enter into them, and, being small, creepe downe theyr vast and large throates before they be aware, and then, putting the crocodile to exquisite and intolerable torment, by eating theyr guttes asunder, and so theyr soft bellies, while the crocodile tumbleth to and fro sighing and weeping, now in the depth of the water, now on the land, never resting till strength of nature fayleth. For the incessant gnawing of the Ichneumon so provoketh her to seek her rest, in the unrest of every part, herbe, element, throwes, throbs, rowlings, tossings, mournings, but all in vaine, for the enemy within her breatheth through her breath, and sporteth herselfe in the consumption of those vitall parts, which waste and weare away by yeelding to her unpacifiable teeth, one after the other, till she that crept in by stealthe at the mouth, like a puny theefe, come out at the belly like a conqueror, through a passage opened by her owne labour and industry.

Of the many symbols in this myth one of the most prominent is vengeance. In fact the ancient Egyptians revered Pharaoh's Mice for their alleged service in crocodile control.

Naturalists and zoologists, in keeping with their commitment to objectivity, scorn the mythical interpretations and incline instead towards the mundane hypothesis that mouth-gaping is a thermo-regulatory mechanism; that is, it disperses excess heat, rather like the panting of a dog. But the fact is that this is as much a myth as the other musings, and it's far less interesting. It is not known why crocs gape. I have seen them do it late at night, which inclines me to regard it as simply a relaxative posture associated with lying ashore. The yellow lining of the mouth may also function as a signaling device connected with lying ashore. There is a tendency for crocs to haul out near others already on the beach.

By day the shallows round Alia looked uniform and innocuous, but at night they became another world. In the patch of torchlight our eyes told us little, and we sensed our surroundings more by feel and smell, and by the special night sounds. Each successive stretch of shallows had its own peculiarities. Some had weedless stretches, hard and sandy underfoot. But these were rare, and in most places, as at Moite, the bottom was a quagmire, booby-trapped with stumps and lava, choked with clutching weed, and pockmarked with deep hippo footprints. ("Where stagnant pools and quaking bogs swarmed, croaked, and crawled with hordes of frogs.")

Northwards the swamp worsened, with many "quaking bogs" from which escape was possible only by swimming. The rifle could take its frequent duckings and still function, but the all-important torch could not. The further we went the murkier it became. Eventually one night we came to an eerie morass of inundated grass and weeds, with an oozy bottom of cold, slimy mud. The faint torchlight showed an endless maze of waterways twisting through dank clumps of vegetation. The wind moaned through the reeds; the still water was black and somber. Wading round clumps of grass we would startle crocs into wild action that momentarily we took for attack. What gloomy haunts there were beyond we never discovered, for it seemed to us that we had chanced upon the mythical dwelling place of the sad-eyed Lady of the Lowlands, into which no man goes.

The Sad-Eyed
Lady of the Lowlands

———

following pages:
Their bellies
gleaming pearly white in
the first rays of the sun

———

Akaeye

———

Peter figured that if he
pushed a tube in
front of him
and hid behind it,
he would be able to swim
right in among
unsuspecting crocs.

———

An uncertain
Wildman on the eastern
mainland shortly
after Guy Poole's murder

———

"By his sneesings
a light doth
shine, and his eyes are
like the eyelids of morning."

———

Richard Lindner:
"And where the slain are
there is she."

To Peter 1973
and Alistair

On our last three trips to Alia, with only 120 crocs to go to reach the quota of 500, we found it increasingly difficult to collect specimens within walking distance of camp. Three schemes got us round the problem. Firstly, as we had done at Moite, we made short flights in the plane north to a big sandspit called Kubi Fora, landing on a dry mudpan just behind the beach. The need to get our kills back to camp for processing before the sun spoiled them tempted us to make unusual demands of our flying machine. I think the most we ever carried—an almost incredible load—was twelve good crocs, plus Peter, the Wildman, myself, and sundry gear—all in the tiny cabin designed for a maximum of three passengers. In this way we got many good muggers, including our all-night record, a monster pebbleworm 15 feet 4 inches long. "Treading" this beast up was something even the Wildman hesitated to do. The water was about five feet deep where it was shot, and it sank immediately. Wading out up to our chests, frankly shivering with fear, we saw a foot slowly break the surface. Clammy as that foot was, it was no more so than the reluctant hand that grasped it. There was no way of telling whether the croc was dead or only stunned; grabbing its foot could very well have unleashed half a ton of carnivorous vengeance.

Our second scheme was a kamikaze invention of Peter's that arose from two observations of crocodile behavior. We noticed that crocs are much warier of disturbances on the land than in the water; and further, that they are easily fooled by strange objects in the water. This is logical, really, because their enemies are mostly terrestrial. It led Peter to experiment with an adaptation of the old croc hunter's trick of crawling towards a "basking" croc very, very slowly, concealed behind a bush which he pushes in front. In his variation, Peter swam towards sleeping crocs pushing an inflated inner tube along in front. The gun lay across the tube, wrapped in kikoys and a broken gun case against the spray. When in range he inched himself up onto a patch of beach and fired. The method was highly successful, with the crocs astonishingly unsuspecting. Peter's greatest triumph came one afternoon when he actually nudged a "watchstrap" out of the way with the rifle barrel to get a shot at a big one beyond. Another time he stopped a nine-footer through the open mouth of a smaller one next door. But it was tedious, cold, and dangerous work; several crocs, far from being afraid, were hostile, and came for him aggressively. On three occasions Peter was driven ashore by such challenges.

The third way we increased our collection rate was simply to hunt further afield, leaving the carcasses tied to drowned bushes for collection

by boat in the early morning. Returning to camp one windy morning with a cargo of crocs, I left the men unloading the boat while I went to prepare my data sheets, etc. About a quarter of an hour later Tukoi announced that the first croc was ready on the scales. As I walked over I felt something was wrong. It took half a minute or so to put my finger on the trouble: there was no boat. I looked around, and out to sea, but

it had vanished. I asked the men what they had done with it. They stared blankly at me and at one another. Looking guilty and crestfallen, they started shuffling about muttering to themselves. They had forgotten to tie up our boat and in no time the wind had blown it far away. The plane on this trip was at Kalokol. We were marooned, and there was nothing to be done. From our camp the wind blew diagonally across the lake about forty miles to the other side. There was little chance of the boat making it without getting swamped. As it happened it did blow across intact, and was found several days later by a Turkana goatherd who walked forty-five miles south to Kalokol to inform McConnell. The latter sailed over to Alia and was as surprised to see us as we were to see him. The incident was an omen of things to come a month later.

CHAPTER 8 THESE SERPENTS SLAY MEN AND EAT THEM WEEPING

*Infamous marauder of the waterways—the perils of
micturition—Shebane's miserable end—picnicker's folly—fearful maimings—
Kwehahura's nemesis—fraud and malice of the sly reptile—crocodili lachrimae—mind not another's
tears—the grisly saga of William Olsen.*

Two thousand three hundred years ago, when the army of Perdiccas was crossing the Nile at Memphis, crocodiles are alleged to have killed 1000 of his soldiers. Though the statistic has probably gained a nought or two with the centuries, the point is made: that man's fear of other animals is grounded in reality. We have already considered some of the psychological implications of attacks from wild beasts. As for crocodiles, few people, even those without direct experience, do not feel antipathy to them, specially when the subject of hostile encounters between crocs and men comes up. As Topsell put it: "The crocodile is a devouring, insatiable beast, killing all that he layeth his mouth on, without all mercy or exorable quality." Every

year in Africa unknown but considerable numbers—perhaps even hundreds—of people are attacked by crocodiles. And this despite the rapid progress made towards exterminating them. Other animals, particularly lions, buffalo and hippo, kill far more humans every year, yet they are not hated for it as much as crocodiles are.

At this point in our tale of Lake Rudolf, before we look at the reflections cast by our work with the crocodiles upon their destiny and ours, it might pay to remind ourselves that the fear and hatred men feel for crocodiles is far from irrational. We have already considered (Chapter 3) the way in which crocodiles influence our unconscious thinking. This is undoubtedly the

most powerful component of our reaction to them. But we also have a more immediate, conscious reaction, a plain physical fear. "When he raiseth up himself the mighty are afraid. . . . Upon earth there is not his like who is made without fear. . . . Lay thine hand upon him, remember the battle, do no more." A consideration of crocodile attacks on man will serve to define the nature of this overt fear.

The wanderer William Bartram, never at a loss for a lurid description, tells us something of what it is like to be alone in a strange place surrounded by threatening saurians. In his *Travels* (1791), he tells how he happened on a place where many large alligators had gathered to feed on easily caught fish that crowded into a narrow channel:

But ere I had halfway reached the place, I was attacked on all sides, several endeavouring to overset the canoe. My situation now became precarious to the last degree; two very large ones attacked me closely, at the same instant, rushing up with their heads and part of their bodies above the water, roaring terribly and belching floods of water over us. They struck their jaws together so close to my ears, as almost to stun me, and I expected every moment to be dragged out of the boat and instantly devoured. But I plied my weapons so effectually about me, though at random, that I was so successful as to beat them off a little. When, finding that they desired to renew the battle, I made for the shore. . . .

Later, having run that gauntlet, he came upon yet another ominous situation:

I began to tremble and keep a good lookout; when suddenly a huge alligator rushed out of the weeds, and with a tremendous roar came up and darted as swift as an arrow under my boat, emerging upright on my lee quarter with open jaws and belching water and smoke that fell upon me like rain in a hurricane. I laid soundly about his head with my club . . .

"Out of his mouth go burning lamps, and sparks of fire leap out. Out of his nostrils goeth smoke, as out of a seething pot or caldron."

A SHOT RINGS OUT! WAMBO-WAMBO, DRAGON-GOD OF THE WAMBESI, QUIVERS--

Men who go to unknown places tend to see things larger than life; reactions to strange phenomena are often exaggerated in the light of later encounters. Thus Bartram was probably describing what he really felt was happening, though we might nowadays think he was embellishing.

Bartram lived to regale us with his exploits. So did many African adventurers who often assumed it was incumbent upon them to have witnessed at least one fatal croc attack when the time came to write up their "diaries." Apart from such yarns there are many authentic eyewitness accounts which serve to illustrate the things that happen when crocs try to kill men. Attacks naturally occur most often when man takes to the water:

Nor should even a substantial boat be thought of as absolutely safe. "The boldness of crocodiles at times is inconceivable. Captain Ross lost the coxswain of one of his barges, who was taken in the act of micturition whilst crouching upon one of the barge's rudder pintles, and this whilst the steamer was under way in the Shire River."

Sitting or standing half in the water is just asking for an attack. About fifteen years ago a particularly gruesome croc attack took place in the Tsavo National Park. An Asian family were sitting on a raft moored to the bank at Mzima Springs, a pleasure spot where tourists can leave their cars and enjoy restful surroundings by the cool spring waters. Several members of the family were dangling their legs over the edge of the raft when suddenly a croc seized one of the men by his leg just above the knee. His family then grabbed him and a tug-of-war ensued which the family won by slowly drawing the victim's leg through the beast's clenched jaws.

"There was the head of a huge crocodile out of the water just swinging over towards the deep with poor Shebane in its awful jaws, held across the middle of his body like a fish in the beak of a heron." (Arthur Neumann, Lake Rudolf, New Year's Day, 1896)

Seventy sharp teeth shredded his leg frightfully, and his screams and the copious blood so demoralized his fellows, that having freed him from the reptile's grasp, none of them thought to stop the bleeding. To the accompaniment of much weeping and wailing he died shortly after from shock and loss of blood—a pathetic accident caused by a mixture of ignorance and panic.

How quick the ponderous-looking crocodile is to exploit an opportunity is shown by a sinister attack that took place on the northern border of the Serengeti National Park some years ago. So dramatic was this incident that it lives on in the region's folklore. A notorious hunter named Kwehahura living in the area defiantly continued "poaching" despite regular arrests by the warden, Myles Turner. Surprised one day by a ranger patrol, Kwehahura took off like a springhare for the bush along the nearby Grumeti river, the haunt of many monstrous crocs. The patrol saw him reach the river and without pausing jump into a large pool, evidently meaning to swim across. Immediately following the splash they heard another, louder splash. Arriving at the brink of the pool they looked down, but saw only wide muddy swirls in the water, which gradually subsided and became still again. Kwehahura had crossed all right—this time to the "other side," to poach forever in the happy hunting ground. The place today is called Kirawira after him, and has been the scene of many other strange events.

Nor is it essential to be in or on the water to provoke an attack. A croc will come out after a suitably vulnerable man. The earliest recorded instance of a croc attack on Lake Rudolf was the bold taking on dry land of Arthur Neumann's cook, Shebane, at the north end of the lake in 1897. Neumann vividly describes the suddenness and finality of the attack, which obviously he himself barely escaped:

Having bathed and dried myself, I was sitting on my chair, after pulling on my clothes, by the water's edge, lacing up my boots. The sun was just about to set, its level rays shining full upon us, rendering us conspicuous from the water while preventing our seeing in that direction. Shebane had just gone a little way off along the brink and taken off his clothes to wash himself, a thing I had never known him to do before with me; but my attention being taken up with what I was doing, I took no notice of him. I was still looking down when I heard a cry of alarm, and, raising my head, got a glimpse of the most ghastly sight I ever witnessed. There was the head of a huge crocodile out of the water, just swinging over towards the deep with poor Shebane in its awful jaws, held across the middle of his body like a fish in the beak of a heron. He had ceased to cry out, and with one horrible wriggle, a swirl and a splash, all disappeared. One could do nothing. It was over: Shebane was gone. The dreadful incident had an insupportably depressing effect on me—a melancholy new year's day indeed.

Of all the characteristics that cause men to fear croc attacks, such as the animal's stealth (or boldness), ferocity, or strength, one in particular stands out—the unexpectedness. The concealment of water, the beast's cryptic looks and its hunting skill combine to make croc attacks sudden and therefore more terrifying.

Crocodiles . . . hide under willowes and greene hollow bankes, till some people come to the waters side to draw and fetch water, and then suddenly, or ever they be aware, they are taken, and drawne into the water. And also for this purpose, because he knoweth that he is not able to overtake a man in his course or chase, he taketh a greate deale of water in his mouth, and casteth it in the pathwaies, so that when they endeavour to run from the crocodile, they fall downe in the slippery path, and are overtaken and destroyed by him.

Men do not care to be caught unawares—even a stumble is blamed on the crocodile. It matters little if one's lack of vigilance is due to ignorance, carelessness, indifference or whatever; to be caught out is humiliating and unnerving.

Crocodile victims fall into three broad categories: the resigned (which includes the majority), that is, those like Kwehahura who for one reason or another consider the risk unavoidable. Secondly, the unaware, those who suffer real accidents of chance. Thirdly, the tantalized, men lured by some compelling aspect of a situation into exposing themselves to attack.

It is difficult for the civilized to comprehend just how resigned most potential victims are to the likelihood of their misfortune. But in fact it is difficult for a man not to be resigned when his life is unavoidably mixed up with wild animals. Throughout human evolution (up to the phase of urban man) our species has been forced into proximity with water and therefore with crocodiles. Man must drink daily; his livestock must too. Probably the earliest settled cultures were fishermen. The first cultivation was probably irrigated. Crocs have been and still are to many a ubiquitous presence—yet most of the time they are invisible. The most ancient (but still widely prevalent) level of cultural interpretation of the external world is animism, in which fear of the unknown and unpredictable is dispelled by attributing human characteristics to objects and animals. Seen in this anthropomorphic light, a crocodile attack was not just a chance episode of instinctive predation. It was rationalized into an intentional attack upon a specific person, akin to an act of human aggression. Often such a croc was held to be a human in disguise. By interpreting the animal's behavior in human terms it became more easily understandable. Such personification of essentially inhuman phenomena still permeates even the most sophisticated cultures; witness our humanization of pets or the popularity of astrology, not to mention thousands of other superstitions.

Animism as a method of interpreting life's enigmas (why should a crocodile attack *me*?) diminishes the element of unknown (which is frightening), replacing it with something explicable. This human capacity for rationalization is the omniscience of thought—the belief by humans in the power of their thoughts. Thus

an unpleasant incident is dismissed by simply thinking up an explanation for it, without the awkwardness caused by objectivity—insisting that the explanation fits all the facts. The objective explanation of the world, that is, science, comes much later, for it requires relatively large intellectual efforts of conceptualization and an accumulation of facts.

Now, the unexpectedness of croc attacks was rationalized by the humans as cunning. People felt the victims had been tricked—how else could such a despicable brute outwit a superior human? This reaction gave rise to the ancient myth of crocodile tears, which supposes crocodiles to be treacherous. "The common proverb also, *Crocodili Lachrimae*, the Crocodile's teares, justifieth the treacherous nature of this beast, for there are not many bruite beasts that can weepe, but such is the nature of the Crocodile, that to get a man within his danger, he will sob, sigh, and weepe, as though he were in extremitie, but suddenly he destroyeth him." Sir John Mandeville warned, "Theise serpentes sley men, an eten hem wepynge." Bartholomew Anglicus maintained, "If the crocodile findeth a man by the brim of the water, or by the cliff, he slayeth him if he may, and then weepeth upon him and swalloweth him up at the last."

As when a wearie traveller, that strayes
By muddy shore of broad seven mouthed Nile,
Unweeting of the perillous wandring wayes,
Doth meete a cruell craftie crocodile,
Which in false griefe hyding his harmeful guile,
Doth weepe full sore, and sheddeth tender tears
The foolish man, that pities all the while
His mourneful plight, is swallowed up unawares
Forgetfull of his owne, that mindes another's tears.

As for the physiological basis, there is none. We can be sure that any tears involved in croc attacks are shed by men, not crocodiles.

The myth of *crocodili lachrimae* touches most surely upon the aspect of fascination, that factor in so many croc attacks that, difficult though it may be to define, must nevertheless be recognized. One cannot always put down the circumstances of a croc attack purely to apathetic resignation or plain ignorance; a positive allure on the victim's part is often apparent. But any guilt is shifted onto the bad crocodile; the blame rests with the beast, or must be made to.

It was in the middle of our survey that we learned of a fatal croc attack that took place not far from Lake Rudolf, in southwest Ethiopia. It was typical of countless croc attacks, and its circumstances emphasize the stark reality of such accidents to those who, ignorant of the ways of the bush, do not believe or appreciate that such things actually do take place. As it

"Sentimentalist!"

happened, a professional hunter, Karl Luthy, was there to witness the incident. Luthy also took the trouble to record what took place, thus providing an unusually authentic and vivid description of the circumstances:

Shortly after noon on April 13, 1966, the DC 3 from Addis Ababa landed at Gambela in southwest Ethiopia. The plane brought six Americans of the Peace Corps, two girls and four boys, who had chosen to spend a short vacation visiting Gambela.

Through the village runs a slow, muddy river, the Baro, on the sandy banks of which I was working that day, building a pontoon on which to ferry my equipment across the river so that my client, an American named Dow, and I could resume our safari to the south. Hot and eager for a swim the Peace Corps came down to the river and I heard them discussing the prospect not far away. But their enquiries of the villagers elicited only a strong warning to stay out of the water on account of a large croc, which it was asserted, had only recently killed and eaten a native child, and later a woman, in the brazenest manner imaginable—by which I mean right in the middle of town, in plain view of a crowd! I, too, strongly warned them against swimming, and for a while they thought better of it.

Not long afterwards I heard a splash and looking up from my work saw one of the Peace Corps in the river striking out for the other bank. At this the others, abandoning all caution, also dived into the water and swam to the other side. For a while they splashed and cavorted in the shallows, maybe 150 yards from where I was working. It was naturally alarming, and very annoying to see them completely ignore my warnings and those of so many well-meaning and experienced people; but I did not wish to intervene again, it was no business of mine and in any case out of my control. Yet it was with considerable relief that I saw five of the six swim back to my side and climb out.

Bill Olsen remained behind, why, I never discovered. I recall seeing him on the far side of the river waist high in the water, his feet on a submerged rock. He was leaning into the current to keep his balance, a rippled vee of water trailing behind him; his arms were folded across his chest and he was staring ahead as if lost in thought. I continued working for a while and looked up again a few minutes later. Olsen had gone—vanished without a trace or a sound, and instinctively I glanced around, a prickle of apprehension spreading over me. But he was nowhere to be seen and I never saw him alive again, although we were to meet face to face much later when I fished his head out of the croc's belly.

Give or take half an hour the croc took Olsen at 3:30 P.M. After that events followed in quick succession. Although I knew instinctively what had happened I had, as yet, no definite proof. At this point the other Peace Corps volunteers came back to the river shouting for Olsen to join them, little knowing that he had in fact left them for ever. I continued to scan the river and eventually, a short distance downstream, a croc surfaced, with a large, white, partially submerged object in its jaws, whose identity was in no doubt.

About 15 minutes had elapsed since Olsen disappeared. The croc then dived to resurface (still carrying the corpse) ten minutes later, now some distance downstream and difficult to see. The Peace Corps were at first incredulous at the news, stubbornly unwilling to believe what was obvious. Olsen had wandered off somewhere, they said, he would be back soon; they clutched at the silliest possibilities rather than accept the bitter facts. Eventually my binoculars arrived and they saw for themselves what was obviously the body of their companion in the jaws of a croc. They went to pieces then, crying, full of remorse and self-incrimination, and I confess that one of them received a sharp rebuke when he ran to me pleading for help.

"Help who?" I shouted. "Help him? He's dead! Help you? I should hit you!"

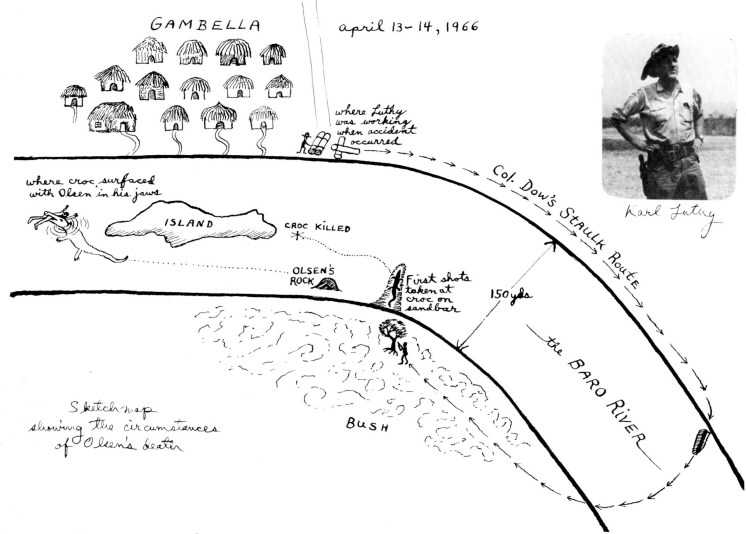

GAMBELLA   april 13-14, 1966

where Luthy was working when accident occurred

Col. Dow's Stalk Route

Karl Luthy

where croc surfaced with Olsen in his jaws

ISLAND   CROC KILLED

OLSEN'S ROCK

First shots taken at croc on sandbar

150 yds

the BARO RIVER

BUSH

Sketch map showing the circumstances of Olsen's death

One does not care to see one's fellow men die such needless deaths, however ignorant they may be.

By this time a crowd of excited people had gathered on the river bank and the commotion caused my client, Colonel Dow, to come with his rifle demanding to know what was going on. On learning the story he wanted to try and shoot the croc then and there, but I persuaded him not to, pointing out that killing the animal now, in midstream, would surely result in Olsen's body being lost, possibly for good. I reasoned that the croc would behave like any other croc; that is, he would haul out of the river early next morning, not too far away, to rest in the morning sun for a while, after the activities of the night.

Sure enough, around seven the next morning, a breathless villager ran up to tell us that a large croc, undoubtedly *the* croc, was lying ashore across the river not 50 yards from where Olsen had been taken. I got my binoculars and located the beast. That this was our quarry was in no doubt, for hanging from his mouth in some macabre reminder of a recent banquet, was a large piece of pale coloured flesh.

We were determined to destroy this croc, not only because it was a menace to the people on the river but also because an undeniable vengeance was in us. This was no circumstantial accident, but a deliberate and vicious attack in our midst and a certain urge for revenge moved us. Dow wanted to be the one to kill the animal so off he went on a careful route which took him upstream on foot for some distance, then across the Baro in a canoe and back down the other side on a painstaking stalk until eventually he

lay directly behind the beast. It was a difficult shot with the croc facing away from him so that its protruding back partially obscured its head. The Colonel shot too high and the bullet struck its neck, temporarily stunning the reptile, but causing only a flesh wound. He then fired four more shots, three of which were well placed, but despite this the croc crawled into the river and disappeared.

I watched all this through binoculars and feared at first that we'd lost the beast. I joined Dow and together we made for a sandbank in midstream, followed by a flotilla of dugouts, carrying the other Peace Corps and as many Amhara and Anuak villagers as could get in the canoes, all very noisy and excited. We stepped out onto the sandbank and began searching the river for some sign of the croc. Quite suddenly it surfaced not ten yards away and Dow, rather hastily, shot and missed. But the animal, mortally wounded took no notice and he was able to fire again, this time hitting the head, sending the brute spinning crazily about its own axis. I rushed forward with several other men and we dragged the carcass from the water onto the sand.

There remained only the gruesome business of opening up the croc, and it was not long before Olsen's fate was established beyond all doubt. We found his legs, intact from the knees down, still joined together at the pelvis. We found his head, crushed into small chunks, a barely recognizable mass of hair and flesh; and we found other chunks of unidentifiable tissue. The croc had evidently torn him to pieces to feed and abandoned what he could not swallow.

"Died: William K. Olsen, 25, Cornell graduate ('65) and Peace Corpsman since last June who taught science in the Ethiopian village of Adi Ugri; after being attacked by a crocodile while standing waist-deep in the muddy Baro river near Gambela, Ethiopia. Five fellow corpsmen heard Olsen shout and saw the beast pull him under; next day police found and shot the crocodile." (Time, April 22, 1966)

The circumstances of Olsen's killing are of some interest in illuminating the way in which crocodiles set about taking their prey. First lf all he disappeared without a sound which suggests that he was not standing on the rock at the final moment—I think he would have had time to scream if he was. It seems to me that he must have started swimming back and was simply pulled under without warning, and held under until he drowned. Secondly, there is the fact that no one saw any sign of the beast before the event although it was flagrantly bold afterwards, illustrating the stealth and cunning with which a crocodile hunts. The croc measured exactly thirteen feet and one inch long, by no means a monster but still powerful enough to catch a human like a fish.

These are the facts of life among crocodiles. So long as one is constantly threatened by savage brutes one is to some extent bound in barbarism; they hold you down. For this reason there is in man a cultural instinct to separate himself from and destroy wild beasts such as crocodiles. It is only after a period of civilization free of wild animals that man again turns his attention on them, seeking in them qualities to cherish.

CHAPTER 9 AUGUST'S BEANS

*Shipwrecked—avoid going over to the majority by
a hair's breadth—Beard swims two miles in rescue bid—praise be to Providence for deliverance—
the true facts about crocodiles—ghetto conditions—the disgraceful
episode of August's beans—
Manifest Destiny—a blundering oracle—emissaries from Technolopolis—the
mingled destinies of crocodiles and men.*

It was our last journey to Alia Bay, and we were only three crocs short of the 500. We knew that Shingle Island was still visited by several large crocs that we hoped would supply our needs. It was no longer possible to go over in the boat, land on one side of the island and surprise crocs asleep on the other, for they knew us well. There was a way to outwit them though: go over in the evening and sleep there until morning, by which time the crocs had forgotten the disturbance of the day before.

Accordingly, one evening I left Peter and the Wildman to spend a cold, damp night on Shingle Island hidden in trenches scooped out of the sand. I was to pick them up the next morning at 9 A.M., giving Peter a chance to shoot anything that came ashore early.

In the morning I set off for the island. The wind was up, blowing twenty to twenty-five miles an hour, covering the lake with whitecaps.

Reaching the island, I found that Peter had shot three good crocs, the first decoying the other two—better than we hoped. We exulted a little at having attained our goal, but anxious to go before the wind got stronger, we immediately loaded up the crocs. At first we thought two trips would be necessary, but on testing the load we reckoned to make it in one. Throughout the survey we had been making such marginal decisions, for time and expense constantly forced us to squeeze in a little extra. Perhaps the thought that we had at last finished dulled our senses that morning so that we failed to observe just how much the wind had freshened in the short time it took to load the boat.

As soon as we left the lee of the island to meet the full force of the sea we realized that we were pressing our luck. But the boat took it and we continued. Then, about 600 yards from the island, the waves got perceptibly steeper

Our dinghy on the slips at Alia Bay— last photograph

scoops.

because of some unseen feature of the lake. The sluggish boat could not follow the fast, high waves. Water began spilling over the transom each time a wave passed, and we jettisoned the crocs. But it was too late. In seconds the stern filled with water and our wretched dinghy sank for the last time. It began its life with us dredged up from the bottom of one lake and ended at the bottom of another.

We realized later that we had sunk almost exactly where Teleki's boat had been destroyed by an elephant eighty years before.

We found ourselves bobbing about in the unfriendly water of Lake Rudolf, far from land, in a rough sea that was rapidly driving us farther out into the lake. The boat had gone down stern first, trapping some air in the bow section that kept it floating with about two feet of the prow sticking above the surface. This gave us invaluable shelter while we decided what to do. We had disconnected the fuel tank, the only thing in the boat that floated: it was well we did, for it saved our lives.

Our first problem was the Wildman. His life in waterless Turkanaland had not encouraged him to learn to swim, and for once his carefree grin was gone as he held onto the gradually disappearing boat and watched to see what we would do. We had only a few minutes in which to teach him the rudiments of swimming before

we drifted too far downwind to make Shingle Island. Having no common language didn't help. We emptied the high-octane fuel from the tank and demonstrated how by holding onto it and kicking he could propel himself along. His wits, sharpened by the occasion, did not fail him, and he got the idea very quickly. There was a moment when we thought he might panic, but we made efforts to calm him, and once under way he kept his head. Shingle Island was by now barely visible 600 yards away through the spray. We gave the Wildman his course and he soon was making rapid progress through the turbulent water. By this time the aviation fuel from the emptied tank was burning us severely, but there was little hope of doing anything about it.

I set off, leaving Peter to make a last minute search in the submerged hull for his diary and the recorded numbers of our Moite crocodile captures. I soon ran into trouble. The waves took my glasses, leaving me unable to see my destination, and the violent reaction of my eyes to the sodary water soon made it difficult for me to see anything at all. Fortunately I had unconsciously registered the direction of the island relative to the set of the sea, so I was able to hold a rough course by swimming at the required angle to the waves. The wind was now blowing about thirty miles an hour, which meant that the air for a foot or so above the waves was full of spray. This, plus my inability to see, made breathing extremely difficult. I gagged often and had to make frequent pauses to regain my breath.

Then I started to panic. Unable to catch my breath at one stage I felt a violent urge to flail about, to struggle widly against a fearful feeling of confinement. I had to concentrate all my conscious resources onto the effort to keep control. I became dissociated from the sea and all physical environment. Then I became aware of a strange thing. My unconscious being that desired to panic began to draw apart from my will. There no longer seemed any but the flimsiest connection between the two. And I myself seemed to witness it all as an onlooker.

Gradually my panic subsided, although I do not think it was any great victory of the will. Rather it seemed as if the panic had run its course, to become for the moment exhausted; all the will did was to inhibit the panic long enough for it to spend itself.

I was by now very weak and numbed. I began to swim again, but slowly and with great effort. I struggled to keep direction though I felt hopelessly lost. I assumed that drowning was inevitable and in my exhaustion could contemplate it with detachment. The fear of death was no longer an issue, for that seemed already decided. Thus I kept swimming, automatically, and for no better reason than that there was nothing else to do. It felt as if an age passed like this, my mind stuck in the realization of my fate.

So when I saw the island's blurred silhouette it had little substance for me, until I sank down underwater and my feet touched bottom and I realized suddenly that I could make it. Then, when I tried to crawl out of the sea I nearly drowned again in the surf, because the breaking waves kept pushing me down as I tried to stand. I could see the Wildman, facing away from me, and tried to call him. But I made no sound; I could not even whisper. Eventually he turned and saw me in the surf and ran to pull me out. Peter came ashore shortly after, also exhausted, but in better shape than I, for he was a strong swimmer. He even had his diary and the croc code numbers from Moite.

Having got back to the island, we now had to think of what to do next. The mainland was two miles away. So long as the wind blew from the east there was no way we could get there against the sea, but Peter thought that he could make it with the aid of the fuel tank if the wind dropped. Luckily, the usual pattern of weather prevailed and the mild westerly sea breeze of the afternoons got up, as we hoped it would, at about 3:30 that afternoon. Peter now felt sure

he could make the mainland with the breeze behind him. I felt equally sure that I could not.

So Peter set off boldly, his progress agonizingly slow. The Wildman of course thought he was crazy—he hadn't the faintest idea what Peter was doing—but wished him luck all the same. Our plan was this: Peter would go to the mainland and there make up a larger float consisting of the tank plus a jerry can. This would be big enough for two of us to hold on to. In the morning when the wind was again blowing offshore he would walk to a point on the mainland immediately upwind of us and swim back to the island. If he misjudged the position of Shingle Island (invisible from his low vantage point for well over half the way), he would be blown past it to face forty miles of open lake. Apart from the navigational hazards there were the crocs; the large ones that used Shingle Island as a daytime resting place could at any time be swimming the same route.

The plan worked, though only just. Peter made the raft, which incorporated some jars of peanut butter and honey, with a flattened jerry can upright to act as a sail, and set off. When he first saw Shingle Island it was a long way off to his left, so that he had to steer the float diagonally across a sea as rough as it had been the day before. But he made it, and we piped him ashore with what ceremony we could muster.

We waited again for the wind to drop, which it did as expected at about 3 P.M. Then Peter and I set off, leaving the Wildman behind

At sunrise a somewhat worried crew carry the components of Peter's raft to a point on the mainland upwind of Shingle Island

———

Having assembled the raft, Peter then set off on the two-mile swim to Shingle Island, which he would not be able to see until he had covered over half the distance.

Back at Ferguson's Gulf

following pages:
The spit at Ferguson's Gulf,
featuring McConnell's
hut, the Curse, and hippo

because there was no handhold for him on the float. After swimming for an hour and a half, we reached the mainland without mishap.

Luckily we had brought the plane over on this last trip, so I was able to fly to Kalokol to get a boat. The next afternoon we returned to Shingle Island in Van's boat, to find an unquenchably cheerful Wildman eager to leave the sandbar on which he had just roosted for three days and nights without food or shelter. He considered the whole affair an excellent adventure. The others, true to form, saw it as the inevitable consequence of consorting with madmen, judging the gap between our foolhardiness and disaster to have narrowed down about as far as it could. For their benefit the Wildman gave a wildly improbable account of our experiences, loudly exaggerating the whole episode, laughing and gesticulating—a delighted man.

In one other way the Wildman personified the Turkana character in his reactions to our mishap. After we had swum to the island and recovered our senses he wandered about it for a bit, digesting the situation. Then, when he realized that for the time being at least we were stuck where we were, he sat down, scooped out a series of holes, and began to play the stones game against himself. For the next two days he played stones for hours on end, no doubt exclaiming at his successes and clucking over his losses. It absorbed him, and when rescue finally came he construed it as entirely natural that it should—here they were in their boat, come to get him. Abandoning his stones exactly as they lay, he stepped off the island without a backward look.

The survey was indisputably over. By taking just one chance too many we had brought it to an abrupt halt three crocs short of our goal of 500. To round it off we had lost our boat, engine, gun, and other equipment.

El Greco

The final phase of the study was now all that remained: an assessment of the population as a whole based on the analysis of data collected from the representative sample of 500 individuals.

Certain basic features of the Rudolf crocodile population could now be described with some confidence. All age groups live on fish, supplemented by virtually any other animal they can catch. They fish mainly at night, in very shallow, *sheltered* water. Nearly all the fish they eat are of one species—tilapia.

After hatching, young crocodiles grow 12-18 inches per year until sexually mature at about 6 years of age. Thereafter growth in length falls off; body weight continues to increase until death at a maximum age of 70 years. The faster growth of males allows them to attain 16 feet and over half a ton weight. Females seldom exceed 13 feet.

The fact of continuous growth permits an average age to be assigned to each length class of male or female crocs. Unfortunately, the impossibility of sexing any but the largest animals (except by internal examination) limits the application of this ageing technique.

Reproduction is seasonal. Mating is most frequent in October, nesting in November, and hatching in February. Large males are territorial. The females are required to attend the nest, or return to it at the end of the 3-month incubation, so as to unearth the hatchlings.

Two other sets of data were essential to complete my population assessment: a census, and an age-structure. I censused the population by counting, from the plane, all visible crocs along the entire 530-mile shoreline. Using this as an index a better estimate of the real number present was obtained by counting in several sample areas of the shore more intensely, and using the factor of increase to raise the whole aerial count. The more intense counts were made by counting eye reflections at night with a light.

The census revealed an interesting fact about crocodiles in general. Though Lake Rudolf is a large crocodile habitat with what may be the biggest single population of Nile crocs surviving, there are surprisingly few adults present. I estimated the entire population (not counting young crocs less than a year old) at about 14,000 individuals, of which only about 5,500 were mature. This fact was even more surprising in view of the strong possibility that the population was overcrowded. What showed up was the dependency of crocodiles on the *shore* of their habitat. They needed the shallows for fishing and the shore itself for resting and nesting. Deep water they shunned, except while traveling. And the avoidance by Rudolf crocs of the windward west shore indicated a dependancy on *sheltered* waters. Disturbances from either the water or the land were equally destructive to the crocs. Rough water forced them to find shelter near land; plundering of their nests and hunting on land they could not escape. Emigration from landlocked lakes such as Rudolf is impossible; thus crocs are actually very vulnerable to depredation, despite their superficial elusiveness and individual toughness.

From what one of the ancients called their "exceedingly prolifical mode of reproduction" it might seem that crocodiles are well adapted to withstand competition from other organisms, including the current plague of hominids. A

single female can produce up to 1000 offspring in her life. I calculated the average annual crop on Rudolf to be about 14,000 hatchlings. But the natural mortality in this yearly host is over 99 per cent: if it were not, the stock of 5000 to 6000 adults would increase. It may be that regardless of how few or how many adults there are in a population of crocodiles, a very high proportion of the young produced inevitably die. And if the number *hatching* is severely reduced (for example, by killing even a comparatively small number of breeding adults), then the number surviving to breed may become very small indeed. According to Peter Matyr, the ancient Babylonian government easily exterminated crocs on the Euphrates by putting a bounty on any *large* crocs killed—thus effectively eliminating the probably small breeding stock and hence the species.

That the seemingly small number of adults on Rudolf was in fact already maximal was suggested by something we have alluded to several times—overcrowding. And this despite the extensive shorelines, particularly on the west side, that supported hardly any crocs. I concluded that Rudolf crocs were overcrowded because several features of their biology showed them to be stunted—a common symptom of overcrowding. Their size at maturity was small, as was the maximum size attained. The average adult female was unusually small, as evidenced by the small average clutch size. These observations were most plausibly accounted for by postulating a retarded growth rate—which means stunted individuals. The age criteria I worked out for the Rudolf population indicated that these crocs were taking twice as long to mature as crocs elsewhere, though the average lifespan was probably the same.

This lowered growth rate was the immediate result of the low rate of food intake, indicated by the high incidence of empty stomachs. What caused the partial starving was much harder to deduce. Perhaps there was a poor variety of food available, forcing them to concentrate on a single food animal—tilapia—which was difficult to catch in optimal quantities. Or, as seemed highly likely, there were too many crocs competing for the same thing.

The topic of overcrowding vexes scientists, not only in animal studies, but in those of man too. The perplexities partly arise out of the unavoidable arbitrariness of what constitutes overcrowding. To those familiar with the outcome of exponential growth, such as that of traditional human economic goals, man appears hopelessly overcrowded. On the other hand, people still convinced of the anthropocentric myth—that man's intrinsic wisdom *will* find a way out—challenge the assertion of overcrowding.

Going back to crocodiles, one can avoid some of the ambiguities of "overcrowding" simply by leaving out any assumptions of the "normal" from estimations of parameters such as growth rate, density, numbers, and reproductive rate. Thus Rudolf crocodiles appeared to be *relatively* crowded, compared to crocs elsewhere. Whether one can call any population absolutely overcrowded depends so much on the choice of criteria that the topic is meaningful to philosophers only.

It is a basic postulate of population dynamics that any population of animals, given favorable conditions, will increase. A population does not increase indefinitely (which is impossible) but tends to stabilize, and even decline. Stabilization is characterized, among other things, by a shift in population structure towards a greater number of older individuals and correspondingly fewer young. The reproductive rate then declines as a result of various, often complex, changes, which are different for different species.

If we make two assumptions regarding the Lake Rudolf crocodile population, we can make a plausible (though conjectural) explanation of its observed peculiarities. Firstly, we assume it to be typical of the species (that is, any croc population in similar circumstances would exhibit similar biological characteristics). Secondly, we assume it to be an old population that has not been heavily hunted or otherwise interfered with by man for a long time. Nothing is known about these crocodiles that invalidates either assumption.

Having made these assumptions, we postulate that an old, stable croc population exhibits stunting of its individuals as a primary response to rising densities. This means a retarded growth rate that delays the onset of maturity, and produces individuals small for their age. Since the *lifespan* is unaltered, the oldest, largest members of the population tend to be smaller than their counterparts in other, faster-growing populations.

This stunting causes a net reduction in the reproductive rate (the population's tendency towards increase), in three main ways: Firstly, for its age, each female yields fewer than an optimal number of offspring because it is small in size (and a croc's clutch size is proportional to its body size). Secondly, its breeding life is shortened (because it took so long to mature). Thirdly, fewer females enter the breeding stock in a given period of time because their growth rate is retarded.

Associated with these three main influences are many other effects, often difficult to measure, that population biologists call *density-dependent*. As conditions get more crowded competition for

the best nesting sites rises. Some females may be forced to nest in places where the offspring have reduced chances of survival. Nesting on the three large islands, around whose inhospitable shores very few (if any) young crocs are likely to live to breeding age, may be such a density-dependent phenomenom.

Another density-dependent consequence of intensifying competition that can be expected is the failure, or behavioral "disinclination," of a female croc to breed every year. It may be that unless a male croc can successfully stake out and defend a territory, it won't breed. Since the number of "plots" is limited, so too is the number of studs—fewer perhaps than can serve all receptive females. Or (and we know far too little about crocs to resolve questions such as these), the territoriality of male crocs may itself be a reaction to crowding—a sort of space-clearing device evolved to ensure the integrity of individual behavior, to protect it from swamping by too many neighbors. Overcrowding induces a generalized kind of apathy, a slowing and weakening of response.

Many more density-dependent phenomena can be expected. For example, increasing numbers of females nesting in the same place means harder competition among the hatchlings for shelter and food. All these effects function as feed-back mechanisms operating to retard the reproductive rate.

We tend to assume, when observing a crowded animal population, that phenomena such as stunting or a declining reproductive rate are symptoms of ill-health. But this is an anthropomorphic view. In crocs, stunting is merely a device to deal with overcrowding. If there are too many individuals in a given population the excess must be disposed of and the trend towards increase reversed. It is but a stage in a natural cycle, the dynamics of evolution. Since crocs are, zoologically, non-violent animals, the deaths of the superfluous must be precipitated indirectly.

Man is no exception to the tendency to increase. In fact, his cultural ideal of economic growth catalyzed by his technological expertise has resulted in a population "explosion" —increase at a dangerously accelerated pace. That man is already overcrowded is obvious if we regard the semi-starvation of over half the world's population as a symptom. Even where food is still in excess other signs of crowding are evident: a density-dependent apathy in urban youth, for example, their cultural dissillusion and disorientation. This apathy is particularly apparent in the infantile regression of many of today's youth—their tendency to perpetuate childhood. This manifests itself in many ways—childish dress and dishevelment, the desire to keep on playing rather than accept the seriousness of adult life. It is evident in social behavior like the extended *crèche* of communal living, the rejection of adult goals, however understandable, engagement in organizations like the Peace Corps, with its ideals of innocence and friendship—of manipulating togetherness. These are retreats into childhood.

An outstanding density-dependent phenomenon is the plea for anti-violence that is so vigorously advanced by urban people. This represents the evolution of a taboo, or rather the extension of a taboo already effective between acquainted individuals to all individuals. It tells the population biologist (and we are concerned here with the biological implications only, not the moral ones) that one of the fundamental human responses to crowding is being strongly stimulated—violence. Man is the most violently aggressive of all vertebrates. In primitive human populations excess individuals were probably eliminated mainly in fights over food and space. Modern man, with barbarism just behind him, still wrestles hard with his aggressive instinct for violence. Its suppression requires constant policing by taboo and law. And the longer violence is deferred, the more destructive it will be when unleashed. Since we are apparently relying wholly on the anthropocentric myth of human invincibility for our continued existence, it is anybody's guess what will be the means by which human populations regulate their densities. We fear and denounce violence as a device to relieve overcrowding because it requires deliberate, conscious action, and to permit or even propose it, is to jeopardize the entire cul-

serpentes." At the other extreme they can aestivate through a drought. Schweinfurth noted this in 1871: "It is surprising in the dry season into what tiny pools and puddles the crocodile will make its way and where buried in the miry clay it will find a sufficiently commodious home."

tural and moral framework of society. Violence on the scale that mankind contemplates is chaos. Starvation or disease, on the other hand, because they are unconsciously inflicted, are more acceptable regulators. Yet anything we do to reduce numbers is aggressive and therefore subject to moral restriction. The more pressing the problem, the stronger is the feedback *inhibiting* the appropriate action. Such is the irony of the human population dilemma.

Returning to the crocodiles, some further aspects of their population dynamics bear consideration. Though the Nile crocodile as a species is sensitive to catastrophe, owing to the smallness of the breeding stock in any population, it is in its zoological adaptation quite hardy. Crocs tolerate 'the weeks of sub-zero temperatures in southern African winters by burrowing underground and hibernating. As Sir John Mandeville put it: "And they ete no mete in all the wynter; but there lizn as in a drem, as don the

Crocs are long-lived, physically robust, fierce, and cunning: yet most of them die before they are old enough to breed. It concerns us to find out the chief agencies of this somewhat paradoxical mortality. Topsell held the answer to be self-evident: "Seeing the friendes of it are so few, the enemies of it must needes be many, and therefore require a more large catalogue or story." Actually, a wide variety of predators will feed on young crocs, from Pharaoh's Mice to marabou storks. The hunter von Hippel cryptically alludes to "those inveterate egg-guzzlers, the elephants. . . ." Monitor lizards, baboons, and hyenas are notorious diggers of croc nests. Even crocs eat crocs. But despite their numerous enemies, it is probable that most young crocs die of starvation or disease, and accidents arising out of the intense competition for food, shelter, and space that must occur in a species in which vast numbers of young are hatched almost simultaneously.

THRILLS IN PLENTY AND JUNGLE ADVENTURES

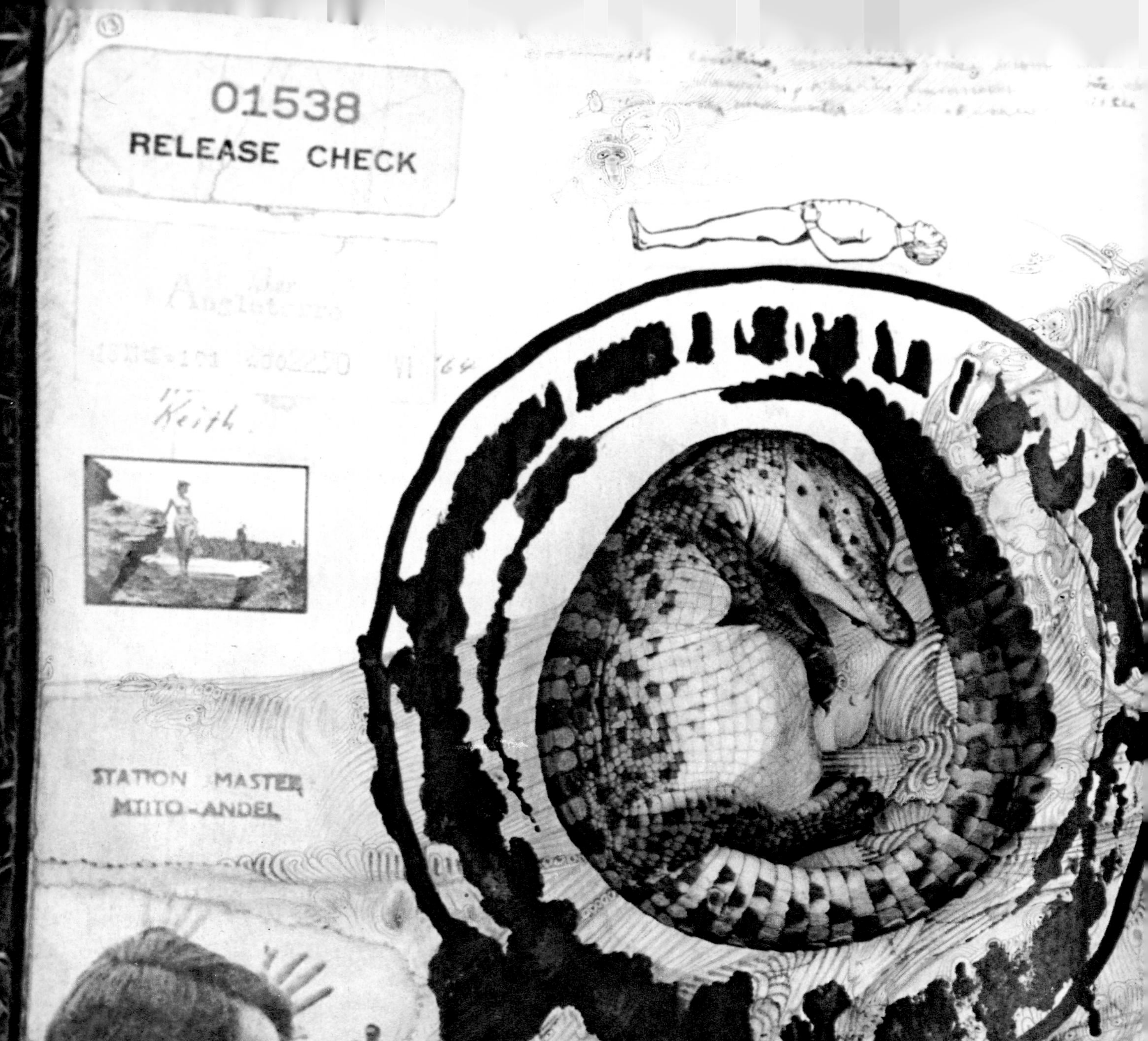

Keith.

STATION MASTER
MIITO-ANDEL

ANOTHER DAY
OVER! ANOTHER
DAY OF LAUGHING,
SMILING, CHATTING.
PRETENDING TO
BE SOMETHING
I'M NOT!

He was so excited that he
ran smack into a lamp post —
and was knocked out.

A few minutes later, a passing motorist found Burgess
dazed, bleeding
stitches put in his wound.

His wife had her baby three
weeks later.

"Of course you realize your nose will never be the same again."

Once grown, a croc has little to fear from predators, except man. There are, though, two herbivores that stand no nonsense from crocs —hippo and elephant. Some ancient Egyptians worshipped a hippo goddess—Hesamut—often depicted in the act of demolishing crocodiles. There is a legend repeated all over Africa of the elephant seized by a crocodile while drinking at a river. Calmly detaching the presumptuous reptile from its leg, the elephant hurled it onto a thorn tree. Impaled on the thorns, the helplessly wriggling croc slowly expired—the laughing stock of hornbills and baboons. One recalls, too, Kipling's tale of the unseemly fracas between the elephant's child and the crocodile. There is clearly strong symbolism in the juxtaposition of these two highly evocative beasts.

These then were some of the thoughts with which we prepared to leave Lake Rudolf. We had completed our count of all the cats in Zanzibar and could retire now to work up the data

"We collected most of our facts relating to the extent of the lake and the course of its shores, a duty which, it will be readily understood, we rigidly performed in our anxious and precarious position"

and report it. Back at Kalokol the sense of going dominated us; nor did we at first lament the end of our time upon the Black Lake. As Sophocles observed: "The long days store up many things nearer to grief than joy. . . ."

The Turkana, too, were ready for our departure. It happened, some time after we paid off our crew, that Elata and Ebei came to see us. We fancied in a moment of benevolence that they came to wish us farewell. Far from it. Without preamble they informed us that we had omitted a month's ration of beans—August's, to be precise. Furthermore, they told us, it was clear that we were plotting to leave without producing said beans. Quickly checking our records we confirmed what we knew anyway: that August's beans had been handed out, and unquestionably devoured.

They were not conning us. They were certain of the omission and positive that we meant to cheat them. But we refused to accept their calculations in favor of our own. How, we asked, had they made theirs? How indeed had we made ours? And what did we propose to do about it? We proposed to do nothing, adding that we considered their allegations to be in extremely bad taste, and that we hoped an apology would be forthcoming. It wasn't, of course, and so they departed, aggrieved and self-righteous, the matter having turned too sordid for their further consideration.

After our indignation had subsided we thought a lot about the wider implications of August's beans. We had worked hard to glean our crocodile information, however little it was. These Turkana had participated in our labors and stood to gain from whatever there was of value in our results. Yet they were concerned only with what they felt we owed them. It was, of course, a rebuke and it was not difficult to perceive its full extent.

To begin with we had to ask ourselves a basic question: What is the purpose of knowledge, or the drive to inquire, if it is not to improve one's situation? And it can improve the lot only of those who *need* more. The biological function of the quest for knowledge is to improve our ability to exploit our environment. Our knowledge of crocodiles ultimately was of potential value only to those far from Lake Rudolf who, feeling overcrowded, needed more resources, more ideas, more space—simply *more*.

The Turkana have no such need. We dangle before their indifferent, "ignorant" eyes juicy carrots grown in the promised land of industrialization, Christianity, and goodwill towards men; yet the Turkana have not the slightest chance of biting those carrots, even if they wanted to, because the promised land is hope-

lessly over-subscribed. The Turkana dream of heroism; we dream of mere survival, and suspect it for a dream, what's more. Yet still we would enlighten the poor savages and convert them to our brand of despair.

And what would our increased knowledge of crocodiles do for *them?* The incompatibility of men and predatory carnivores remains; our findings could not alter that. Knowledge dispels the *evil* of crocs—for those who bother to acquire it—but our facts would not change the Turkana's outlook. For them, crocodiles would remain evil, hostile denizens of the lake. Nevertheless, no Turkana would ever attempt to exterminate crocs. They do not *hate* them. It takes a civilized, cultured, overcrowded man to hate crocs, or love them, or exploit them, or exterminate them.

When all was said and done, the Turkana envied us only our guns and our plans. Among men for whom violence is still functional and honorable our guns were professionally admired as fine weapons, though to us they were merely tools. And our vast array of plans and arrangements were impressive. We were, they conceded, ingenious fellows.

Sometimes it seemed as if the Turkana indifference was a mockery of us. Nothing so disparages an offering as plain disinterest. Then again their scorn appeared to be absolutely genuine, as if they really had no use for us, could not comprehend what strange ailment made us invite them to join us in our restlessness. Karen Blixen perceived this when she wrote: "Like the spurfowl, the natives might be mimicking a fear of us because of some other deeper dread the nature of which we could not guess. Or in the end their behavior to us might be some sort of strange joke, and the shy people were not afraid of us at all. The natives have, far less than the white people, the sense of risks in life. Sometimes on a safari, or on the farm, in a moment of extreme tension, I have met the eyes of my native companions, and have felt that we were at a great distance from one another, and that they were wondering at my apprehension of our risk. It made me reflect that perhaps they were in life itself, within their own element, such as we can never be, like fishes in deep water, which for the life of them cannot understand our fear of drowning. This assurance, this art of swimming, they had, I thought, because they had preserved a knowledge that was lost to us by our first parents; Africa, amongst the continents, will teach it to you: that God and the Devil are one. . . ."

Perhaps it is the destiny of the Turkana to be obliterated by the pale-faced culture that so envies them their wilderness and their "untapped resources." The "enemy" ordered them to pay regular tribute and quit fighting. This enemy also told them to bestir themselves, to combat famine with fishing instead of old-fashioned magic and moans. Politicians exhorted them to elect and become Deeply Committed Citizens. Missionaries urged them to accept the guilt of original sin and beg God by numbers for mercy. Doctors pronounced them sick and herded them into hospital. Traders taught them to trick each other with money. A famous folk singer even came while we were there and confided that the answer was blowing in the wind. . . .

The enemy insisted on taking away his "unsafe" raft and giving him a plastic boat. Then plastic shoes, a plastic apron to replace his foreskin, a harmless plastic fishing net instead of his spear. We would turn him into a marvelous

plastic-fantastic warrior out of the sheer kindness of our civilized wisdom.

The beautiful America, the Walden of the Red Indian, was civilized thus. We were cruder then, if no less or no more aggressive. We razed their wilderness with such brutality that the "savage" Indian stood amazed, aghast at the incredible spectacle. The exterminating angels were more civilized than he; their culture was more refined. Their descendants, more civilized still, are beginning to regret their barbarity now that their own destiny seems less sacred. Nevertheless, they continue to shrug off their handiwork as Manifest Destiny, to claim that they are raising the barbarian from savagery into humility, showing him how to live a better, industrialized, prolific life. "Who shall say what prospect life offers another?" So busy are we with our economic, social and scientific benevolence that we do not stop to think what we are really doing. Imagine, for a moment, a state of human existence so

sublime that men's consciences are clear. Why should there not be a remote wilderness where hunters pursue and are pursued? Where crocodiles eat people and people eat crocodiles? Why not a flat earth to contain the wilderness, and a life of no spiritual importance? Why shouldn't warriors throw their spears into the unplummable depths of an inscrutable lake, rather than trawl for fish in its croc-free waters? Why should there not be famine and fighting and pestilence—and spiritual peace?

It seems to be the destiny of all Walden Ponds, Lake Rudolf included, to be consumed by technological man. It is not for the Turkana to say yea or nay. He does not even have to submit or flee. He will not be butchered for his balkiness or haughtiness, as the Indian was. Instead he will be inundated with benevolence. Sociological religious, political, economic, scientific, medical and technological benevolence will flow over him like lava: a creeping, choking, inexorable mantle of civilization will bury him forever. The crocodile, because of its helpless hostility to man, will be traded with, made into a public spectacle, and finally exterminated without even the benefit of benevolence. The prophecy of Leonardo da Vinci will be fulfilled: "A countless multitude will sell publicly and without hindrance things of the very greatest value, without license from the Lord of these things, which were never theirs nor in their power; and human justice will take no account of this."

And when the wilderness has been sold out, the inevitable remorse will set in. But that which has been obliterated can never be reconstituted. It cannot be remade as a national park, because gazetted paradises are as artificial as the laws behind them, the sentiments around them, and the robots imprisoned within them.

It was our destiny that we who lamented the decline of the Turkana and the crocodile, the great free spirits of the wilderness, should actually participate in their going. For we were emissaries from Technolopolis (benevolent, of course); we could not be disloyal to our kind and still be of that kind. Whatever we found to marvel at, respect, or admire in Lake Rudolf and its people could not change our identity. But what we could not do was convince ourselves of the value of our offerings. Just what was it that sickened us to our task, that aroused in us the wish to leave it all alone?

Like the crocs of Rudolf that stunt themselves by their own fecundity, we men of Technolopolis are beginning to stunt. Not physically—we are too *clever* for that—but spiritually. It is our sensitivity that withers. And men *know* what ails them. In a sense it is knowledge itself that is

the virus, in particular a certain item of knowledge. John Stuart Mill foresaw the problem: "If the earth must lose that great portion of its pleasantness which it owes to things that the unlimited increase of wealth and population would extirpate from it, for the mere purpose of enabling it to support a larger population, I sincerely hope, for the sake of posterity, that they will be content to be stationary long before necessity compels them to it."

But we have not been content to be stationary, and the realization of what necessity may compel arouses in us a longing for the kind of life we think we see around Lake Rudolf. As soon as we understand the origin of this longing we perceive also that reality will make a mockery of the wish for an untouched widerness. All species of people and animals are relative to their time and circumstances. The Turkana is a myth. The wild crocodile is a myth. For the moment they are living myths, self-perpetuating images, legends in their own lifetimes. But they can exist only on their own; they cannot be sustained or copied, or incorporated by another culture, however ingenious. *They cannot be preserved because we know how to preserve only one kind of thing—a dead thing.* A crocodile is a crocodile only while it is a fierce beast of prey, free to come and go as it pleases, to take its chances with other hunters, to fight and die as its instincts direct in the wilderness of its choice. So too with the Turkana. He is nothing without his sharpened spear, his cattle, his arrogance, and the privacy of his wilderness.

It is monstrous, really, the technological impertinence of industrial man that supposes he is in command of nature, capable of ordering the destinies of all things. The naive faith of the tyrants of megalopolis in the magic of their technology is nothing more than the escalation of witchcraft; it is the anthropocentric myth—that man is the nub of nature, and that all things are his. We are drunk with industrial mead.

In our contemplation of the destinies of crocodiles and men, and the influence of studies such as ours on the course of events, we wondered at the business of wildlife conservation. Already there was talk of fencing off the northeast shore of Lake Rudolf as a national park—a development that would entail, among other things, the eviction of the nomads who grazed the hinterland.

Perhaps the most striking thing about the human compulsion to save animals is that it only evolves in dense, affluent societies. Where people exist at low densities, or in poverty, the concept of game saving is unknown. It does not arise because there is no *emotional need* of it. It

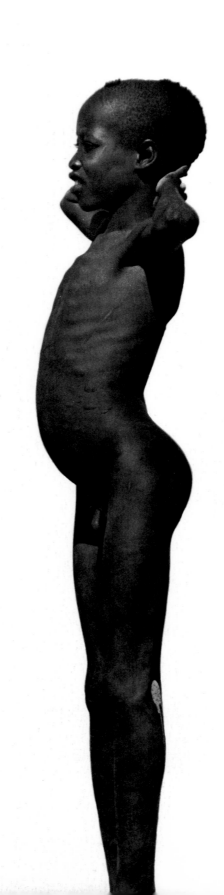

is not that "primitive," simple folk automatically practice conservation, as starry-eyed game savers often assert; it is simply that the question never arises. Such people live spontaneously as their instincts direct them, in a quite fortuitous harmony with their world.

Conservation is guilt. It springs from fearful introspection, the awful tension between what we *would* do if we obeyed our instincts, and the prohibition of our moral sense. Our urge is to strike out at the people overrunning us, to fight for what we covet, to destroy what we fear and hate—but these aggressive actions and thoughts are culturally taboo. So we invert these dangerous, frightening impulses and counter them with their opposites. Instead of destruction we insist upon preservation. Instead of killing we cry out: Save!

And so the fantasy of a nature untouched by man grows like a fetus shielded from reality in a warm womb of nebulous benevolence. We brandish this benevolence as proof of our gentleness—we who toy with nuclear cataclysm. The wilderness becomes a magical mystery tour through which the animal lover trips and flits

his way to tearful Disney tunes, drunk with the incestuous wonders of old Mother Nature. Conservationists fawn before reality like submissive dogs exaggerating their vulnerability, pleading: "Don't bite me—lick me."

There is a popular expression to describe the vaguely defined sentiments of conservationists—"deeply concerned." Comfortable, affluent, powerful, *well-informed*, racially tolerant, educated, democratic, *crowded* people are the kind most susceptible to the affectation of deep concern for wildlife. All over the western world they can be seen squatting hopefully beside their TVs—watching the animals; or driving breathlessly round national parks—watching the animals; snapping hungrily with cameras—watching the animals; squinting earnestly through binoculars—watching the animals. All of them feel deeply, deeply concerned about wildlife.

But what are they watching for? Is it some sort of answer? Do they really believe that the poor, dumb, doomed beasts are going to share a revelation with them? ("Will he speak soft words unto thee? Will he make a covenant with

Hippo "poachers"

thee?'') Why is it that between them and the animals there is always a glass shield? Dark glass, plate glass, frosted glass, smoked glass; glass with cross-hairs, glass with CONCERN etched into it, glass with DESPAIR scratched all over it. They are so near, yet so far. If only they were to insert a mirrored glass, they would find themselves staring at their own earnest, puzzled, *desperate* faces. The riddle would be solved. They would realise that the concern is for *their* fate—not that of the animals. It is so simple really; solve mankind's problems and the predicament of the animals will automatically vanish. But no amount of concern for the animals

is going to make any difference to their destiny or ours.

The more we thought about Lake Rudolf and the forces eroding its dignity and solitude, the more we inclined towards Thoreau's exclamation: "So much for blind obedience to a blundering oracle." In so many respects it is impossible not to see modern man as a vast, lumbering blunder. We place such implicit faith in our economic, social, and political paradigms. We reject categorically the possibility that they are as mythical as the savage's flat earth. He sees flatness and takes for granted the veracity of his vision. We see prosperity following upon

Merille

economic growth—and take for granted the veracity of our vision. The fact that the savage has never seen the edge of the world does not shake his belief in its existence. We who have never seen the end of the world ironically overlook the possibility of its imminence.

Perhaps it was the very difficulty of our time and work on Lake Rudolf that reminded us of the reality behind the romance that was there as well. To see only the beauty of the wilderness was something we were not fitted to do. It takes a poet to overlook the harshness and the struggle, to see only the admirable and beautiful things. Often only the poet can find these things. The great pastorals—*Walden, Out of Africa*—they are peculiarly personal experiences not easily

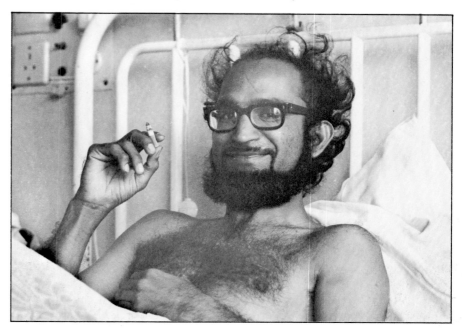

shared. Thoreau, after a mere two years of Walden, confessed that he left for as good reason as he came; nor did he ever try to return.

Karen Blixen was a visitor to Africa who did her Walden for a while, then retreated when the going became impossible. She went out of Africa far more surely than into it. Her house now is a school for cooks. Her cook, her Kamante, is a blurred shadow of an unrepeatable memory; yet he will die in Africa, where he was born. And he will go without ever having felt the urge to learn one word of the language in which the romance of his life was written.

These people knew, as only intuitive people can, just how far they could go along the stepping stones without falling. As poets they made legends when they eulogized that which they chose to remember. Their recollections are immortal sentiments, so delicately phrased that less sensitive men are entranced to a degree never attained in their own experiences.

Mulji Modha recovering from a croc attack on Central Island

Yes, their poetry is immortal. But their ponds dry up in the drought of mankind's seasons.

There were moments when we found our minds casting back over the days on the east shore. We remembered the beautiful, delicate evenings when everything seemed for just a few short minutes to exult in living. The geese make brief, meaningless flights hissing and honking at one another; pelicans pass by on aimless journeys, skimming the backs of the crocodiles sliding wakefully off the sandbars. The topi that spent the day hunched dismally on the lava, its back to the wind, gets up now, and walks briskly away.

We thought of the hippo in Moite Bay that would be plunging and snorting, eager to emerge and begin the night search for grass. The leopard on Moite would be stretching as he gazed across the lake and watched the sun go down. The big perch would be floating up to the shallows out of the cool green depths where they had spent the hot day. Soon there would be the mysterious clump and splash that the Turkana said was a hunting perch darting at its prey, but which one never could witness. Gradually the shallows would swirl and splash with crocodiles searching for fish.

He appointed the moon for seasons; the sun knoweth his going down.
Thou makest darkness, and it is night, wherein all the beasts of the forest do creep forth.
The young lions roar after their prey, and seek their meat from God.
The sun ariseth, they gather themselves together, and lay them down in their dens.
Man goeth forth unto his work and to his labour unto the evening.

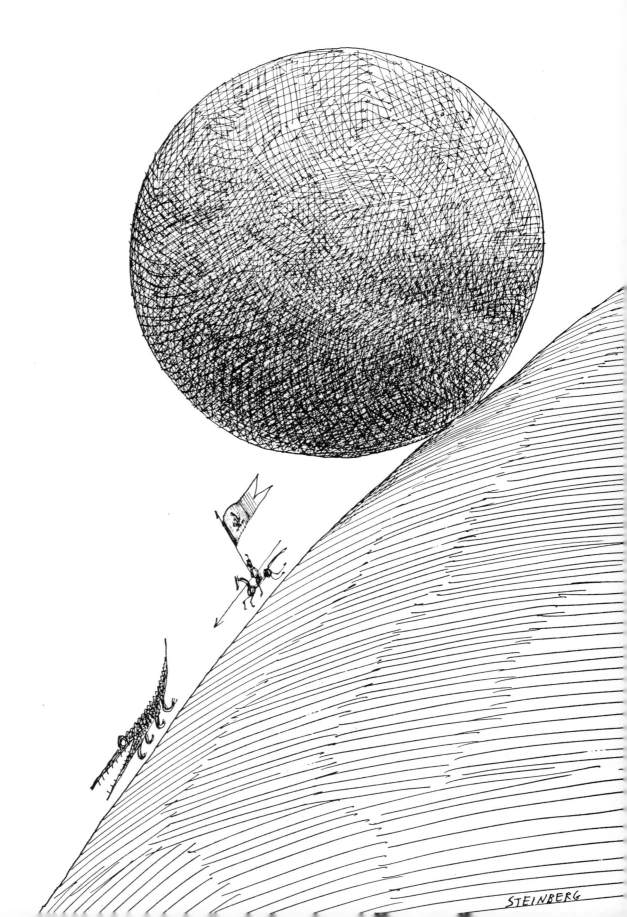

STEINBERG

At rest behind a 185-pound lunch.

Measuring a 14-footer.

The El Molo "ngombe" learns to hold its breath, put its head under water and graze on weeds.

15 feet 9 inches.

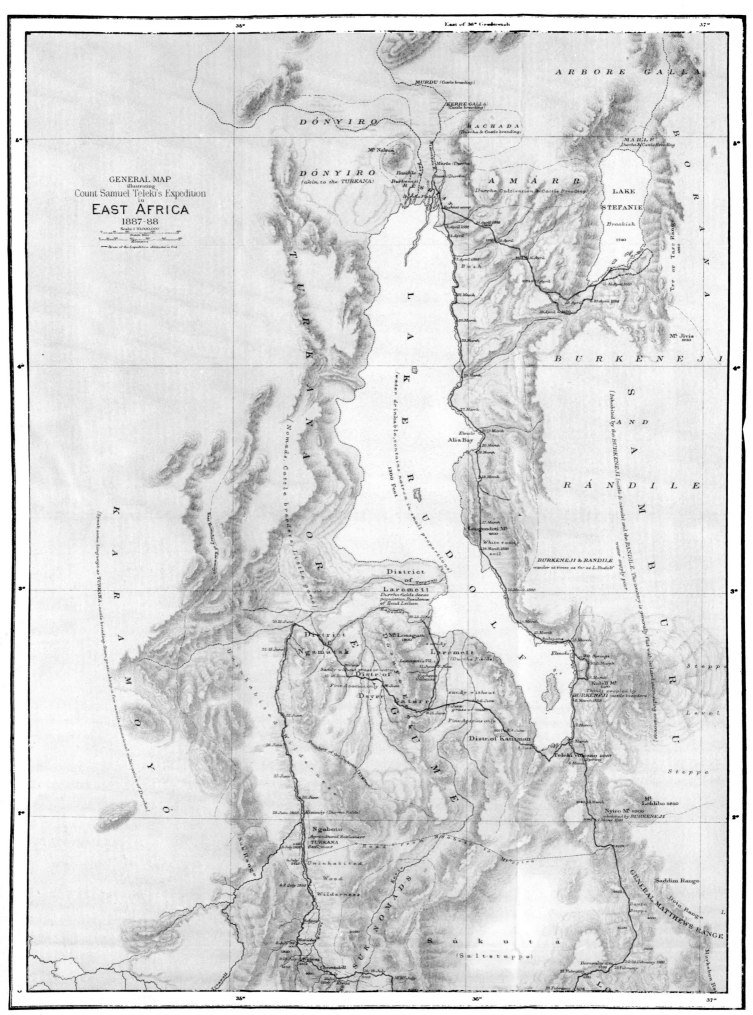

GENERAL MAP
illustrating
Count Samuel Teleki's Expedition
in
EAST AFRICA
1887-88
Scale 1:10,000,000

Longmans, Green & Co. London & New York

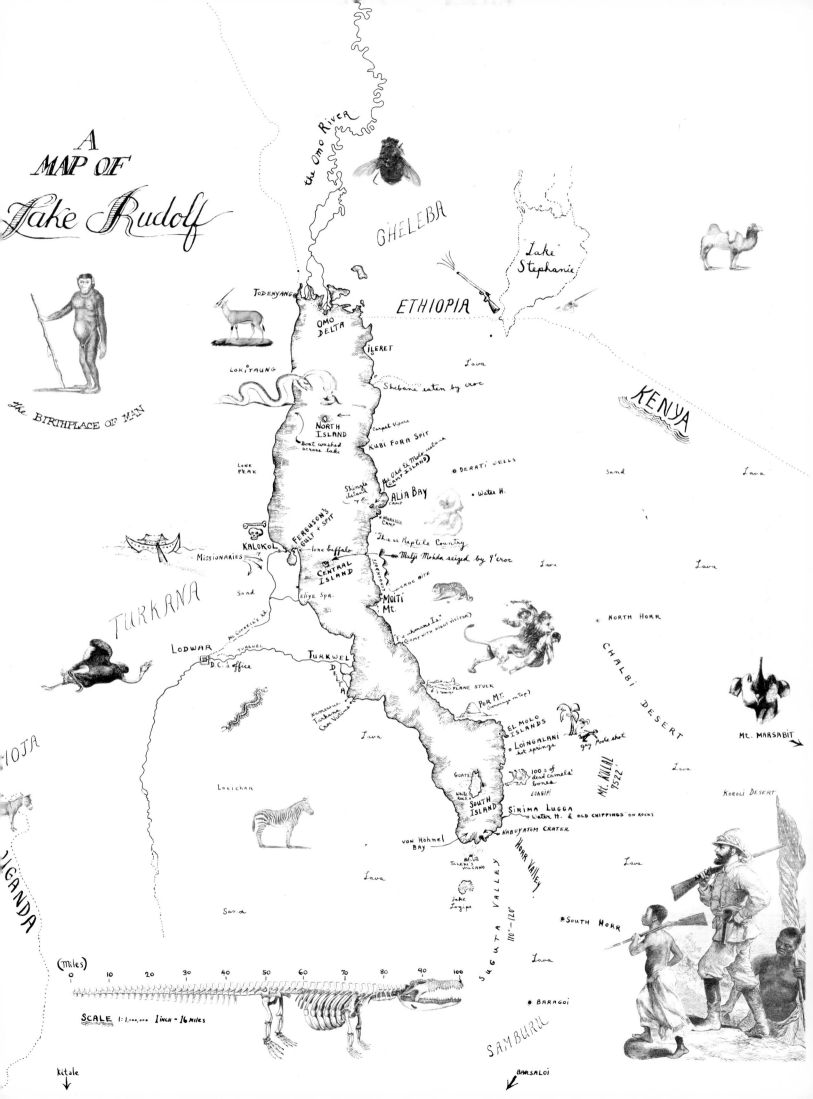

A MAP OF Lake Rudolf

The BIRTHPLACE OF MAN

SCALE 1:1,000,000 1 INCH = 16 MILES

BIBLIOGRAPHY

The titles cited refer to the Nile crocodile (excluding most taxonomic and paleontological references, but including references to other crocodilians of relevance to population studies) and to the exploration of Lake Rudolf.

Abercromby, A. F. "Crocodile burying its food." *Journal of the Bombay Natural History Society*, 28 (1922), 55.

Adams, A. L. *Wanderings of a Naturalist in India.* Edinburgh: William Hodge, 1867.

Adamson, J. "Rock engravings near Lake Rudolf." *Journal of the East African Natural History Society*, 19 (1946), 70–71.

―――――. "The island of no return." *Country Life*, (1955), 1040–1042.

―――――. "Hohnel island (South island) in Lake Rudolf." *Geographical Journal*, 122 (1956), 478–482.

Aelianus. *On the Characteristics of Animals.*

Ahrenfeldt, R. H. "Two British anatomical studies on American reptiles (1650–1750). 1. Hans Sloane: Comparative anatomy of the American crocodile." *Herpetologica*, 9 (1953), 79–86.

Anonymous. "Rhino vs. crocodile." *Northern Rhodesia Journal*, 1 (1950), 13.

―――――. "Outsize crocodiles." *Northern Rhodesia Journal*, 1 (1952) 45.

―――――. "Crocodiles are useful in food fish dams." *South African Shipping News and Fishing Industry Review*, 7 (1952), 75.

―――――. "Big crocodiles." *Northern Rhodesia Journal*, 2 (1955), 8.

Arambourg, C. "Observations sur la bordure nord du Lac Rodolphe." *C.r. hebd. Séanc. Acad. Sci., Paris*, 197 (1933), 856–860.

―――――. "Les formations prétertiaires de la bordure occidentale du Lac Rodolphe (Afrique Orientale)." *C.r. hebd. Séanc. Acad. Sci., Paris*, 197 (1933), 1663–1665.

―――――. "Mammifères Miocènes du Turkana Afrique Orientale." *Annales Paléontologique*, 22 (1933), 123–147.

―――――. "Découverte d'un gisement de Mammifères Burdigaliens dans le bassin du Lac Rodolphe (Afrique Orientale)." *C.r. Séanc. Soc. géol. Fr.*, 14 (1933), 221–222.

―――――. "Les résultats géologiques de la mission de l'Omo (1932–1933)." *C.r. Séanc. Soc. géol. Fr.*, 15 (1934), 63–64.

―――――. "Les formations eruptives du Turkana." *C.r. hebd. Séanc. Acad. Sci., Paris*, 198 (1934), 671–673.

―――――. "Esquisse géologique de la bordure occidentale du Lac Rodolphe." *Mus. nat. d'Hist. nat. Mission sci. de l'Omo, 1932–1933*, 1 (1934), 9–16. Paris: Editions du Musée.

―――――. "Contribution à l'étude géologique et paléontologique du bassin du Lac Rodolphe et de la basse vallée de l'Omo. Pt. 1: Géologie." *Mus. nat. d'Hist. nat. Mission sci. de l'Omo, 1932–1933*, 1, 157–230. Paris: Editions du Musée.

―――――. "Les Hippopotames fossiles d'Afrique." *C.r. hebd. Séanc. Acad. Sci., Paris*, 218 (1944), 602–604.

―――――. "Contribution à l'étude géologique et paléontologique du bassin du Lac Rodolphe et de la basse vallée de l'Omo. Pt. 2: Paléontologie." *Mus. nat. d'Hist. nat. Mission sci. de l'Omo, 1932–1933*, 1 (1947), 231–562. Paris: Editions du Musée.

―――――, P. A. Chappuis, and R. Jeannel. "Historique et itinéraire de la mission." *Mus. nat. d'Hist. nat. Mission sci. de l'Omo, 1932–1933*, 1 (1935), Paris: Editions du Musée.

Aristotle. *Historia Animalium.*

Attwell, R. I. G. "Crocodiles feeding on weaver-birds." *Ibis*, 96 (1954), 485–486.

―――――. "Crocodiles at carrion." *African Wild Life*, 13 (1959), 13–22.

Attwell, R. I. G. "Possible bird-crocodile commensalism." *The Ostrich*, 37 (1966), 54–55.

Austin, H. H. "Journeys to the north of Uganda. II. Lake Rudolf." *Geographical Journal*, 14 (1899), 148–152.

―――――. "From Njemps to Marich, Save and Mumia's (British East Africa)." *Geographical Journal*, 14 (1899), 307–310.

―――――. "Through the Sudan to Mombasa via Lake Rudolf." *Scottish Geographical Magazine*, 18 (1902), 281–302.

―――――. "A journey from Omdurman to Mombasa via Lake Rudolf." *Geographical Journal*, 19 (1902), 669–690.

―――――. *Among Swamps and Giants in Equatorial Africa.* London: Arthur Pearson, 1902.

―――――. *With Macdonald in Uganda.* London: Edward Ar-

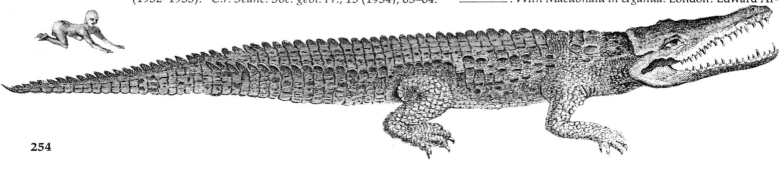

nold, 1903.

Aylmer, L. "The country between the Juba river and Lake Rudolf." *Geographical Journal*, 38 (1911), 289–296.

Baker, J. R. "The evolution of breeding seasons." In *Evolution*. Oxford: University Press, 1938.

Baker, S. W. *The Nile Tributaries of Abyssinia.* London: Macmillan, 1871.

Barbour, T. "An historic crocodile skull." *Copeia,* (1924), 16.

Barker, R. de la B. "Crocodiles." *Tanganyika Notes and Records,* (1953), 76–78.

Barton, J. "Turkana grammatical notes and vocabulary." *Bulletin, Society of Oriental Studies, London University,* 2 (1921), 43–73.

————. "Notes on the Turkana tribe." *Journal of the Royal African Society,* 20 (1921), 107–115.

Bartram, W. *Travels.* New York, 1791.

Beadle, L. C. "Scientific results of the Cambridge expedition to the East African lakes, 1930–1 IV." *Journal of the Linnaean Society (Zoology),* 38 (1932), 157–211.

Bellairs, A. *Reptiles.* London: Hutchinson, 1957.

Benedict, F. G. *The Physiology of Large Reptiles.* Washington: Carnegie Institute, 1932.

Bicknell, W. *The Natural History of the Sacred Scriptures, and Guide to General Zoology.* New York, 1877.

Bigalke, R. "The longevity of wild animals in captivity." *South African Journal of Natural History,* 6 (1929), 297–302.

————. "Note on the egg of the Nile crocodile." *Proceedings of the Zoological Society of London,* (1931), 555–559.

Blake, D. K. *Crocodile Farming in Rhodesia.* Rhodesia: Department of National Parks and Wildlife Management. 1970.

Blake, W. *Illustrations of the Book of Job.*

Boake, B. "The nest of the crocodile." *Zoologist,* 5, (1870), 2002–2004.

Bonnet, H. *Reallexikon der Aegyptischen Religionsgeschichte.* Berlin: Walter de Gruyter, 1952.

Boreman, T. *A Description of above 300 Animals.* London, 1794.

Bothwell, Dick. *The Great Outdoors Book of Alligators.* St. Petersburg, Fla.: Great Outdoors Publishing Co., 1962.

Bottego, V. (See general index to the first 20 vols. of the *Geographical Journal* 1893–1902 in Vol. 26 for published results of Bottego's journey to Lake Rudolf in 1896.)

Brander, D. "Stones in crocodiles' stomach." *Field,* 146 (1925), 537.

Brazaitis, P. "The determination of sex in living crocodilians." *British Journal of Herpetology,* 4 (1968), 54–58.

Brock, J. *Krokodile.* Stuttgart: Alfred Kernan, 1970.

Brooke, J. W. "A journey west and north of Lake Rudolf." *Geographical Journal,* 25 (1905), 525–531.

Brown, B. "The largest crocodile." *Natural History,* 49 (1942), 260–261.

Buel, J. W. *Heroes of the Dark Continent.* Philadelphia: Historical Publishing Co., 1890.

————. *Great Achievements of the Century.* Philadelphia: Historical Publishing Co., 1898.

————. *Conquering the Dark Continent.* Philadelphia: Historical Publishing Co., 1899.

————. *Living World.* Philadelphia: Historical Publishing Co., 1900.

Burrage, B. R. "Nile crocodiles attacking small boats." *British Journal of Herpetology,* 3 (1967), 82–83.

Bustard, R. H. "A future for crocodiles" *Oryx,* 10 (1969), 249–255.

Butter, A. E., and P. Maud. *Geographical Journal,* 22 (1904), 552–579.

Cansdale, G. *Reptiles of West Africa.* London: Penguin Books, 1955.

Carpenter, C. D. H. "Can crocodiles swallow their food under water?" *Nature, London,* 122 (1928), 15.

Carpenter, H. D. *A Naturalist on Lake Victoria.* London: Nisbett, 1920.

Carter, D. *The Symbol of the Beast.* New York: 1957.

Castle, W. M. "A survey of deaths in Rhodesia caused by animals." *Central African Journal of Medicine,* 17 (1971), 165–167.

Cavendish, H., and H. Andrew. "Through Somaliland and around and south of Lake Rudolf." *Geographical Journal,* 11 (1898), 372–381.

Chabreck, R. H. "Methods of capturing, marking and sexing alligators." *Cyclostyled report of the Louisiana Wildlife and Fisheries Commission,* 1963.

————. "The movement of alligators in Louisiana." *Cyclostyled report of the Louisiana Wildlife and Fisheries Commission,* 1965.

————. "Methods of determining the size and composition of alligator populations in Louisiana." *Cyclostyled report of the Louisiana Wildlife and Fisheries Commission,* 1966.

Champion, A. M. "Teleki's volcano and the lava fields at the southern end of Lake Rudolf." *Geographical Journal,* 85 (1935), 323–341.

————. "In search of Teleki's volcano." *Journal of the East African Natural History Society,* 12 (1935), 118–129.

————. "The physiography of the region to the west and south-west of Lake Rudolf." *Geographical Journal,* 89 (1937), 97–118.

————. "The volcanic region around the southern end of Lake Rudolf, Kenya Colony." *Zeitschrift Vulkanische,* 17 (1937), 163–172.

Chapman, C. M. "Survey of the crocodile population of the Blue Nile." *Geographical Journal,* 136 (1970), 55–59.

Chappuis, P. A. *Als Naturforscher in Ostafrika, Schilderung einer Expedition zum Mt. Elgon, Rudolfsee, Omo-fluss.* Stuttgart: E. Schweizerbartsche Verlagsbuchhdlg, 1935.

Chenevix-Trench, C. *The Desert's Dusty Face.* London: William Blackwood, 1964.

Churchill, W. S. *My African Journey.* London: Holland, 1908.

Cirlot, J. E. *A Dictionary of Symbols.* Philosophical Library, 1962.

Claudianus. *de Raptu Proserpinae.*

Clemens Alexandrium. *Protrepticus.*

Collins, R. O. "The Turkana Patrol." *Uganda Journal,* 25 (1961), 16–33.

Copley, H. "A short account of the freshwater fishes of Kenya." *Journal of the East African Natural History Society,* 16 (1941), 1–24.

Corbet, P. S. "Notes on the insect food of the Nile crocodile in Uganda." *Proceedings of the Royal Entomological Society, London (A),* 34 (1959), 17–22.

————. "The food of a sample of crocodiles (*Crocodilus niloticus*) from Lake Victoria." *Proceedings of the Zoological Society of London,* 133 (1960), 561–571.

Cott, H. B. "The status of the Nile crocodile in Uganda." *Uganda Journal,* 18 (1954), 1–12.

————. "Ecology and economic status of the crocodile in Uganda." In, Record of Symposium on African hydrobiology and inland fisheries. *Pub. 6. Commission of Technical Co-operation in Africa South of the Sahara. Bukavu,* (1954), 119–122.

————. "Is it curtains for the crocodile?" *Listener,* BBC London, 1957.

————. "Scientific results of an enquiry into the ecology and economic status of the Nile crocodile in Uganda and Northern Rhodesia." *Transactions of the Zoological Society, London,* 29 (1961), 211–356.

————. "The status of the Nile crocodile below Murchi-

son Falls." *I.U.C.N. Bulletin*, 2 (1968), 62–64.

————. "Nile crocodile faces extinction in Uganda." *Oryx*, 9 (1968), 330–332.

————. "Tourists and crocodiles in Uganda." *Oryx*, 10 (1969), 153–160.

Croulet, C. "A taste of the tropics." *Bulletin of the Philadelphia Herpetological Society*, 11 (1910), 1–5.

Cumming, R. Gordon. *A Hunter's Life in South Africa*. London: John Murray, 1850.

Cunnington, W. A. "Fauna of the African lakes." *Proceedings of the Zoological Society of London*, 93 (1920), 507–622.

Cuvier. *The Animal Kingdom. 9. The Class Reptilia*. London: Whittaker, 1831.

Daudin, F. *Histoire Naturelle (Reptiles)*. Paris, 1802.

Deraniyagala, P. "Some scientific results of two journeys to Africa." *Spolia Zeylanica*, 25 (1948), 31–32.

De Sola, C. R. "The crocodilians of the world." *Bulletin of the New York Zoological Society*, 36 (1933), 3–24.

Devalle, G. "Sulle sponde del lago Rodolfo." *Universo Firenze*, 21 (1940), 53–65.

Ditmars, R. *Reptiles of the World*. London: Macmillan, 1949.

Donaldson-Smith, A. *Through Unknown African Countries*. London: Cox, 1898.

————. *Geographical Journal*, 16 (1900), 600–621.

Downing, H., and P. Brazaitis. "Size and growth in captive crocodilians." *International Zoo Year Book*, 6 (1966), 265–269.

Druce, G. C. "The symbolism of the crocodile in the middle ages." *The Archaeological Journal*, S2 16 (1909), 21–43.

du borg de Bozas, M. "D'Addis Ababa au Nil pour lac Rodolfe." *Géographie*, (1903), 91–112.

————. *De la mer Rouge à l'Atlantique à travers l'Afrique Tropicale*. Paris: 1906.

Dyson, W. S., and V. E. Fuchs. "The El Molo." *Journal of the Royal Anthropological Institute*, 68 (1937), 327–338.

Earl, L. *Crocodile Fever*. New York: Knopf, 1954.

East African Freshwater Fisheries Research Organization, "Chemical analyses: Lake Rudolf." *East African Freshwater Fisheries Research Organization (Append A1)*, 27 (1954).

Edmund, A. "Tooth replacement phenomena in the lower vertebrates." *Royal Ontario Museum, Life Sciences Division Contribution*, No. 52, 1960.

————. "Sequence and rate of tooth replacement in the crocodilia." *Royal Ontario Museum, Life Sciences Division Contribution*, No. 56, 1962.

Emley, P. D. "The Turkana of Kalosia district." *Journal of the Royal Anthropological Institute of Great Britain*, 57, (1927), 157–201.

Evans, L. T. "Structure as related to behavior in the organization of populations in reptiles." In W. F. Blair's *Vertebrate Speciation: A University of Texas Symposium*.

Austin: University of Texas Press, 1961.

Farragiana, A. *Bollettíno della Reàle Società Geographica Italiàna*, 1908.

Flower, S. S. "The Egyptian plover, *Pluvianus aegyptius*: its name, distribution, known and reputed habits." *Avicultural Magazine*, (n.s.), 6 (1908), 139–144.

————. "Contributions to our knowledge of the duration of life in vertebrate animals. III, Reptiles." *Proceedings of the Zoological Society of London*, 98 (1925), 735–851.

————. "Notes on the recent reptiles and amphibians of Egypt, with a list of the species recorded from that kingdom." *Proceedings of the Zoological Society of London*, 106 (1933), 735–851.

————. "Further notes on the duration of life in animals." *Proceedings of the Zoological Society of London*, 107A (1937), 1–39.

Fox, W. "The proper names of the Alpine chough and of the Egyptian crocodile." *Science*, 13 (1901), 232.

Fryer, G. "Predation and its effects on migration and speciation in African fishes: a comment—with further comments by P. H. Greenwood, a reply by P. B. M. Jackson and a footnote and postscript by G. Fryer." *Proceedings of the Zoological Society of London*, 144 (1965), 301–322.

Fuchs, V. E. "The geological work of the Cambridge expedition to the East African lakes, 1930–31." *Geological Magazine*, 71 (1934), 97–112; 145–166; 837–838.

————. "The Lake Rudolf Rift Valley Expedition, 1934." *Geographical Journal*, 86 (1935), 114–142.

————. "Foreword to Admiral von Höhnel's manuscript." *Journal of the Royal African Society*, 37 (1938), 16–20.

————. "The geological history of the Lake Rudolf basin, Kenya Colony." *Philosophical Transactions of the Royal Society (B)*, 229 (1939), 219–274.

————. "Pleistocene events in the Baringo basin, Kenya Colony." *Geological Magazine*, 87 (1950), 149–174.

Gadow, H. *Amphibia and Reptiles*. London: Macmillan, 1901.

Gans, C. (Editor). *Biology of the Reptilia*. London: Academic Press, 1969.

Geographical Notes (1889). "Count Teleki's discoveries in Eastern Africa." *Scottish Geographical Magazine*, 5 (1889), 96–100.

Gervais, M. P. *Atlas de Zoologie*. Paris, 1844.

Gesner, K. *Historiae Animalium*. (1551).

Gosse, P. H. *Natural History (Reptiles)*. Boston, 1850.

————. *Romance of Natural History*. Boston, 1861.

Gould, C. *Mythical Monsters*. New York, 1886.

Grabham, G. W. "A crocodiles nest." *Nature, London*, 80 (1909), 96.

Graham, A. *The Lake Rudolf Crocodile Population*. Report by Wildlife Services Ltd. to the Kenya Game Department, 1968.

Green, L. *Secret Africa*. London. Stanley Boyd, 1936.

Gregor, G. "Farming crocodiles in Kabwe." *Horizon*, 11 (1969), 4–9.

Gregory, J. W. *The Rift Valleys and Geology of East Africa.* London: Steeley Service, 1921.

Grenfell, B., A. Hunt, and J. Gilbart-Smyly. *The Tebtunis Papyri.* London: Frowde, 1902.

Gulliver, P. H. "A preliminary survey of the Turkana," *Communications from the School of African Studies,* No. 26, University of Capetown, 1950.

—————. *The Family Herds.* London: Routledge and Kegan Paul, 1955.

Hambly, W. D. "Serpent worship in Africa." *Field Museum of Natural History,* 21 (1931), 1–83.

Hamblyn, E. L. "A note on Lake Rudolf." *East African Freshwater Fisheries Research Organization* (1962) *App. H,* 46–47.

Hamilton, H. C., and W. Falconer. *The Geography of Strabo.* London: George Bell, 1887.

Harrison, J. J., A. E. Butter, P. G. Powell-Cotton, W. F. Whitehouse, and D. Clarke. "A journey from Zeila to Lake Rudolf." *Geographical Journal,* 18 (1901), 258–275.

Herodotus. *The Histories.* Penguin, 1954.

Hillaby, J. *Journey to the Jade Sea.* London: Constable, 1964.

Hippel, E. V. "Stomach contents of crocodiles." *Uganda Journal,* 10 (1946), 148.

Hoare, C. "Studies on Trypanosoma grayi. 3. Life-cycle in the tsetse fly and in the crocodile." *Parasitology,* 23 (1931), 449–484.

—————. "On protozoal blood parasites collected in Uganda, with an account of the life cycle of the crocodile haemogregarine." *Parasitology,* 24 (1932), 210–224.

Hobley, C. W. "On crocodiles." *Journal of the East African Natural History Society,* (1919), 407–410.

—————. "Further notes on crocodiles." *Journal of the East African Natural History Society,* (1921), 61–62.

Hoey, A. C. "Lake Rudolf." *Journal of the East African Natural History Society,* (1911), 27–31.

Höhnel, L. R. von. "Ostaquatorial-Afrika zwischen Pangani und dem neuentdeckten Rudolf-See. Ergebnisse der Graf S. Telekischen Expedition 1887–1888." *Petermanns Mitteilungen Erganzungs,* 21 (1890), 1–44.

—————. "Zum Rudolf-See und Stefanie-See." *Schr. Ver. Verbreit. naturw. Kennt. Wien,* 30 (1890), 1–34.

—————. "Beiträge zur geologischen Kenntnis des östlichen Afrika." *Denkschr. Akad. Wiss. Wien,* 58 (1891), 447–464.

—————. *Zum Rudolf- und Stefanie-See. Die Forschungsreise des Grafen Samuel Teleki in Ost-Aquatorial Afrika 1887 und 1888.* Vienna: Holder, 1892.

—————. *Discovery of Lakes Rudolf and Stefanie.* London: Longmans, 1894.

—————. "The Lake Rudolf region. Its discovery and subsequent exploration. 1888–1909." *Journal of the Royal African Society,* (1938), 21–45; 206–226.

—————. "Uber veranderungen im Teleki-vulkangebiet." *Petermanns Mitteilungen,* 84 (1938), 84–88.

Holland, W. P. "Volcanic action north of Lake Rudolf." *Geographical Journal,* 68 (1926), 488.

Howcroft, T. P. "Crocodile and geese." *Lammergeyer,* (1968), 53.

Hubbard, W. D. "Crocodiles." *Copeia,* (1927), 115–116.

Hulme, F. E. *Natural History Lore and Legend.* London, 1895.

Huxley, J. S. "Sacred crocodiles of Lake Victoria." *Review of Reviews,* 82 (1930), 120–122.

Innocente, A. *Animali Quadrupedi.* (1771–1775).

International Zoo Year Book. "A recent survey of longevity records for reptiles and amphibians in zoos." 6 (1966), 487.

Jackson, P. B. M. "Why do Nile crocs attack boats?" *Copeia,* (1962), 204–205.

Jeremine, E. "Roches volcanique de la bordure occidentale du Lac Rodolphe." *C.r. hebd. Séanc. Acad. Sci., Paris,* 198 (1934), 673–675.

Joanen, T. "Nesting ecology of alligators in Louisiana." *Louisiana Wildlife and Fisheries Commission, La.,* 1969.

Johnson, M. *Over African Jungles.* London: Harrap, 1935.

Johnstone, H. *The Uganda Protectorate.* London: Hutchinson, 1902.

Jung, C. G. *Answer to Job.* New York: World Publishing, 1960.

Kälin, J. A. "Crocodilia" in Piveteau's *Traité de Palaeontologie.* Paris: Masson, 1955.

Kimura, W., and H. Fukada. *Crocodiles of the World.* Tokyo: 1966.

King, F. W., and P. Brazaitis. "Species identification of commercial crocodile skins." *Zoologica,* 56 (1971), 15.

Kirk, R. L., and L. Hogben. "Studies of temperature regulation. II. Amphibia and reptiles." *Journal of Experimental Biology,* 22 (1946), 213–220.

Kvam, T. "The teeth of Alligator mississipiensis. IV. Tooth succession." *Nytt. Magasin for Zoologi,* 5 (1958), 43–78.

Kymdell, W. "Crocodile, dogs, and waterbuck." *Lammergeyer,* (1968), 53.

La Gironiere, P. de. *20 years in the Philippines*. Boston, 1854.

Lambron, W. A. "Notes on habits of certain reptiles in the Lagos District." *Proceedings of the Zoological Society of London*, (1913), 218–224.

Lang, H. "Congo crocodiles, lizards and turtles." *Copeia*, (1919), 29–30.

Lange, K., and M. Hirmer. *Egypt*. London: Phaidon, 1956.

Lavauden, L. "Les grands animaux de Chasse de l'Afrique français. XII. Crocodiles." *Faune Colon. franc.*, Paris, 5 (1934).

Leisegang, H. *The Mysteries*. New York, 1955.

Livingstone, David and Charles. *Narrative of an expedition to the Zambesi and its tributaries; and the discovery of the lakes Shirwa and Nyassa*. London: John Murray, 1865.

Loveridge, A. "The Nilotic crocodile" *Copeia*, (1928), 74–76.

————. "Attack on man by an estuarine crocodile" *Copeia*, (1944), 128.

Loveridge, J. P., and D. K. Blake. "Techniques in the immobilization and handling of the Nile crocodile." *Arnoldia*, 5 (1972), 1–4.

Mallowan, M. "Animals in art. V. Egyptian." *Geographical Magazine*, (1948).

Mann, N. J. "Report on a fisheries survey of Lake Rudolf, Kenya." *Report of the E. Afr. Freshwat. Fish. Res. Org.*, (1962/63), 62–83.

McIlhenny, E. A. "Notes on incubation and growth of alligators." *Copeia*, (1934), 80–88.

————. *The Alligator's Life History*. Boston: Christopher Publishing House, 1935.

Mertens, R. *The World of Amphibians and Reptiles*. New York: McGraw-Hill, 1960.

————, and H. Wermuth. "Die Rentzen Schildkröten, Krokodile; und Brückenechsen" *Zoologische Jahrbücher (Systematik)*, 83 (1955), 323–440.

Mitchell, S. A. "A survey of the crocodile population of the Sinamwenda river and bay, lake Kariba." *Cyclostyled report of the University College, Salisbury, Rhodesia*, 1968.

Modha, M. L. "The ecology of the Nile crocodile, *Crocodylus niloticus* Laurenti, on Central Island, Lake Rudolf." *East African Wildlife Journal*, 5 (1967), 74–95.

————. *The Ecology of the Nile Crocodile, Crocodylus niloticus Laurenti, on Central Island, Lake Rudolf*, M.Sc. Thesis, University of East Africa, 1967.

————. "Basking behaviour of the Nile crocodile on Central Island, Lake Rudolf." *East African Wildlife Journal*, 6 (1968), 81–88.

Mook, C. "Individual and age variations in the skulls of recent crocodilia." *Contribs. to the Osteology, affinities and dist. of the Crocodilia*. Cont. No. 4. *Bulletin of the American Museum of Natural History*, 44 (1921), 51–66.

————. "Notes on the post-cranial skeleton in the crocodilia." Cont. No. 5. *Bulletin of the American Museum of Natural History*, 44 (1921), 67–100.

————. "Skull characteristics of recent crocodilia, with

notes on the affinities of the recent genera." Cont. No. 10. *Bulletin of the American Museum of Natural History*, 44 (1921), 126–268.

————. "The Evolution and Classification of the Crocodilia." *Journal of Geology*, 42 (1934), 295–304.

Murray, R. M. "Foods and feeding (*Crocodylus niloticus*)." *Lammergeyer*, 2 (1962), 69.

Neill, W. T. *The Last of the Ruling Reptiles*. New York: Columbia University Press, 1971.

Nelson, P. R. "The Nile crocodile." *Chicago Natural History Bulletin*, 33 (1949), 6–7.

Neumann, A. *Elephant Hunting in East Equatorial Africa*. London: Rowland Ward, 1898.

Nicander, *Alexipharmaca*.

Nicodemus. *Apocryphal Gospel*.

Oberhummer, E. "Ludwig Ritter von Höhnel." *Petermann's Geographische Mitteilungen*, 88 (1942), 183–184.

Ogilby. *Africa*. (1670).

Oppian. *Cynegetica*. New York: Loeb's Classical Library.

Owen, T. R. H. "Notes on the feeding and other habits of the crocodile." *Sudan Wild Life and Sport*, 2 (1951), 33–35.

Parker, H. W. "Reptiles and amphibians collected by the Lake Rudolf Rift Valley Expedition, 1934." *Annals of the Magazine of Natural History*, Series 10, 18 (1936), 594–609.

Parker, I. S. C., and A. Graham. "A crocodile census of the Rufiji river between Shaguli and the Ruaha junction." *Report by Wildlife Services Ltd. to the Tanzania Game Division, Dar-es-Salaam, Tanzania*, 1965.

Parker, I. S. C., and R. M. Watson. "Crocodile distribution and status in the major waters of western and central Uganda in 1969." *East African Wildlife Journal*, 8 (1970), 85–103.

Paton, D. *Animals of Ancient Egypt*. London: Macmillan, 1925.

Peabody, F. C. "Annual growth zones in living and fossil vertebrates." *Journal of Morphology*, 108 (1961), 11–62.

Pellegrin, J. "Mort d'un alligator présumé avoir vécu 85 ans à la ménagerie des reptiles." *Bulletin, Musée National d'Histoire Naturelle*, 2nd Series, 9 (1937), 176–177.

Penley, E. W. "Superstition among the Turkana: a southern Turkana heaven." *Man*, 30 (1930), 139–140.

Perkins, E. A. T. "The crocodiles of Nabugabo." *Uganda Journal*, 11 (1947), 69.

Philostratus. *Vita Apollonii*.

Pienaar, U. de V. "Predator—prey relationships amongst the larger mammals of the Kruger National Park." *Koedoe*, 12 (1969), 108–176.

Pitman, C. R. S. *A Game Warden among His Charges*. London: Nisbet, 1931.

_____. "About crocodiles." *Uganda Journal*, 8 (1941), 84–114.

_____. "The amazing muscular reflexes of a dead crocodile." *Uganda Journal*, 9 (1942), 81.

_____. A Game Warden Takes Stock. London: Nisbet, 1942.

_____. "Pigmy crocodiles in Uganda." *Uganda Journal*, 16 (1952), 120–124.

_____. "Further notes on aquatic predators of birds." *Bulletin of the British Ornithological Club*, 77 (1957), 89–97; 105–110; 122–126.

_____. "Nile crocodiles versus Spurwing goose." *Bulletin of the British Ornithological Club*, 81 (1961), 112.

Pliny (trans. Holland). *The Historie of the World. Commonly called the Natural Historie of C. Plinius Secondus*. London.

Plutarch. *Moralia*.

Poole, D. G. "Notes on tooth replacement in the Nile crocodile." *Proceedings of the Zoological Society of London*, 136 (1961), 131–140.

Pooley, A. "Nile crocodiles, notes on the incubation period and growth rate of juveniles." *Lammergeyer*, 2 (1962), 1–5.

_____. "Crocodile farm." *Black Lechwe*, 4 (1965), 5–6.

_____. "Preliminary studies on the breeding of the Nile crocodile in Zululand." *Lammergeyer*, 10 (1969), 22–44.

_____. "Some observations on the rearing of crocodiles." *Lammergeyer*, 10 (1969), 45–57.

Pooley, A. "The burrowing behaviour of crocodiles." *Lammergeyer*, 10 (1969), 60–63.

_____. "Rearing crocodiles in Zululand." *African Wildlife*, 23 (1969), 314–320.

_____. "Conservation of the crocodile in Zululand." *Animals*, 13 (1970), 76–79.

_____. *Conservation of the Nile Crocodile*. Natal Parks Game and Fish Preservation Board, 1971.

Pope, C. H. *The Reptile World*. New York: Knopf, 1955.

Potous, P. *No Tears for the Crocodile*. London: Hutchinson, 1956.

Powell-Cotton, P. *In Unknown Africa*. London: Macmillan, 1904.

Raven, H. C. "An incident in the feeding habit of *Crocodilus niloticus*." *Copeia*, (1921), 33–35.

Rayne, H. *The Ivory Raiders*. London: Macmillan, 1923.

Reese, A. M. *The Alligator and its Allies*. New York: Putnam's, 1915.

Rich, F. "Scientific results of the Cambridge expedition to the East African lakes, 1930–31. 7. The Algae." *Journal of the Linnaean Society (Zoology)*, 38 (1933), 249–275.

Richardson, J., and D. Livingstone. "An attack by a Nile crocodile on a small boat." *Copeia*, (1962), 203–204.

Robinson, P. *The Poet's Beasts*. London: Chatto & Windus, 1885.

_____. *The Poets and Nature, Reptiles, Fishes & Insects*. London: Chatto & Windus, 1893.

Rose, W. *The Reptiles and Amphibians of Southern Africa*. Capetown: Maskew Millar, 1950.

Rosiwal, A. "Uber gesteine aus dem gebiete zwischen Usambara und dem Stefanie-See." *Denkshr. Akad. Wiss., Wien*, 58 (1891), 465–550.

Ross, R. "The algae of the East African great lakes." *Vehr. int. Verein. theor. angew. Limnol*, 12 (1955), 320–326.

Rutledge, J. "Crocodile farm." *Black Lechwe*, 7 (1969), 4–7.

Saint-Hilaire, G. "Sur deux espèces d'animaux nommes Trochilus et Bdella par Herodote, leur guerre, et la part qu'y prend le crocodile." *Mémoirs du Musées de Paris*, 15 (1827), 459–474.

St. Leger, J. "Mammals collected by the Lake Rudolf Rift Valley Expedition, 1934." *Annals of the Magazine of Natural History*, S10, 19 (1937), 524–531.

Savage, J. M. "Crocodilia." *McGraw-Hill Encyclopedia of*

Science and Technology. New York: McGraw-Hill, 1960.

Schmidt, K. P., and R. F. Inger. *Living Reptiles of the World*. London: Hamish Hamilton, 1957.

Schuette, G. W. "Crocodile's prey." *Lammergeyer*, (1968), 52.

Schweinfurth, G. *The Heart of Africa*. London: Low, Marston & Searle, 1874.

Seidl, F. "Beobachtungen an cinem *Caiman crocodilus. Aquaria und Terraria* (Z), 16, 88–89.

Selous, F. C. *African Nature Notes and Reminiscences*. London: Macmillan, 1908.

Siah, Y. "Siamese crocodiles." *Game bird breeders Gazette*, 11 (1962), 53.

Smellie, W. *Philosophy of Natural History*. London, 1799.

Smith, H. "Evolutionary lines in tooth attachment and replacement in reptiles." *Kansas Academy of Science Transactions*, (1958), 61–62.

Smith, M. A. "Crocodilus siamensis." *Journal of the Natural History Society of Siam*, 3 (1919), 217–227.

Stejneger, L. "Crocodilian nomenclature." *Copeia*, (1933), 117–120.

Stevenson-Hamilton. *The Lowveld, its Wildlife and its People*. Edinburgh: Oliver and Boyd, 1912.

Stigand, C. H. *To Abyssinia Through an Unknown Land*. London: Cassel, 1910.

Stoneman, J. "Notes on growth and feeding of *Crocodylus*

niloticus." *Occasional papers (2) of 1969 of the Uganda Fisheries Dept.*, 1969.

Stoneman, J. "Crocodile industry in Uganda." *Occasional papers (2) of 1969 of the Uganda Fisheries Dept.*, 1969.

"T. C." *The new Atlas of Travels and Voyages in Africa and America through the most reknowned parts of the World.* 1698.

Tenaille, G. "La trituration des aliments par l'estomac des crocodiles." *Bulletin, Musée Nat. d'Histoire naturelle, Paris,* 13 (1941), 408.

The physiologus.

Thorp, J. *The Glittering Lake. An Autobiography of a District Officer, Kenya, 1937–43.* Rhodes House, Oxford. MSS. Afr. 974.

Thunberg, C. P. *Travels in Europe, Africa and Asia.* London, 1796.

Timbs, J. *Strange Stories of the Animal World.* Boston, 1866.

————. *Eccentricities of the Animal Creation.* Boston, 1869.

Timotheus of Gaza. ca. A.D. 500. *On Animals.*

Topsell, E. (1658). *History of Four-footed Beasts and Serpents.* Reprinted by DeCapo Press, 1967.

Villiers, A. "Tortues et crocodiles de l'Afrique noire française." *Institut Française d'Afrique Noire, Initiations Africaines,* (1958), 1–354.

Viosca, P. "External sexual differences in the alligator." *Herpetologica,* (1939), 154–155.

Voeltzkow, A. "Ueber Biologie and Embryonalentwickelung der Krokodile." *Sitzber. Akad. Berlin,* (1893), 347–353.

————. "Beitrage zur Entwicklungsgeschichte der Reptilien. Biologie und Entwicklung der ausseren Korperform von Crocodilus madagascariensis Grand." *Abh. Senck. Naturf. Gesell.,* 26 (1899), 1–150.

Voiage & Travaile of Sir John Maundevile, Knight. London: Woodman, Lyon & Davis, 1725.

Watson, R. M., A. Graham, R. Bell, and I. Parker. "A comparison of four East African crocodile populations." *East African Wildlife Journal,* 9 (1971), 25–34.

Wellby, M. S. "King Menelik's dominion and the country between lake Gallop (Rudolf) and the Nile valley." *Geographical Journal,* 16 (1900), 292–306.

————. *Twixt Sirder and Menelik.* London: Macmillan, 1901.

Welman, J. B., and E. B. Worthington. "The food of the crocodile." *Proceedings of the Zoological Society of London,* 113 (1943), 108–112.

Wermuth, H. "Systematik der rezenten Krokodile." *Mitteilungen der Zoologische Museum (Berlin),* 29 (1953), 375–514.

————. "Farbwechsel und Lernfahigkeit bei Krokodilen." *Aquarien und Terrarien-Zeit,* 16 (1963), 90–92.

————. "Das Verhaltnis zwischen Kopf-, Rumpf-, und Schwanzlange bei den rezenten Krokodilen." *Senckenbergiana (Biologie),* 45 (1964), 369–385.

————, and R. Mertens. *Schildkroten—Krokodile—Bruckenechsen.* Jena: Fischer Verlag, 1961.

Werner, H. *A Visit to Stanley's Rearguard.* London: Longmans, 1897.

Whitehouse, P. *To Lake Rudolf and Beyond.* London: Chatto & Windus, 1900.

Wickenburg, Count. *Geographical Journal,* 22 (1903), 698–700.

————. "Account of a journey from Jibuti to Lamu." *Petermann's Mitteilungen,* 9 and 10, 1930.

Worthington, E. B. "The lakes of Kenya and Uganda." *Geographical Journal,* 79 (1932), 275–292.

————. *Science in Africa.* Oxford: University Press, 1938.

————, and C. K. Ricardo. "Scientific results of the Cambridge expedition to the East African lakes 1930–1. No. 15. The fish of Lake Rudolf and Lake Baringo." *Journal of the Linnaean Society (Zool.),* 39 (1936), 353–389.

ACKNOWLEDGMENTS

There are many to whom we extend thanks. To Bob McConnell and Mike Newton, who added crucial impetus in a time of need; and to Bob again for his year as nurse, host at sand parties, cucumbers, salt, etc.... To Ian Parker, whose initiative was the origin of the survey. To Betty Childs for her exceptionally intelligent editing. To John Brogna, David Ford, Betsy Beach, Peter Schub, Bob Bear, and Carol Ann Oberholtzer, who attended to things in New York. To Lexington Labs in New York City (Phil Pessoni, the Moraleses and George) and Nairobi Photofinishers in Kenya (Musa Quiraishy) for developing, enlarging, storing, delivering, helping in every way with highest quality performances. To Jane Graham, who worked hard on the manuscript. To Richard Lindner and Charles Addams for their unique and highly esteemed art works. To Andy Warhol for Hellman's, Ritz, and Skippy canvases. To Saul Steinberg and the *New Yorker* for permission to reproduce the cartoon on page 243 under their copyright. To the Munich Pinakothek for permission to reproduce Rubens' "Die Nilpferd Jagd." To Karl Luthy and Jay Mellon for details of the Gambella incident. To Dr. Oscar Owre of the 1958 Maytag Expedition to Lake Rudolf and the Viscaya Science Museum (Miami) for their cooperation. To Dick Cole, Naomi Simms, Bella Reeves, Bill and Ruth Woodley, Bill Holden, Tony Partridge, and all hosts and helpers in the crocodile years. To Lokwar the Wildman, Elata, Tukoi, Ebei, and Atikukeni, who shared in the hardest work.

Special thanks to RAPOPORT printers, specifically to Sid Rapoport and Tom O'Brien for their patient genius

A.G. and P.B.

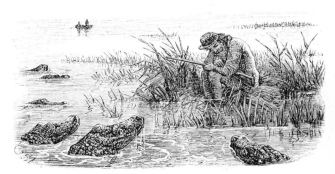